Cheers -
Crack a Fosters for

THE BUNYIP ARCHIVES

A NOVEL BY

James E. Schutte

This book is a work of fiction. Names, characters, places and incidents are either the product of the author's imagination or are used fictitiously. Any resemblance to actual events or locales or persons, living or dead, is entirely coincidental.

BASKERVILLE Publishers, Ltd.
7540 LBJ/Suite 125, Dallas, TX 75251-1008

Library of Congress Catalog Card Number: 92-070844
ISBN: 0-9627509-8-0

Manufactured in the United States of America
First Printing

To DeeDee

with love and hope

So all our studies we will sink;
The Bunyip is the Missing Link
Between the Monkey and the Man;
We'll find that Bunyip if we can.
—J. H. Nicholson
Opal Fever, 1878

1

"I've caught me a bunyip! A bloody bunyip!"

Paul McDaniel bolted upright in his bed, the chill quiet of the Australian Outback night shattered by a beer- and adrenalin-charged voice. The shouts were close and growing nearer, booming over the engine roar of a fast-approaching vehicle. Between shouts, the driver hammered an endless series of beeeep beeeep beeeeps on the horn.

Headlights glowed through the parchment window shade across the room. The twin yellow circles were coming straight at Paul, and they were getting too big too fast. Just as he gasped with fear that he might be run over where he lay, Paul heard the crunch of tires braking hard against gravel. He sighed in relief as the vehicle skidded to a halt a few feet short of the window.

"Come on out, Perfesser! Y'say bunyips is mythical? Well, I got one for yer!" yelled Freddy Brennan, Paul's closest friend and most relentless tormentor. Where Freddy went, mischief followed close behind.

More blasts of the horn.

"Here we go again," Paul muttered to himself. All he asked of life was a chance to do his research so he could complete his Ph.D. Then he'd click his heels together three times and wake up back at the University of Kansas. Until then, he needed to get along with the locals. And frequently that meant humoring them through their idiotic pranks. But within limits. Take the time somebody slipped him a bottle of cold piss in the guise of buying him a beer. Paul yanked the man, considerably larger than himself, overhead and threw him across the bar. After that, people understood that the jokes would only be tolerated so far.

"Y'say yer don't believe in bunyips? That they ain't real? Well, c'mon out, Perfesser, an' shake hands with one."

Still more of that goddamn horn.

The ancient bedsprings beneath him groaned in protest as Paul groped the air overhead until he caught the cord and, with a tug, lit the room's single, bare light bulb. The clock on the upended crate by the bed read 3:13.

Paul pulled on his jeans, then stumbled over cardboard boxes and torn linoleum to the front door of the two-room miner's shack that served as both home and field station. Judging from Freddy's enthusiasm, he'd thought up a real corker this time. And Paul would endure it with his usual good humor.

"C'mon, Perfesser. Come see me bunyip." Mercifully, Freddy had stopped pounding his horn once the light came on.

A young American kangaroo enthusiast made an irresistible target for the deranged humor of the Outback, and Paul had reluctantly become the main source of amusement for the 147 hard-drinking denizens of Woolloona. But the endless barrage of jokes and pranks had worked in his favor too. When Paul had first come to Woolly last year, no one had wanted much to do with him. Although only 28 at the time and still a graduate student, he was dubbed "Perfesser" out of that peculiar combination of deference and contempt that those with too little education have for those with too much. But Paul had quickly established himself as a "reg'lar bloke" by being ever the good sport who joined in on the laughter and drinking.

"Hurry, Perfesser. It's an honest-to-gawd bunyip."

"Hang on, Freddy. I'm coming," Paul yelled through the closed door. His voice carried a deliberate air of resignation. If he was going to put up with this nonsense, he at least wanted to make it obvious that he was on to the joke.

The warped front door, stuck shut to the unwitting, snapped open in response to a sharp, well-practiced yank. Warily, Paul emerged to face the pranksters. Freddy immediately seized his arm and began dragging him toward the fiberglass camper shell covering the bed of a battered yellow Toyota pickup.

"C'mon, Perfesser. Yer just gotta see this."

Freddy was in rare form tonight, Paul observed, amazed at his captor's exuberance. Freddy had a childlike enthusiasm for carrying everything, especially practical jokes, beyond excess. Paul found this trait endearing, but also excruciating in day-to-day practice.

"Yer gotta see it, Perfesser. A bloody bunyip."

At 6-foot-4 and well over 300 pounds, Freddy was a head taller than Paul and twice his weight. He had a round, ruddy face, a flowing red beard and a cherubic smile usually eclipsed from view by a can of Foster's Lager. In all, he reminded Paul of a youthful, hop-scented Santa Claus.

"Yer'll never believe what I've got over here, Perfesser."

"Is it a bunyip?" Paul asked dryly.

"Gawd, yes. A dinkie-die bunyip. Yer just won't believe it."

"I'm *sure* I won't."

It seemed to Paul that people around here were obsessed with bunyips. Anywhere else in Australia, they were simply the mythical Outback version of Bigfoot, the Yeti, or what have you. But here in Woolly, such stories were taken seriously. Most Woolloonians ("Woollunatics," Paul called them, only half in jest) even claimed to have encountered a bunyip or two. But considering that they all seemed to live in the hazy nether world of perpetual intoxication, it amazed him that bunyips were the only thing they hallucinated. As they approached the truck, Freddy thrust his flashlight into Paul's hands.

"Here, Perfesser, have a look." He reached for the hatch of the camper shell.

Paul braced himself, having learned from previous experience. Some drunk in a gorilla suit, probably George Newstead, almost certainly waited in the back of that truck. Once the hatch opened, George would jump out, grab Paul, then scream like a banshee while delivering a back-cracking bear hug.

Finally, after Freddy and George had laughed until they'd puked themselves out, they'd invite Paul to help them finish off whatever beer they had left. Then they'd run and tell the entire town of Woolloona about scaring the shit out of the Perfesser.

Though he'd never admit it, even to himself, Paul actually enjoyed these bizarre little escapades. They interrupted a tedious and very lonely daily routine. And they almost always yielded a few cold beers.

Freddy snapped the hatch open and Paul stepped back instinctively, holding the flashlight like a sword in front of him. Sure enough, a dark, hairy, human-like form crouched in a far corner of the truck bed. But if it *was* someone in a gorilla suit, it couldn't have been George. George was almost as large as Freddy. The figure in that truck was no bigger than a child.

"Who the hell *is* that?" Paul asked cautiously.

"Who? No, no! Yer've got it all wrong, Perfesser. This ain't no joke. That's a bunyip there, a dinkie-die bunyip." A massive arm around his shoulders pulled the still-suspicious Paul closer to the truck bed. He could feel Freddy tremble. Had to be from excitement, he thought. The only other possibility, DTs from alcohol withdrawal, could be ruled out by the aroma of Freddy's breath.

With his chest now touching the still-closed tailgate,

Paul trained the narrow flashlight beam on the dark form crouched against the cab. It faced them, its back wedged into the corner and knees pulled to the shoulders in a pathetic attempt to get as far away from the men as possible.

It sure looked like a child—maybe a lost aborigine who'd been living wild in the bush. Yet the entire body except the face was sparsely covered with inch-long reddish-brown hair. Even a feral child wouldn't grow hair like that. But it wasn't a gorilla suit, either. Light brown skin lay clearly visible under the hair. Unless Freddy had help from a makeup artist, the individual in front of them was for real. Whoever it was.

Paul's suspicion gave way to curiosity. He scanned the body with the flashlight, trying to make sense of what he saw. Training his light on the crotch, Paul spoke at just above a whisper. "I think it's a girl, Freddy. Can't tell for sure, though. Hair's too thick right there. And look at how swollen the belly is for such a skinny little kid. Probably malnutrition. Or worms."

"Maybe she's pregnant," Freddy volunteered, voice lowered to a coarse whisper.

"Possibly. But then you'd expect some tits, and I don't see any. In fact, oddly enough, I don't even see any nipples." The beam inched upward, lighting a face frozen into a wide-eyed mask of fear. "Easy, girl. Nobody's gonna hurt you," Paul said softly. Then to Freddy, "I wonder if it's an aboriginal kid with some weird genetic disorder."

"She ain't no aborigine! She's a—"

"Well, she's certainly not a *normal* aborigine. Maybe she's got a gland problem of some kind. Maybe—"

"I'm telling yer, Perfesser, she ain't no bloody abo! She's a bunyip!"

Something caught Paul's attention. "That's strange. Look at her eyes, the way they glow blue-green in the light." He moved the beam slowly back and forth across her face.

"Yer means the eyeshine?"

"Yeah. Usually, you see it in nocturnal animals. The pupil stays wide open when the animal looks at a bright light. Light reflects off the back of the eyeball and causes the shine."

"So whattayer sayin'?"

"I'm not sure," Paul continued in growing confusion. "See, in human eyes, the pupils shrink almost immediately in bright light. That shuts out the excess light. Which means that humans . . . don't . . . have . . . eyeshine."

The creature's abdomen heaved convulsively as the margins of a crease in her belly parted to reveal the shiny pink skin inside. Paul stood silent for several seconds, trying to comprehend. Then it hit him. He spoke in low, measured tones of shock and disbelief.

"My God, Freddy . . . she's got a pouch . . . a marsupial pouch."

The margins of the pouch spread wider, and a small, reddish-brown head emerged. A tiny, bewildered face stared back at Paul and Freddy, its eyes glowing blue-green in the flashlight beam.

"I *told* yer it was a bloody bunyip!" Freddy roared triumphantly. "An' there's its joey to prove it! Whattayer say now, Perfesser?"

But Paul had nothing to say, nothing at all. He could only stare in open-mouthed astonishment.

A scientist does not easily absorb facts that contradict his basic understanding of the world, and it took many minutes for the new reality to percolate through Paul's brain. He was actually looking at a bunyip. Not a mythical creature, but a very real, human-like marsupial that carried its young in a pouch like a kangaroo. Paul tried to remember if any of the stories ever mentioned that they were marsupials. Apparently, the Woollunatics weren't quite as crazy as he'd thought, although that still left them listing dangerously to port.

Paul's thoughts drifted toward the professional possibilities. In front of him sat the dream of every aspiring biologist, a new and *very* unusual life form. He and Freddy were about to become world-famous, and the scientific papers Paul generated from this discovery would guarantee him a secure place in the academic world. Heady thoughts for a graduate student facing an overcrowded job market.

But Paul's euphoria was muted by pity as he watched the tiny mother desperately shove her child back into its fragile sanctuary. Whatever the bunyip was, and whatever her value to science, they had no right to hold her captive. They'd have to let her go.

But not just yet.

"Where did you find her?" Paul asked, finding his voice.

"By a billabong nor'west o' here. Caught her with a can of Foster's, I did." Freddy still trembled with excitement.

"I was huntin' wild pigs from a blind I'd staked out. Hadn't seen nothin' fer a couple hours, and yer *know* I'd had me a few beers by then. So I decided to climb back in me truck fer a nap. Must've left a full tube o' beer behind, 'cuz when I came back to the blind, I found this here bunyip sprawled out with an empty beer tube in her hand. She was too drunk to run away, so I carried her to me truck and brought her here."

"I want a closer look at her," Paul said, "but as scared as she is, she'd probably panic. I wish we had some way to sedate her."

"One sedative, comin' up." Freddy cheerfully headed for the cab of the truck and returned a few seconds later with a can of Foster's. He popped the top, then placed the can as close to the bunyip as his reach allowed. "Yer already knows what to do with this, young lady." He closed the hatch. "Let's you an' me have a sedative too, Perfesser."

Unable to see inside the camper, the men listened and waited anxiously for something to happen. After several minutes they heard the hollow clink of a can being dropped. Moments later came a dull thud.

"I reckon our little friend's medication has taken effect." Freddy reopened the hatch. Sure enough, the bunyip now lay spread-eagled in the far corner. Freddy lowered the tailgate and carefully pulled her out.

"Let's put her on my bed for now," Paul suggested, leading the way inside.

Once Freddy had laid her down Paul gently examined the bunyip, checking out every feature. He wanted a closer look at the joey too, but it stayed huddled out of sight in the pouch. After several minutes Paul turned to Freddy.

"I'd never believe this if I weren't actually touching her. Absolutely incredible! Except for the pouch, she's human-like in almost every detail, right down to the shape of her teeth. But she's a goddamn marsupial. Not even related to us. The closest evolutionary ancestor she shares with humans was probably some dinosaur."

"Don't make much sense to me neither, Perfesser."

"I mean, it has to be some type of collateral evolution," Paul continued as he struggled, more for his own benefit than for Freddy's, to develop a logical explanation. "See, when unrelated animals face similar evolutionary pressures, they can evolve in the same direction. Just like whales developed fish-like bodies from living in the ocean. Here in Australia, there's a marsupial mole that looks and acts a lot like the moles we have back in America. You've also got marsupial cats and marsupial mice, even used to have a marsupial wolf."

"Right-o," Freddy joined in. "Furthermore, there us'ta be a marsupial analog o' the placental saber tooth felines o' the Pleistocene."

Although Freddy played the role of a simpleton to the hilt, beneath the façade was a self-educated naturalist of incredible intelligence. "An' durin' the early Holocene following the extinction o' the Pleistocene megafauna—"

"Wouldja cut it out!" Paul exploded. "One minute you're a drunken illiterate and then suddenly, with no warning, you know more about this shit than I do. Stop switching roles in the middle of a conversation!"

"Sorry, mate," Freddy replied with a sly grin. God, how he must love doing that.

"Anyway," Paul continued, recovering his stride, "if the ancestors of these creatures evolved in an environmental niche similar to the one that produced humans, I guess there's no reason why they couldn't have developed in a human-like direction also. In fact, a few years ago a paleontologist named Dale Russell argued that if the dinosaurs hadn't died out, they'd have evolved a large-brained humanoid of their own. The guy even came up with pictures of what it would look like. If a dinosaur could become man-like, why not a marsupial? But wherever our little guest came from, the real question is, what are we gonna do with her?"

The first step was to document her existence.

"We could shoot some photos, then take her back to the billabong an' release her," Freddy suggested.

"Won't work. Remember all the troubles those early naturalists had in proving the existence of the duck-billed platypus? Even when they sent skins of the animals back to Europe, the whole thing was rejected as some elaborate hoax. The only way anybody's gonna believe us is if we bring the scientific community face-to-face with a real, live bunyip."

"We can't just haul her off to Sydney," Freddy protested. "Poor thing'd die o' fright."

"Yeah, and too much early publicity might backfire on us," Paul added. "There are bound to be others where she came from. God knows what might happen to them if their whereabouts became public knowledge."

The first step would be to bring in Charles Andrews, Paul decided. Not only was Andrews the world's most renowned expert on marsupials, but as administrator of Paul's grant, was his boss. And Andrews would not appreciate learning of Paul's discovery from the media. Still, the decision to summon Andrews to Woolly was not made lightly. Andrews was infamously short of patience. God help Paul if anything went wrong.

Paul went to his radio transmitter and was able to reach the district communications base of the Royal Flying Doctor Service. They patched him into a telephone link with University of Sydney. It was now 7:30. Andrews would already have been in his office for an hour.

"Good morning. Professor Andrews speaking."

"It's Paul McDaniel. You've got to come to the field station immediately. I have something incredible to show you!"

"Well, it'll have to wait a couple of weeks. I'm leaving for my European lecture tour in two hours. I'm only in the office to take care of a few last-minute details."

Paul cleared his throat and braced himself. He could challenge authority when necessary, but was never comfortable when putting his career at risk. "I'm telling you this *can't* wait! You've got to get here immediately."

"What's going on there? Gotten yourself in some kind of trouble?"

"No, there's no trouble. And I promise you that what I have here is worth delaying your trip for."

"So? What is it?"

"I can't tell you. Somebody might be listening in on this frequency. You've got to just trust me and come immediately."

A long pause, then Andrews spoke with a voice that betrayed rising irritation.

"What kind of idiot do you take me for? Have you been drinking?"

It took Paul several minutes to prevail upon Andrews to delay his trip. Still unconvinced, Andrews agreed only to reschedule his flight until that evening. He knew a pilot who could get him to Woolly that afternoon and still make it back to Sydney in time for the later flight. The conversation closed on an ominous note.

"Let me warn you, Paul. I expect nothing short of the greatest scientific discovery of the decade. You'd better not disappoint me."

Paul checked his watch for the dozenth time in ten minutes. Half past noon.

"Damn it, Freddy, where are you? You promised to be back an hour ago."

His friend, who made a bare living from odd jobs, had taken a load of supplies to a sheep station several miles away.

Andrew's high-pitched voice crackled over the two-way radio. "Paul, the pilot tells me we'll be landing in ten minutes. Don't keep me waiting."

He didn't request an acknowledgment and obviously assumed that Paul was monitoring the transmission.

Paul paced between the kitchen and the bedroom while the bunyip slowly regained consciousness. She lurched upright on the bed, then leaned over the side and puked.

Paul grabbed a newspaper and scooped the mess onto it with a magazine. The bunyip lay back down with her forearm across her eyes.

"What am I gonna do with you?"

There was no way she could ride with him to the airstrip, since his only transport was a motorbike. But he didn't feel safe leaving her behind, either. She'd soon be sober enough to run away.

The only solution was to tie her up.

He carried her into the front room, which served as both

kitchen and laboratory. Setting her upright in one of the two battered wooden chairs that came with the shack, Paul secured her with strips torn from an old sheet.

He headed for the door, suddenly aware that his left foot tingled, as if falling asleep.

Across the room, the bunyip's expression reflected utter misery. Paul decided to check her bindings. The one around her left ankle was too tight. He retied it, then checked the others one last time. All were fine. The tingling in his own foot had also disappeared.

Satisfied that the bunyip was both secure and not too uncomfortable, given the circumstances, he stepped outside and mounted his motorbike, then headed for the airstrip.

Paul's shack lay halfway between the airstrip and town, a couple of miles from each over the dusty path through the scrub that passed for a road. He watched the plane begin its descent, relieved that he'd make the strip before it landed.

The plane came to a halt and a short, gray-haired man with a dour expression emerged. He still wore his trademark black vested suit with a red bow tie, and seemed oblivious of the desolate world of heat and dust he'd just entered.

"Now where's this great discovery of yours?" Andrews demanded.

"It's back at the field station. I'll just have to show to you. You wouldn't believe me if I told you."

Andrews sighed with annoyance and mounted the motorbike. Paul revved the engine and took off. Any conversation would be pointless until after they arrived at the field station. They roared along wordlessly, an immense plume of red dust billowing behind.

As soon as they arrived, Andrews jumped to his feet and began dusting himself off. In another context, this fastidious little man caked with dust would have made an amusing sight. But no one poked fun at Charles Andrews to his face. Paul parked the bike and invited Andrews to follow him.

As he looked up, Paul's heart took a sudden leap. The front door of the shack was open. He distinctly remembered shutting it. He sprinted ahead to check on the bunyip.

"Oh, shit!"

Inside sat an empty chair with strips of sheeting littered about it. Paul rushed in and checked to see if she might be still hiding somewhere inside. No such luck.

Andrews stood in the doorway, confused. "What's going on? What's the problem?"

"I had a bunyip here. An honest-to-God bunyip. And now she's gone."

"A *bunyip*?" Andrews asked, dumfounded. "Did you say *bunyip*?"

"Yeah. They really do exist. They're a kind of human-like marsupial. I had one right here. It must have gotten away." Paul realized how totally insane he must sound, but he had to keep trying. "I swear to God! There was a bunyip sitting in this chair just a few minutes ago."

Andrews shook his head in exasperation, then spoke with cold, rational hostility. "Mr. McDaniel, you have either lost your bloody mind or you have just pulled the most foolhardy stunt in the history of modern education. In either case, you are now without a job."

"Professor Andrews, you've got to—"

"Belt up!" Andrews yelled, losing control. "Start packing your bags, young man. You're sacked! Fired! The moment I get back to Sydney, I'm calling the bursar at the university and ordering your grant and salary terminated. Now take me back to the plane. I've got to catch a flight to Paris."

"Calm down, damn it. The bunyip can't have gotten very far. My friend, Freddy, is the best tracker I've ever met. He'll help us find her again."

"I'm not putting up with this foolishness another minute." Andrews wheeled around and began marching toward the airstrip.

Paul had never felt so helpless. Seven years of post-graduate study hung in the balance. Within hours his grant would be terminated, his project destroyed. Even if he recaptured the bunyip later, it would be weeks before he could show it to Andrews.

His only hope lay in finding the bunyip immediately and beating Andrews to the airstrip with it. The professor would have to slow down in this heat, and that gave Paul maybe an hour to head him off. Freddy might have stopped over at his own house. Paul jumped on his motorbike and sped toward it.

Freddy lived in a corrugated tin-covered shack much like Paul's at the outer edge of Woolly. As he approached, Paul spotted a yellow pickup parked out front.

He skidded to a sideways stop and dropped the bike, then ran for the door and burst inside.

"Freddy, we've got problems!"

"I know, mate. Ran out o' beer, yer did. But no worries. Ol' Freddy's got plenty."

"No, you don't under . . . " Paul stopped short. "Oh, my God."

Freddy sat at one end of the kitchen table clutching his ubiquitous can of Foster's. At the other end of the table, wearing a blue child's dress and also clutching a can of Foster's was . . . the bunyip.

"What in hell is going on here?" Paul asked incredulously. "You were supposed to be at my place, both of you."

"Sorry, mate, but I got there just after yer left. Saw yer drivin' off. So I came in and untied our little friend here. I could tell she was thirsty. Dunno how, but I could. An' I can always handle a cold one meself. But yer didn't have no beer in the bloody fridge. Can't expect us to stay in a place with no bloody beer! I figured that once yer noticed yer was outta beer, yer'd know where to look for us," Freddy said matter-of-factly.

He then pointed to the bunyip. "Whattayer think of her

dress? Belonged to me daughter, Melissa. Had to cut a hole in it, 'course, so the joey could look out. Looks nice on her."

The bunyip nodded slightly and fell face forward onto the table, dropping her beer to the floor.

"Tch, tch, tch," Freddy clucked in mock disapproval. "Look at that. Only one beer and she's passed out cold. I think I'll name her Maude, after me ex-wife. She was a quick drunk too, a reg'lar two-pot screamer. Y'know, little Maude likes me. I can tell. Maybe she thinks I'm family." He laughed, tugging at the thick red hair on his own forearm.

Paul was boggled. In the space of twelve hours he'd been confronted with an inebriated mythical creature, lost his job, destroyed his career and was now listening to a drunken degenerate discuss his familial resemblance to some mutant wombat.

"Freddy, how much time would I need to bash your head in with a can of Foster's?" he asked as he picked up the bunyip.

Freddy stopped for a moment and pondered before answering. "Well, mate, y'know me skull's about as thick as they come. So if yer usin' an empty tube, I doubt yer could—"

"A full one, God damn it!"

Freddy wrinkled his brow and calmly redid his mental calculations. "Now that *might* work. Even then, yer in fer at least ten minutes o' bloody hard work."

Paul carried the bunyip out the door, struggling to regain his composure. "We'll have to put it off till later, then. We've got to get to the airstrip *right now*."

He propped the bunyip upright between the seats of Freddy's pickup. Then he helped Freddy, who was nearly as drunk as Maude, into the passenger seat.

As the speeding truck approached the airstrip, Paul observed the plane already preparing for takeoff.

"Damn! He's leaving already."

He pressed the accelerator all the way to the floor. Freddy's head bounced off the ceiling with every chuckhole they hit. They were now just short of the runway. In a few seconds, Paul would be able to block the plane's takeoff. Then, without warning, the pickup's engine died. Desperately, Paul tried to restart the vehicle as it coasted to a halt. The needle on the fuel gauge pointed well below the E.

"Freddy, when this is over, remind me to murder you."

"After twelve beers and that ride, mate, I think yer've already done it."

Paul was too distracted to notice that Freddy's complexion had taken on a greenish tinge.

By now the plane had finished taxiing to the far end of the runway and was revving up for takeoff. Paul burst from the cab and sprinted toward the runway.

"Stop! Stop!" he yelled, waving his arms for attention.

The pilot released the brakes and headed down the runway. Paul pushed himself even faster.

"Stop, dammit, stop!"

The roar of the propellers drowned out his yells. The plane continued to pick up speed.

He'd come close enough to the runway that the pilot should be able to see him, yet the plane kept going faster. Was Andrews so angry that he'd made the pilot ignore Paul's obvious plea?

"Stop! Don'tcha see me? Stop!"

Within seconds, the plane would be airborne. He kept his eyes on the aircraft, and didn't see the animal burrow that caught his left foot and sent him sprawling face down onto the packed gravel at the edge of the runway.

"Oh, God, no!" he cried. He scrambled to his feet, blinking back the blood- and mud-stained sweat streaming into his eyes.

He started to run again, but by now the plane had passed. The pilot couldn't see him any more. Paul was about to give up in despair when the propeller roar dropped as the pilot cut the engine. They were stopping!

Paul rushed to the plane. He made it there just as Andrews emerged.

"What in bloody hell are you trying to pull this time?" Andrews demanded, ignoring the various shades of red that now covered Paul's face.

Paul could only pant for breath while pointing to the yellow pickup in the distance.

The two of them made their way to the vehicle while Paul implored every known deity that nothing more go wrong. No such luck. As they drew near, he could see that the cab was empty. He bolted ahead.

"Please don't do this to me *again*," he prayed.

They were gone. He checked the camper. No luck.

"Shit!"

Paul looked apologetically at Andrews, who glared at him in stony silence. Andrews was about to turn back when Paul heard a familiar sound rising from behind a bush about fifty feet away—Freddy retching.

"Follow me," Paul yelled, sprinting toward the bush. He arrived and turned to Andrews, coming up from behind.

"There. Just as I promised," Paul said with profound relief.

Andrews surveyed the strange sight. There they were. Maude, still in her little blue dress, with Freddy right beside her. Two hairy red, pot-bellied figures, both on their hands and knees, puking their guts out onto the dirt and sand. He turned back to Paul.

"So which one's the bunyip?"

2

They entered the field station with Paul already doubting the wisdom of having brought Andrews to Woolloona. If Maude was at all typical of the bunyips, they were entirely too vulnerable to risk being "discovered" by humans. But Paul couldn't back out now. He could only resolve to return Maude to the wild at the earliest opportunity.

The heat and excitement had finally caught up with Andrews, who draped his over-garments on one of the kitchen chairs and rolled up his sleeves. "Let's take a look at what we have here," he said as Paul laid Maude back on the bed.

She'd stopped puking but was still haunted by her recent indulgence.

So was Freddy, who'd made the return trip inside the camper. He was still back there, hanging over the tailgate while desperately trying to aim his heavings downwind. The insufferable heat had left him drenched with sweat and his dehydration had concentrated the stench of his stomach's former contents. Bacchus always took revenge against the careless imbiber, but in Freddy's case it seemed more like a personal vendetta.

"Yer always threatenin' to kill me, Perfesser," Freddy pleaded on their return to the field station. "So why don'tcher do it now, when yer best mate could use a nice, therapeutic assassination?"

"At this stage, it'd be redundant," Paul said reassuringly. "But in the unlikely event that you don't die from the hangover, I promise to strangle you sometime tomorrow."

"D'yer swear to it?"

Freddy would fight his demons by himself. Paul's attention was focused on Maude and Andrews.

"First, let's get rid of this ridiculous dress." Andrews pulled the garment off Maude.

The professor did a quick once-over, then began probing her roughly with his fingers. He did most of his research with a scalpel and wasn't used to working with live specimens. Maude squirmed uneasily.

"Hold her front paws for me," Andrews commanded.

Paul hesitantly complied.

But they aren't "paws," he thought. With a thumb and four fingers and flat nails instead of claws, these were hands. Maude didn't resist him, but clasped Paul's hands firmly with her own. He thought of the times, many years ago, when his little sister had held onto him like that. The grip conveyed the trust of someone small and vulnerable.

Paul felt a sudden wave of revulsion. He wasn't protecting Maude, he was subduing her. Even as she began to extend her trust to him, he was betraying it.

"Dammit, Paul, she's squirming again. Hold her still."

"Easy," Paul insisted. "You're scaring her."

"I'm trying to be careful, but this might be the only specimen of its kind we'll ever get to examine. It's our job to accumulate as much data as possible."

Maude's hands squeezed tighter against Paul's as Andrews' fingers worked their way toward her pouch.

Paul had to stop this before she panicked. "Wait. I know a better way. We can x-ray her in the clinic over at the old silver mine. The mine's been closed for a couple of years, but they still keep the offices going. I've been using their x-ray machine for my kangaroo studies. We can find out a lot more about her anatomy that way than from a superficial examination."

"Sounds good. But we've got to work in secret until we're ready to announce our findings."

Andrews' easy acquiescence restored Paul's confidence that the situation was still under control. "No problem. The only ones left at the mine are the watchmen, and they're used to my coming and going. We can put Maude's dress back on her, and I'll get a hat for her too. If anyone asks, I'll just tell him that I'm giving you and your daughter a tour of my research activities."

Andrews seemed appalled at the thought of posing as Maude's father, but agreed anyway. They'd need the truck, but Freddy was still in the camper unloading his stomach. Paul helped his friend into the field station and situated him on a chair directly in front of the water evaporation cooler. After emptying an assortment of kangaroo bones from a large plastic bucket, he handed the bucket to Freddy who accepted with a grateful nod. Paul then sprayed the room thoroughly with a can of air freshener. As the thickly sweet perfume settled in, he decided that he preferred the smells emanating from Freddy.

Paul carried Maude to the truck and sat her between himself and Andrews during the drive to the mine offices. Still lethargic, she had a hard time keeping her buttocks centered between the bucket seats. Paul wrapped his free arm around Maude to steady her, and she responded by moving closer to him until she sat almost on his lap.

Four hours later the trio returned to the field station with a thick sheaf of developed x-rays. Darkness was falling, and no one had eaten since lunch. A now-functional Freddy was sent to Newstead's Hotel and Bar to pick up some meat pies, Australia's bland, gooey and uniquely vindictive contribution to the fast food market.

"Let's take a look at these x-rays," Andrews said with

enthusiasm as he slid the first film onto the light table bolted to the far wall of Paul's kitchen.

Paul wondered what to do with Maude. She'd sobered up a little but showed no signs of fright or panic. She'd submitted passively while Paul posed her for the x-rays and now sat quietly on the floor like a bored but obedient child. Her large, soft brown eyes revealed no hint of worry. After a while, she walked over and opened the refrigerator, poked around for a few moments, then closed the door and sat back down. Paul remembered that he was still out of beer.

"Look at this," said Andrews, oblivious of all but the x-rays in front of him. Paul looked over the man's shoulder. "You can see her joey right here." Andrews traced the outlined skeleton with one finger. Then he pointed to a blurry, crescent-shaped shadow about the size of a man's little finger. "What do you suppose that is?"

Paul studied the image. "Looks like another joey, but much smaller than the other one."

"Yeah. I wonder what it's doing there? Why would she have one large joey and another the size of an embryo? The pouch is barely big enough for the one."

"Maybe it's an advanced form of embryonic diapause, like the kangaroo's," Paul ventured.

"That involves a dormant embryo in the mother's uterus, one that doesn't begin developing until after the larger joey leaves the pouch."

"Yeah, but the whole point of it is to speed up the reproductive process. Maybe the bunyips go a step further and have a dormant joey already in the pouch."

Andrews paused a moment, stroking his chin. "Yeah, that makes sense. Good thinking. But we can't be sure from just the x-ray. We need a look inside the pouch. You hold her, Paul, while I do the search."

"Let's do it tomorrow. She's been through an awful lot in just one day, and I'm afraid we're gonna hurt her."

"All we need is a quick peek," Andrews insisted. "Just hold her for a moment while I have a look."

Andrews was, after all, the boss. Paul gently lifted Maude off the floor and sat her on his lap, positioned so that Andrews could get to her pouch. She relaxed and leaned against his chest, holding his hands with her own.

"Get a tight hold on her front paws, Paul. She probably won't like us touching her babies."

Paul could already feel her tensing up. Andrews reached for her abdomen, and Maude jerked against Paul's embrace, struggling to break free. He held her firm, but started feeling panicky himself.

"Stop!" Paul commanded. "We're gonna hurt her."

But Andrews, unaccustomed to taking orders from a graduate student, pulled the pouch open and pushed the larger joey to one side for a better view as Maude writhed to break free.

"I said stop. You're scaring her." Paul yelled. Andrews still couldn't see clearly, so he grasped the larger joey with one hand and pulled it out. The joey was about a foot long and looked very much like a miniature human two-year old except for the short, reddish-brown fuzz covering all but the face.

Maude flailed her legs in panic. Andrews didn't cooperate, so it was up to Paul to put an end to this.

"Let go of her, damn it!" he yelled angrily as he stood up to carry Maude away. Her foot caught Andrews' shoulder, knocking him off balance. He fell backward, pulling hard against the margins of the pouch. Paul felt a sudden, ripping pain in his own abdomen and, caught off guard, released his grip on Maude.

She sprang forward in full fury, and buried her teeth in Andrews' neck as she grabbed her child back. The professor screamed, releasing his grip on the joey. Maude's teeth were tightly fastened, and Andrews needed both hands to push her off. Finally Maude's bite tore loose, and she was sent reeling across the room and into the opposite wall. She hit with a thud and collapsed unconscious to the floor, dropping her offspring.

Paul rushed to Maude's limp body. Her eyes were open, staring into the void. He put one hand on her chest to feel for breath while his other hand fumbled to find a pulse in her wrist.

"Shit! I don't even know where a bunyip's arteries are."

He tried for a pulse in her thigh, then her neck. No response anywhere. "Damn it, you can't be dead."

Andrews, desperately trying to stanch the blood that now flowed from his neck, attended to his own problems.

Paul instinctively began resuscitation. He alternated between breathing for Maude and pushing against her heart.

Freddy, get back here, he thought. If only Freddy could read minds.

Less than a minute later, Freddy's truck skidded to a halt out front. Paul heard a rush of feet on the porch, then the door exploded inward, ripped off its hinges by the impact of a giant shoulder.

On seeing Maude's prostrate body, Freddy stepped toward Andrews.

"You murderin' little bastard," he roared. "I *knew* there was somethin' wrong goin' on here!"

"No, I swear it was an accident!" With one hand Andrews pointed to the blood-soaked towel he held tightly against his neck.

"Freddy, come help me. See if you can find a pulse."

The red-haired giant probed the bunyip's neck where the carotid artery would presumably run. "I can't find nothin'."

"Okay, you breathe for her while I continue the heart massage," Paul commanded.

The minutes ticked away as Paul pushed rhythmically against the bunyip's chest.

Sweat streamed down his face and dripped onto his

hands, which grew increasingly numb. His arms ached from exhaustion, but he somehow forced them to keep pushing.

"Come on, Freddy, find us a pulse, damn it!"

Freddy felt her neck for the dozenth time, shook his head, then resumed breathing for her.

Paul forced his emotions away and concentrated on the mechanical action of keeping his arms in motion.

Freddy said something, but it didn't register. Paul kept pumping.

Finally, a huge hand pushed him slowly back.

"She's dead, Perfesser. Ain't nothin' more we can do."

"No, Freddy, we can't just—"

"She's dead, mate." Freddy spoke with soft deliberation, his blue eyes rimmed with tears.

Both men knelt silent and motionless for a couple of minutes, allowing the horror to sink in. Freddy was about to speak when the joey, who'd been crouching in a corner, slowly walked over and knelt by his mother. With tiny, desperate hands he tugged at her lifeless face. When she failed to respond he stretched out alongside her, hugged her neck and buried his face in her cheek. His chest heaved, and soft, muffled sobs broke the silence.

"I'm going to throw up." Paul headed for the doorway. What really sickened him was his own role in what had happened.

Andrews had finally brought his bleeding under control. Maude had bitten loose a thumb-sized flap of skin on his neck, but hadn't damaged any major blood vessels.

From the menacing way Freddy was looking at him, Andrews must have sensed the big man's inexhaustable capacity for violence.

"I didn't do it intentionally," Andrews insisted. "She had her teeth in my neck. She could have opened an artery, and I'd have bled to death if I didn't get her off!"

Freddy didn't move but continued to glare silently at the man. Slowly, as if a sudden move might provoke an attack,

Andrews pulled the first aid kit out of Paul's day pack and bandaged his wound.

"Look, I'm sorry for what happened," Andrews said on Paul's return. "I realize it's my fault. Things just got out of hand. I know you're both upset, and need some time to yourselves. I'm going to take a walk. I'll be back in a couple of hours. Then we'll discuss what needs to be done."

Andrews turned and walked out, stepping over the shattered remains of the door.

"We both needs a beer, an' yer still out," Freddy said as Andrews disappeared into the night. "Let's go to my place. I even got some milk for the joey. We'll take Maudie with us too. I ain't leavin' her behind fer no more o' yer bloody 'scientific research.'"

Freddy already held the joey. Paul, too angry with himself to speak, silently picked up Maude's body and carried it to the truck. He drove while Freddy sat cradling the joey. Maude's body lay stretched out across both men's laps.

The first round of beers went very quickly, also the second. They still hadn't eaten, so Paul agreed to pick up the meat pies that were still waiting for them at Newstead's. He decided to walk, as he usually did when he needed some time to himself.

On his return, Paul was puzzled to hear a deep, hearty laugh coming from the shack. Unsure of Freddy's mental state, he opened the door just wide enough to look in. There sat Freddy in his dilapidated reading chair in the far corner of the kitchen. Sitting on his lap, tugging his beard and tickling him was . . . Maude.

"What . . . is . . . going . . . on?" Paul asked in utter bewilderment as he stumbled inside.

"Perfesser, yer just won't believe what happened."

"Try me."

"As soon as yer left, little Maudie here just snapped back to life like nothin' happened. Dunno if she was in shock or playin' dead, but she's full of life right now. She stuffed the joey back in her pouch, headed straight fer the fridge an' got herself a beer."

Paul was close to overdosing on surprises.

Although Freddy remained jovial, Maude's expression became serious. Gingerly, Paul stepped toward her.

"Careful, Perfesser. Somethin' tells me she ain't too happy with you."

When Paul was close enough, he slowly extended his hand to touch her. She backed off for a few seconds. Then, with a speed and force that surprised both men, Maude's hand shot forward and slapped his arm away with a stinging blow.

Paul was stunned. Not by the blow—he half expected that—but by her facial expression. Only someone you've betrayed can look inside you with such hard-eyed intensity that it sears your very soul. He'd only seen that look once before, from Sheila, right before she turned around and silently walked out of his life. In *The Inferno*, Dante said that the spirit of whoever betrays a friend is cast instantly into hell while his earthly body is taken over by a demon. Paul feared that something in him had proven Dante right.

"This day has lasted too long already," Paul said, trying to hide his shame. "Why don't you keep them here for the night? I'll go back to my place and explain to Andrews what's happened. We can pick this up in the morning."

"Fine, but you tell that little bastard that the next hand he lays on Maude gets broken off!"

Paul righted his motorbike, which still lay on its side in Freddy's yard, and headed home. Things were getting out of hand, he realized. In addition to protecting Maude, he'd now have to keep Andrews and Freddy apart. He pulled up to the field station and noticed that the remains of the front door had been propped up to cover part of the doorway. He edged into the front room where Andrews sat at the kitchen table, writing.

Andrews looked up and spoke soberly. "Paul, I'm truly sorry about—"

"Maude's alive and well," Paul broke in. "Seems she was playing possum on us. She's over at Freddy's drinking beer right now."

Andrews leaned back with a rare smile. "Wonderful! We certainly wouldn't want to kill the first and only specimen in captivity."

Paul worried that his boss still referred to Maude as a "specimen," and definitely didn't like thinking of her as "in captivity."

Andrews wasted no time in getting down to business. "I've already started making notes for a press release and an official communiqué we'll publish in *Nature*. I don't dare risk taking the bunyip with me to Sydney just yet, so we can expect some initial skepticism. The x-rays will dispel some of that, but we'll need photos, too. Do you have any?"

"No, but I've got a camera. We can take some shots tomorrow."

"Fine. I'm sure my pilot is back in his bed in Sydney by now. I'll radio word for him to pick me up tomorrow around noon. You'll keep the bunyip here until I can bring some CSIRO officials in to verify our discovery."

Paul liked the plan. As a government agency, the Commonwealth Scientific and Industrial Research Organization not only had clout in the scientific community but could act quickly in the legal arena to ensure that the bunyips were protected from human exploitation.

"What about Freddy? I'd have a hard time taking care of Maude without him."

"We'll hire him on your grant as a research technician. That way, he won't be running all over the country, and we'll have some control over him."

Obviously, Andrews lacked even the slightest understanding of Freddy's nature. But what the hell?

"After the CSIRO people see her, we'll have to let Maude go," Paul said firmly.

"That remains to be seen." Andrews looked at his watch. "It's almost midnight, and we've got a lot of writing to do in the next few hours. I'll cover the anatomical descriptions. Why don't you make us a cup of tea, then get to work on the story of how the bunyip was found?"

After setting a tea billy to boil, Paul retrieved his rusting Underwood from the shelf and went to work. Eight hours later, the pair had assembled a working draft.

Andrews skimmed the typed copy. "Very good, Paul. Now get your camera, and let's take some photos of her."

Paul began to feel ill at ease on the way back to Freddy's. Unattended, Freddy had a way of getting into trouble. Paul hadn't slept since Maude came into his life and was too exhausted to contend with much.

For once, his fears proved unfounded. They entered the kitchen to find Freddy sitting in his chair with Maude on his lap, reading to her about the dietary preferences of rabbit-eared bandicoots. Both had a can of Foster's in hand.

"You've got her drinking beer for breakfast?" Paul asked.

"I never drinks beer before noon, mate," Freddy winked. "Until then, I only has hop juice. And I've cut Maudie here back to half a tube per sitting."

"Good idea. By the way, do bunyips really care what bandicoots eat?"

"I doubts it. I thinks she just likes the sound o' me voice."

Freddy readily agreed to help pose Maude for the photos. For her part, Maude didn't seem to mind as long as Freddy was the only one touching her. After the third roll of film had been shot, Andrews insisted that they take a couple of shots of the joey, whom Freddy had named Alex. Paul hesitated, but Freddy assured them it would be no problem as long as the two men kept their distance. Freddy stroked

Maude's abdomen for a few seconds. The pouch opened and Alex crawled out into his mother's arms while Paul recorded the entire sequence on film.

"Hand me the camera, mate, and I'll get a picture o' the inside of her pouch," Freddy offered. Maude herself held the pouch open for the photo.

Freddy confirmed that there was indeed a dormant joey in there—hairless, pink, and looking very much like a human embryo. Its mouth had fused to one of Maude's two teats, where the men assumed it would remain until Alex left the pouch for good.

Andrews had one final request. "Take a picture of me with the bunyip."

Although clearly displeased, Maude didn't mount a serious protest as long as Freddy kept one hand on her. With the photos done, Andrews turned to the matter of Freddy's employment. Freddy was delighted to accept the offer, since he already spent virtually every free minute helping Paul anyway. The fact that he'd be tripling his income didn't hurt either.

"But we can't hold Maude prisoner forever," Freddy insisted. "We's gotta take her home soon."

"Not until after we've eliminated even the slightest doubt about her existence," Andrews replied.

Two hours later, Andrews boarded the plane back to Sydney.

"Y'know, mate, I jist realized somethin' that bothers me," Freddy said as soon as Andrews had taken off.

"That the only face to appear with Maude in any of those pictures is Andrews'?"

"Yeah."

Paul still felt uneasy when he went to bed that night. But he had to trust Andrews. What choice did he have?

The next day, the two men sat at Freddy's table finishing off another batch of meat pies. Maude had refused hers, as she had any other food offered her. She now sat quietly in the corner staring back at the men.

"I wonder what she does eat?" Paul asked.

Just then an eight-inch lizard scurried across the floor. With astounding speed, Maude sprang to her feet and snatched it with both hands. She bit the head off, then smiled happily while she chewed and swallowed it. She returned to her seat and, nibbling with feminine daintiness, proceeded to consume the entire carcass—bones, skin, claws and all.

"This is just a theory, mind yer," Freddy replied as he turned back to Paul, "but her diet might include small reptiles."

"How do you come up with these brilliant hypotheses?"

"Dunno, mate. It's a gift, I reckon."

Paul was pleased that Maude insisted on catching her own food. It would keep her from growing too dependent on them and make it easier to return her to the wild.

The trio returned to Paul's the next morning so that he could finish his monthly field report while Freddy repaired the front door. Freddy had just finished his task, which included fixing that idiot door so it didn't stick any more, and was getting ready to read to Maude from the *Atlas of Vertebrate Anatomy*. Suddenly Maude dropped her beer and ran into the bedroom, slamming the door behind her.

"Wonder what's gotten into her?" Freddy asked.

The men heard a truck pull up front, then footsteps on the porch. Seconds later the front door swung open and a severed kangaroo head bounced across the kitchen floor, splattering clotted blood in every direction.

"There's twenty more on the truck, Perfesser. Hope yer've gots th' cash handy." Years of sun and hard living were cured into the leather of Nate Townsend's face, aging him well beyond his three and a half decades. In one hand he held the stomach containing the kangaroo's last meal.

"I think Maudie had the right idea," Freddy said, joining her in the bedroom.

"Sounds like you had quite a 'roo shoot," Paul commented to fill the gap.

Nate's face twisted into a scowl. "Yeah, but don't think we does it on yer account, Perfesser. The pittance yer pays us ain't hardly worth the effort of bringin' this shit back to yer."

"Glad to hear it." Paul made no attempt to hide the sarcasm.

'Roo shooting was a fact of life in the Outback, Paul rationalized. And if people were going to kill them anyway, he might as well learn something from their carcasses. The heads provided teeth, from which he could tell the age of the kills. The contents of the stomachs told him what they were eating. By adding his own data to the information available from vegetation maps, Paul hoped to help explain why the grey and red kangaroos were actually increasing in number while most other marsupial populations were declining.

He stepped outside where one of Nate's hired hands, a youth of about twenty, unloaded the gory cargo amidst a swirling blizzard of flies. With lusterless eyes and a thick lower lip overhanging a receding chin, the kid looked utterly devoid of intelligence.

No one was sure exactly how Nate and his crew made their living. Rumor had it that they stole things and rustled livestock, but that had never been proven. It was none of Paul's business in any case. What mattered was that Nate always provided him with useful specimens. Paul needed to match stomachs with the appropriate heads. Usually that meant that he had to tag along on a roo shoot and butcher the carcasses himself. But Nate was so skillful with a knife that, in less than a minute, he could remove an animal's head and stomach without cutting the esophagus connecting them. Born to better circumstances, he might have become famous as an anatomist, neurosurgeon or Mafia hit man. Regardless of what Paul thought of Nate Townsend as a person, he liked the convenience of doing business with him. He reached for his wallet and pulled out three bank notes, which were grudgingly accepted into a blood-caked palm.

Two days later, Freddy and Maude sat in Paul's bedroom listening to the radio as the afternoon news came on.

"We begin this afternoon's program with a remarkable story. University of Sydney Professor Charles Andrews has astounded the scientific world by capturing a creature that was, until today, presumed to be mythical. We take you now to the University of Sydney, where a press conference is about to begin."

"Perfesser, get in here."

Paul pulled back from his microscope, wiped his hands, and stepped into the bedroom.

"I wish to announce my discovery of a new and fantastic life form," Andrews began.

"*His* discovery?" Freddy asked.

"Shhh!"

"Colloquially referred to as the bunyip, this animal is, in fact, a remarkably human-like marsupial. I have just presented evidence of my discovery to officials of the CSIRO, who are here to confirm that, whilst they have not yet seen the bunyip themselves, I have substantially documented its existence."

The two listened in frozen silence as Andrews rambled on.

"He was supposed to bring them CSIRO blokes here before anything was made public," Freddy said at the end of the broadcast. "But then he'd have to share the credit with us. Instead, the bludger stole it all for hisself. Didn't even mention our bloody names."

Paul still wasn't ready to believe he'd been betrayed.

"Maybe he figured that giving out our names would only help others locate the bunyips. After all, he didn't—"

"Belt up, mate. I'm sick o' hearin' yer make excuses fer them blood-suckin' bastards what calls themselves 'intellectuals.' Yer bends over 'cuz yer reckon that's the only way you'll gets yer bloody doctorate. But me, I don't owe them spine-bashers nothin'."

Paul slumped dejectedly in his chair. "Well said," he replied quietly.

Although he didn't quite comprehend it, Paul knew there was a place called the Real World—a place where you didn't worry about tenure, where nobody gave a damn about your publications, and where family obligations were more important than committee assignments. Best of all, it was a place where senior faculty didn't rule like gods. He wasn't sure that Freddy lived in the Real World, but he knew for certain that he, himself, didn't.

Freddy interrupted his thoughts. "Yer know what bothers me most 'bout that news conference? The part where he talked about what keeps the smaller joey dormant: that the mother prob'ly secretes some kind of hormone in her blood that prolongs a bunyip's childhood."

"Yeah! That bothered me too. Must've been the way he said it. Some moron might infer that the hormone, if it even exists, is some kind of youth elixir. I have a feeling that those words are about to cause us a lot of grief."

3

Three days after Andrews' announcement, Paul still hadn't heard from him. What was going on? Did he actually think that Paul and Freddy would just stand by and let him steal the credit? Paul tried repeatedly to contact him, but the professor's secretary said he'd dropped out of sight. She was trying to get in touch with him herself.

Finally, a telegram arrived via the district radio communications base.

"Andrews says he'll be coming to Woolly with five important guests early Tuesday morning. Sounds like you'll have a busy day, Paul," said the familiar voice he recognized as belonging to Sally, one of the operators. Although Paul and Sally had never met, they talked to one another like old friends.

"I'll have plenty to show them."

Tuesday was still five days away. Why the delay?

"By the way, is that the same Professor Andrews who claims to have captured a bunyip?"

"What on earth are you talking about?" He'd always been a rotten liar, so he'd learned to evade.

"Guess you haven't heard. There's a bloke in Sydney who claims to have captured a bunyip. Says it's some kind of human marsupial. Even showed pictures of it on the telly."

"That's the craziest thing I've ever heard," Paul said with a loud and deliberate laugh.

"That's not even the half of it," Sally continued. "The tabloids in Sydney claim that bunyip blood contains some kind of a youth serum, that the professor himself said so."

"Imagine that." He tried to force a laugh, but this time it wouldn't come.

"Say, you're quite the popular fellow, Paul. Someone just handed me another message for you. It's from a Dr. Y. K. Lee. Says he's coming to Woolly this Monday and wants to meet with you."

"Sure it's for me? I don't know anyone by that name."

"It's addressed to Paul McDaniel, care of the Marsupial Ecology Research Project, Woolloona."

Whoever this Dr. Lee character was, Paul had a sick feeling he was looking for bunyips.

Friday morning found Paul at his microscope, examining plant remains from kangaroo stomachs. Maude seemed intrigued when he'd pulled the first stomach out of his fridge, but her curiosity turned to obvious amusement when he opened it with a scalpel and began picking through the contents. She shook her head and turned away from the table with a smirk and a roll of her eyes. Now she sat quietly in the far corner playing with Alex.

Paul would identify the plant fragments, then relay his observations aloud to Freddy, who inscribed them into Paul's field notebooks with an elegant Spencerian script.

"Perfesser, has yer noticed lately—"

"—that we're finishing each other's sentences? No, you're—"

"—imaginin' it. Yeah. 'Cuz otherwise we'd—"

"—be reading each other's minds. And that's—"

"—impossible. Right-o. That's my opinion too, Perfesser."

Paul thought to himself that life had been getting very weird lately.

"Yeah, it is gettin' sorta weird, ain't it?" Freddy said without looking up.

Paul rubbed his neck to ease the mounting tension. Establishing credibility as a scientist was hard enough without involving himself in some kind of psychic mumbo-jumbo.

Monday started badly. Paul's refrigerator, still crammed with the specimens Nate had delivered several days earlier, had stopped working sometime during the night. Paul and Freddy were now scrambling to finish their analysis before the stuff ripened.

The shack already reeked of an odor somewhere between rotting meat and vomit. Paul had opened the windows for ventilation, and swarms of hungry flies now blackened the patched window screens.

Paul paused a moment to wipe the sweat from his face with a bandana. As his eyes closed, he had a vision of a red-haired girl, about six, running across the room. She had bright green eyes and chubby, freckled cheeks. She wore the same blue dress that Freddy had earlier put on Maude. "Hi, Daddy, I'm home!" the girl called out happily. Then she was gone.

Paul looked over at Freddy, who stared off into the distance with a sad, misty-eyed expression.

"Was that Melissa?" Paul asked quietly.

Freddy gave him a bewildered look. "How did yer—?"

"Lotta strange things going on around here," Paul shrugged. He looked over at Maude, who sat quietly on the floor staring back at him, her lips curved in a secretive little smile.

"That was me Melissa, all right," Freddy sighed. "She'll be twelve next week. Ain't seen her in a long, long time."

Paul knew that Freddy's wife disappeared with Melissa

five years earlier. Freddy didn't talk about them much, but the story was common knowledge around Woolloona.

"C'mon, pal, let's take a break," Paul said, heading for the door. A few minutes sitting on the porch might lighten both men's spirits.

Maude stayed inside and used the opportunity to help herself to the beer supply. She'd passed out on Paul's bed by the time the men returned a half hour later.

Just after lunch, there was a knock. Paul opened the door to find a distinguished-looking Oriental man in his mid-40s standing on the front porch. He wore a neatly-pressed white silk suit with a blue dress shirt, open at the neck.

"Good afternoon. I'm Dr. Y.K. Lee," he said in a faultless Oxford accent. "You, I presume, are Mr. McDaniel?"

"Yes, I am," Paul said, extending his hand. Dr. Lee seemed cordial enough, but his dead-fish handshake worried Paul. His dad had always told him to never trust a man with a limp grip, especially a damp one. He invited Lee inside and introduced him to Freddy, who also seemed wary.

"What can we do for you?" Paul asked.

"I'd like to discuss your bunyip."

"My what?" Paul laughed. "Did you say *bunyip*?"

"Oh, come now, Mr. McDaniel. You know what I'm talking about. In fact, I'd wager that the bunyip is probably in the very next room."

"What makes you so sure of all this? Are you one of Professor Andrews' associates?"

"No, just a businessman from Singapore. I was in Sydney at the time Professor Andrews announced his discovery. As soon as I read the newspaper accounts, I decided to find out where the bunyips were."

"What makes you think I know?"

"Simple deduction. Obviously, he didn't discover a

bunyip in his lab in Sydney. In fact, I quickly came to the conclusion that the professor wasn't the one who discovered it at all. The university catalog indicates that he has a full lecture schedule, so it's unlikely that he'd be spending much time in the field. Logically, someone who works for him in the Outback must have made the discovery. So I asked around until I learned which of Andrews' grants currently maintain employees in the field. Turns out that your MERP project was the only one."

Paul and Freddy exchanged worried frowns.

"Okay, let's assume, just for the sake of argument, that there's a bunyip in the back room," Paul evaded. "What's it to you?"

"As I mentioned earlier, I'm a businessman. Although I was trained as a physician in England, I found that the, uh, pharmaceuticals industry, shall we say, was infinitely more profitable than the practice of medicine. Along with other ventures, I developed a supply business—one that provides traditional Chinese folk healers with the various herbs and other ingredients they use in their concoctions. Not exactly the kind of medicine I trained in, but a very profitable one nonetheless. My operation is now the major supplier for herbalists in Chinatowns in every major city in the free world. I've come here because you have something for which a very lucrative market can be created—a *very* lucrative market."

Paul's stomach tightened. "Which is . . . ?"

"Bunyip blood. The word is already being spread that bunyip blood is a modern-day fountain of youth. Those rumors can make you gentlemen rich."

"Surely you don't believe that the blood of—"

"I'm only a merchant, Mr. McDaniel. What I believe has nothing to do with anything. My customers are convinced that powdered rhinoceros horn will cure a variety of ills, and they're willing to pay incredible amounts of money for it. So I sell it to them. Should you have such a horn lying about, I'd gladly buy it for twice your annual salary. But were you to offer me one of the pills that I'd make from that very same horn, I'd laugh in your face."

"I think you'd better leave," Paul warned.

"Whilst yer can still walk," Freddy added.

"Hear me out first," Lee replied. "Humans sell their own blood for money all the time. And everyone benefits, even the donor. We certainly don't want to bleed the bunyip to death. That would be killing the goose that lays the golden egg. All we do is remove a little bit of blood every week. You could even use the money to fund your research. What harm in that?"

Paul slammed his fist against the table, struggling to contain his anger. "The harm is in creating a demand that outstrips the supply. The rhinoceros is nearly extinct thanks to those worthless products you so cynically manufacture from its horn. I'll be damned if I'll help some Chinese snake oil salesman get rich by killing off another species. Now I'd suggest you get out of here very quickly."

"I'm prepared to pay you one hundred dollars per cubic centimeter of blood," Lee continued as if Paul hadn't even interrupted. From his pocket he pulled a small disposable syringe and unsheathed the needle. From another pocket he produced a thick wad of bank notes which he placed on the table. "Think of it. All this cash is yours just for letting me fill this one little syringe."

As he spoke, the bedroom door opened and in stumbled Maude, who was beginning to sober up. She walked over to Freddy and reached for his beer.

He pulled the can away from her. "Yer've had enough."

"And this must be our little goose," Lee said with a grin. "Let me show you how easy it is to get rich."

Lee stepped toward Maude, and Freddy raised out of his chair.

"Back off, Freddy, he's mine!" Paul shouted as he

drove his fist full force into Lee's mouth, knocking the man backward into the opposite wall.

"Easy, Perfesser. That's enough," Freddy said in a calming voice. Freddy had a big man's self-confidence around violent situations, and Paul relied on his judgment to keep confrontations from going too far.

Paul stood in place as Lee got up, pulled a handkerchief from his pocket and began dabbing the blood that dribbled down his chin. Then Paul grabbed the wad of bills from the table and stuffed them inside Lee's shirt, ripping off a couple of buttons in the process.

He pushed Lee ahead of him. "The door is this way."

"Very well, gentlemen," Lee replied. "I understand that unemployment is high around here. I'll have no trouble finding others who aren't as particular about how they make their money. And those others might not be so concerned about the welfare of the bunyips that you're trying so admirably to protect."

When they reached the doorway, Paul shoved Lee hard and sent him sprawling into the dirt. He slammed the door and returned to his chair. For a long moment he and Freddy looked at each other in knowing silence. Maude pulled herself up on Paul's lap and hugged him.

"I won't let anybody hurt you or Alex ever again," he promised, relieved that she'd finally forgiven him. "I hope you understand that."

"She does, mate. She does."

"Yeah, but now what? Lee's right about one thing. There are plenty of people around here who'd be willing to collect bunyip blood for the kind of money he's paying."

Freddy picked up Paul's calculator and began punching in numbers. "Well, let's see. Let's assume that all the bunyips is about Maude's size. Now if a seventy-kilo man has about three an' a half liters o' blood, then someone her size would have . . .

He frowned at the result. "You're right about the

money, Perfesser. At a hundred dollars a cc, ever' bunyip has about a hundred and fifty thousand dollar inventory circulatin' through his veins. People's gonna go to a lotta trouble an' risk for that kinda money. And they ain't gonna stop at fillin' no 10 cc syringe, neither."

An idea dawned on Paul. "Y'know, Freddy, you and I are the only ones so far who know exactly where the bunyips live. Even Andrews has only a vague idea. Maybe if we took Maude home and let her loose, this whole thing might blow over like some UFO sighting."

"True, but Andrews is gonna be here tomorrow with them CSIRO blokes. He'll sack your arse for sure if Maude ain't here."

Silent a long time, Paul considered his options. He had no easy outs. It all boiled down to a choice between his job and his conscience. Without asking, Freddy knew Paul's decision the instant he made it.

"So we're takin' her back then. What about yer research?"

"Been thinking about it lately. I might be able to squeak by and finish my dissertation with the data I already have."

"What if yer can't?"

"The point of getting a Ph.D. isn't just to prove you know a bunch of stuff," Paul replied with grim resolution. "It's also to show that you're capable of figuring things out. If I can't even find a way to finish my degree at this point, then I guess I don't really deserve one."

He winked at Freddy. "Hey, maybe I could get a job as *your* assistant."

"By Gawd, yer've gots the right skills, mate. Yer can sweat an' stink an' drink beer with the best of us."

"And the worst of you. In any case, it's our last chance to put a stop to this shit. Let's get it over with before I change my mind."

The decision didn't sit easy. Paul wasn't a gambler by nature, especially with his career. He resisted the temptation to call Jim Knox, his advisor back in Kansas, for clearance. Paul alone was responsible for undoing the damage, even if it jeopardized his future. He only wished that he could force himself to stop worrying about it.

They went to Newstead's and filled their cooler with ice and beer, and the truck's tank and spare petrol cans with fuel. They also picked up a bag of meat pies and snacks. The billabong lay a good five hours' drive away, and they didn't expect to see any other humans until their return.

Finally, by late afternoon, they were all loaded up. Maude opened the truck door and seated herself on the perch that Paul had created by stuffing a blanket in the space between the bucket seats.

"So tell me about the blonde girl yer've been day-dreamin' about," Freddy said as he pulled himself behind the wheel.

"What girl?"

"Dunno her name, mate. But lately, whenever yer stare off in the distance, like yer always doin', I get a mental picture o' this blonde girl. She's a real beaut with a big set o' knockers. She's got an Aussie accent, an' says things like, 'I love you, Paul.' Who is she?"

Paul looked at Freddy in wide-eyed wonder. "You . . . can . . . see . . . ?"

"Jist like yer saw me Melissa th' other day. Like yer says, mate, lotta strange things goin' on these days. Now if we was—"

"—going crazy, we'd be spouting some nonsense that the bunyip—"

"—might have somethin' to do with this. But we ain't—"

"—losing our minds. We're just experiencing—"

"—a lotta unusual coincidences. Right-o, Perfesser. So yer gonna tell me about 'er?"

"Her name's Sheila, and it's a long story."

"Good, 'cuz we gots a long drive ahead of us. Go get a coupla beers from the back, then come tell me 'bout Sheila."

Paul retrieved the beers and started to close the hatch.

"Oh, Perfesser?"

"Yeah?"

"Bring a couple fer me too."

Paul returned with an armload of beers. He was smiling, his mind already drifting back to a simpler, happier time. "We met during our junior year at the University of Kansas. It amazed me that anyone could be that pretty. She didn't even wear makeup. She was a big girl, almost as tall as me, and she had shoulder-length blond hair, piercing blue eyes, and breasts that—I swear to God!—defied gravity. But I didn't pay much attention to her at first. I figured she was so far out of my league that . . . well, why torture myself? Besides, everyone said she was a lesbian because she avoided men and never went anywhere without this other girl, Bronwyn, at her side. The two of them had been together since high school, and Bronwyn was the only real friend Sheila had. See, Bronwyn was the first to figure out that Sheila wasn't the prick teaser everyone assumed she was back then . . ."

* * *

The only child of an Outback couple who lived a hard scrabble existence raising a few head of sheep, Sheila Mayor grew up a loner in a place where self-reliance was paramount. Like most children of Outback graziers, she did her first eight years of schooling in her own living room over a two-way radio. The lessons came from the School of the Air, broadcast from the district communications base of the Royal Flying Doctor Service.

Sheila never really knew anyone her own age until, at her parents' heartbroken insistence, she moved in with her aunt and uncle to attend high school in the large mining town of Silver Hill. Money was tight for the family, especially her aunt and uncle who were on pension, and Sheila wasn't able to buy school uniforms as fast as she outgrew them. And the sight of her increasingly voluptuous figure straining against the seams of skin-tight clothing forced the already volatile glands of her male classmates into warp drive. The boys assumed that her tight clothing was a deliberate effort to titillate them, and responded with crude come-ons and cruder jokes. This, in turn, fostered jealousy and hatred from the girls. Even her first name, Aussie slang for any pretty girl, became a weapon against her. Already shy, Sheila retreated further into herself. Her withdrawal was misinterpreted by her peers as aloofness. In the middle of more people than she'd ever seen before, this bashful little girl from the country had never been more alone.

Bronwyn Thompson was Sheila's opposite and fellow outcast. Tall, big-boned, boisterous and unmercifully oversexed, Bronwyn craved the kind of attention that Sheila tried to avoid. Yet her uncanny resemblance to an overweight Mick Jagger was something of a hindrance to such ambitions.

Far from being resentful of Sheila's striking appearance, Bronwyn saw the potential for exploiting it. She already understood that the pubescent male was a slave driven by two deceptively harmless-looking glands that dangled ever so innocently between his legs. Yet those nefarious little hormone factories, having only recently learned their craft, now worked with maniacal obsession dumping their prurient excretions into the bloodstream. The inevitable build-up of these obscene concoctions led to a condition similar to that of an engine cylinder filled with fuel and compressed air. All that was needed was a spark to set the piston in motion.

Once this process had started, the boys were driven by such dire biological imperatives that few dared be choosy about how they released the overpowering forces from within. And Bronwyn simply wanted to help them vent some pressure. Unfortunately, she wasn't able to produce the spark needed to get things going. That was where Sheila came in.

The idea for a partnership occurred to Bronwyn when she watched Sheila take a stretch in algebra one day. Sheila pulled her shoulders back with her arms behind her head and yawned. An innocent maneuver, but the force of her breasts pushing against the already too-tight bodice sent a button flying across the room. Sheila immediately turned crimson and bent over her desk, pretending not to notice. But the two boys on either side of her did notice. They leered and smirked with the obnoxiousness peculiar to adolescent males. At the same time, they put their books in their laps to hide the growing bulges in their pants. After class, Bronwyn noticed that those boys were the last to leave their seats. When they finally did get up, both continued to hold their books in the same strategic position.

Bronwyn immediately struck up a friendship with Sheila, and invited her to spend the weekend. Sheila accepted, seeming surprised that the first person to befriend her would be the richest girl in school. Sheila might not have accepted so readily had she known that the weekend would be spent without adult supervision. Bronwyn's mother was dead, and her father was out of the country on business, as he usually was. This lack of supervision allowed Bronwyn the freedom to fine-tune her already remarkable propensities for mischief.

Sheila was awed by the massive red brick home. It was the first time in her life that she'd slept in a building that wasn't covered with corrugated tin. The private swimming pool was something she'd only seen before in movies. On Saturday morning, Bronwyn announced that one of their classmates, Bruce, would be joining them for a swim that afternoon.

"Not that awful boy who always stares at my chest?" Sheila asked in horror.

"Well, yeah, but don't worry. I'll take care of him."

What Bronwyn didn't tell her was that she'd tried to get Bruce over on several occasions, and he only accepted this time because Sheila was going to be there.

As they prepared to go swimming, Sheila noticed that the top to her suit no longer fit. Not to worry, Bronwyn assured her, handing her a white tee-shirt.

"This is even better," Sheila said as she pulled the shirt over her bare chest. "Now Bruce won't be able to see my bosom quite as well."

"That's right," Bronwyn replied. If Sheila didn't know what happened to white cotton when it got wet, that was her problem.

Bruce arrived in the middle of the afternoon. He was a reasonably attractive boy to those not put off by his complexion. While the trio romped and played around the pool for several hours, Sheila seemed unaware that Bruce could observe every detail of her bosom through her shirt. She jumped and played and wrestled with him like some vision out of his wet dreams. Bronwyn realized that this was no doubt the first opportunity Sheila ever had to cavort like the teenager she was. She seemed to enjoy it thoroughly. She even joined in when Bronwyn brought out the beer.

When darkness came, Bronwyn made a suggestion that she dearly hoped Sheila couldn't handle. "Let's skinny dip," she said, then pulled off her suit and dumped it by the side of the pool.

"Good idea." Bruce did likewise and looked hopefully at Sheila.

"I . . . I . . . have to go to the dunny," Sheila stammered. She pulled herself out of the water and headed for the bathroom.

"I hope she'll be back," Bruce said.

"I'm sure she won't. After all, she's a good girl." Bronwyn came up beside Bruce and pressed a firm, bare breast against him. "I, on the other hand, am a bad girl . . . "

"You did that on purpose," Sheila said scornfully after the boy left. "You just wanted me here so you could lure Bruce over. The minute my back was turned, you had sex with him."

"Did you want to screw him?"

"Of course not."

"Then what are you worried about?" Bronwyn shrugged. "Look, you've had a great time today. Don't say you haven't. Nobody pushed you to do anything you didn't wanna do. If I screwed a boy you don't even like, so what?"

"You're awfully bloody sure of yourself, aren't you?"

"Maybe so. But the way I see it, we're both unpopular, even if it is for different reasons, and we both need a friend. You and I could have a lotta fun together. And as wild as things might get, you don't have to worry about losin' your cherry till you're ready. If a boy gets too hot and bothered for your liking, I'll be only too glad to take him off your hands."

"What about my reputation?"

Bronwyn's eyes narrowed slyly. "What good has it done you so far? Look, you can either have a good reputation and a rotten time or a rotten reputation and a great time. I mean, what's the reward? A tombstone that says 'Here lies Sheila Mayor. She died a good, proper virgin?' Know what mine's gonna say? 'Here lies a slut. We had to cremate her to wipe the smile off her face!'"

Sheila's ever-serious expression froze at the sheer audacity of Bronwyn's remark. Finally, a smirk began. Which became an embarrassed giggle. Which grew to a laugh that she couldn't conceal even with both hands clasped over her mouth.

Sensing victory, Bronwyn closed in for the kill. "Y'know, you'd definitely benefit from some bad influence."

Sheila could barely restrain her laughter. "And I reckon you'll provide plenty of that."

"The dinkie-die worst in the whole world. I swear to it."

Thus had begun an improbable friendship that would last a lifetime . . .

* * *

"So how'd two Outback lasses wind up at the University of Kansas?" Freddy asked.

"During their senior year in high school, when Bronwyn's father was out of town as usual, they sponsored a pool party for the boy's rugby team. All it took was the sight of Sheila in a bathing suit to start the hormones flowing, and Bronwyn did all the rest. Three days later, when the boys went to take their morning piss, they found their little dicks plugged with pus."

Freddy roared with laughter, shaking so hard that he nearly drove the truck off the trail. Paul had to steady the wheel with one hand until he regained control. "So Bronwyn gave the entire team a dose of the clap?" he asked at last.

"Yeah. Her old man was pretty upset too. Decided to get rid of her by sending her to a college as far away as he could find. He'd have probably put her in the University of Ulan-Bator if the Mongolians would have had her. He finally settled on Kansas. When Bronwyn refused to go without Sheila, he offered to pay Sheila's way through college as long as Bronwyn agreed not to come home for four years."

"So is that how yer met Sheila? Bronwyn used her as bait to reel yer in for herself?"

"Not exactly." A sad longing now weighed on Paul.

"So tell me how yer met 'er, then."

"Another time. Right now, I'm hungry."

Paul reached into the bag and pulled out a meat pie. To both men's surprise, Maude did likewise. Paul demonstrated how to take a bite and suck the gravy out, and Maude followed suit.

"So little Maudie's developed a proper Aussie taste for meat pies," Freddy observed.

"God knows why. Personally, I'd rather eat raw lizards. It's just that meat pies are easier to catch."

Paul was amused, but also disturbed by Maude's mimicry. She was getting entirely too familiar with humans for her own good.

"Here we are, mate. Maudie's billabong," Freddy said at long last. Just ahead, lit by the truck's headlights, the trail they'd been following passed through a thicket.

The empty beer cans in the camper rolled and clanked as the truck came to a stop. Nobody had kept count of the beer consumption, but none of the three was feeling any pain. Still, Freddy suggested that they toast each other with one more. Paul walked around to the rear of the truck, opened the hatch, and dug a beer out of the ice chest. The three of them passed it around. Then Freddy led the way through the trees until they were standing at the very place where he first found Maude.

"Let's get this over with before we're all blubberin' like babies," Freddy said.

"I'm gonna miss you, Maude," Paul whispered as she returned his farewell hug.

"Me too," Freddy said when his turn came. "You take good care o' yerself, little lady."

But after the hugs, Maude simply stood with her hands behind her back, smiling at them.

"Go back where you came from. Leave." Paul ordered.

Maude responded with a quizzical look.

"You're free. Go."

She wrinkled her forehead in confusion.

Paul turned her about by the shoulders, then gave her a little push and a light slap on the bottom. "Go, damn it!"

Finally, with a shrug, Maude headed into the scrub and disappeared.

"You drive home," Freddy said.

They walked back to the truck. Paul closed the camper hatch and slid into the driver's side. He turned the truck around, then braked suddenly.

"Did you see that?" Paul asked.

"See what?"

"Over there." Paul pointed off to one side. "I thought I saw a flash of red, like the reflector on a tail light."

"I think yer eyes is playin' tricks on yer, Perfesser. There ain't another car or truck within fifty miles of us."

"I guess you're right." Paul tried to suppress his uneasiness. He took off again, fresh doubts creeping into his mind. Would Maude, or any of the bunyips, be safe in the wild anymore? Or would the recent publicity destroy their world forever? Paul forced himself to concentrate on keeping the truck centered in the tracks.

Between the beer, the nagging doubts, and the emotional burnout, it was hard to tell right from wrong anymore. It would be even harder to tell Andrews what had happened. More than anything, Paul needed sleep.

It was daylight by the time they made Woolloona. They'd stopped along the way and slept a couple of hours on the blankets Freddy kept rolled up behind the seats.

Paul dropped Freddy off at his place and went to the field station, hoping to grab a quick shower before he had to confront Andrews and company. No such luck. He turned the radio on to find that the pilot was already trying to contact him. The plane was approaching the airstrip.

He arrived just as Andrews and companions had finished unloading their gear.

"This is my graduate assistant, Paul McDaniel," Andrews said as Paul emerged from the truck. Andrews appeared almost jovial, and Paul dreaded the change in mood he was about to create. Perhaps he should just quit on the spot and get the hell out of there right now.

"Gentlemen," Andrews continued, "one of you can squeeze in up front with Paul and me. The rest of you will have to get in back for the short ride to the field station. Now, Paul, I'll introduce you around in just a minute. But first, where's the bunyip?"

Paul cleared the very throat he was about to slit.

"Well, Professor Andrews, some things have happened recently."

"What things?" Andrews demanded. "No, never mind. Just tell me this: Where's the bunyip?"

"She's . . . she's . . . "

"She's right here," said one of Andrew's companions cheerfully.

Paul turned around to observe that the man had just opened the camper hatch and was peering inside. Paul rushed over. Sure enough, there was Maude, sprawled out amid the empty beer cans. He remembered leaving the camper hatch open while he and Freddy set Maude free. Apparently, she'd just doubled back and crawled right in with the beer supply.

He closed his eyes and shook his head. He'd been spared the immediate crisis, but that only left a much larger one waiting somewhere down the line. What words could express the combination of relief and horror he felt at this moment?

* * *

At Newstead's Hotel and Bar, a guest room door opened in response to a knock.

"I've found out what yer wanted to know," said Nate Townsend. He grinned broadly as Dr. Lee reached for his wallet.

4

The deadliest thing in Australia, Paul had discovered, was the hospitality. Sure, Australian waters were home to the great white shark. Yes, there were man-eating crocodiles, two kinds of deadly spiders and God knows how many venomous snakes. They all took their toll. But the sane needed little guile to avoid such obvious perils.

Hospitality, on the other hand, was a subtle killer made all the more insidious by the Aussie's custom of sharing his vices. He didn't just have a smoke. He passed the pack around so that his mates, too, could spend their final days in an oxygen tent coughing up little bits of putrefied lung tissue. When it came to alcohol, an Aussie didn't just buy himself a drink. He bought a round of cirrhosis for his mates' livers too. Not just one round, mind you. No self-respecting Aussie escaped his mates' relentless camaraderie until ready to stagger off in search of a logical place to puke. Such rigorously enforced merriment made nonsmokers and nondrinkers, who were incessantly forced to reject their mates' lethal generosity, conspicuously antisocial. Smoking and drinking in Australia were not sins, but vital symbols of one's commitment to lay waste to health and sanity in the name of fellowship. In Australia, and especially here in the lonely Outback, hospitality was the ultimate carnivore.

Little Maude was the latest to be consumed. After less

than two weeks among humans, she'd forsaken her birthright of freedom and independence among her own kind for beer and meat pies at Freddy's. Now she sat in the back of Freddy's truck awaiting the probing inquiries of the CSIRO agents, and Paul wondered what she would sacrifice next.

He and Andrews were alone in the front seat on the drive back to the field station, since all five of their guests insisted on riding in back with Maude.

Paul took advantage of the privacy to confront Andrews. He spoke calmly, hiding his anger until he'd heard his boss out. "I noticed that Freddy's and my names—"

"—weren't on the news reports," Andrews interrupted. "I know, and I'm sorry about that. But I got to thinking about things on the way to Sydney. If I gave out your names, everyone in Woolloona would know where the bunyips are. And they'd tell. Next thing you know, everyone on earth would know where to find the bunyips. Imagine what would happen next. We have to keep the two of you out of the public eye until we can protect the bunyips from the added publicity."

It was a logical explanation and the one Paul had anticipated. He thought back to Freddy's earlier comments. He'd called Andrews a "spine-basher"—a parasite.

"Don't worry, Paul. You'll both get credit for your efforts in the scientific literature, where it really matters. I've already given you first authorship for the *Nature* communiqué, and Freddy's name is second. Your names will also appear first on the articles that follow."

This revelation left Paul thoroughly confused. First authorship of the scientific articles was no minor concession, and would provide Paul with exactly the career boost he needed. No question about that. Was it just a sop to keep him and Freddy quiet so that Andrews could continue to monopolize the coverage in the popular press?

There was no way of determining Andrews' motive, Paul decided. He pulled the truck in front of the field station.

All he and Freddy could do was act in the bunyips' best interests. At this point, even that would be hard to assess.

As soon as the truck had been unloaded, Paul headed over to pick up Freddy. His friend awaited him on the front porch and, judging from his expression, was already aware of the situation. Eventually, they were going to have to sort out the nature of their mind-link.

"I dunno what to do, neither," Freddy said in answer to Paul's unspoken question.

"Now that the others have seen the bunyip, everything is pretty much out of our hands," Paul surmised.

"Yeah. Reckon we'll just have to go back to yer place an' see what them gov'ment blokes has in mind."

For three long, busy days the CSIRO scientists and naturalists crawled over one another like ants in the tiny field station. Maude was allowed enough beer to keep her mildly tranquilized while the agents measured and photographed every conceivable detail. After a complete medical exam, they took a wax impression of her teeth, samples of her hair and blood, scrapings from the inside of her cheek, fingernail parings and, whenever she took a crap, they even scooped that up and put it in a jar. Of course, everyone wanted a photo of himself with Maude sitting on his lap and Alex peeping out of the pouch.

Maude remained complacent through it all, even when Andrews touched her. Maybe it was just the beer, but Paul could also sense a generally benign attitude among the gathering, something they used to call "good vibrations." Maybe Maude felt it too. In fact, he realized, she might be the one transmitting her own feelings of well-being to him. He thought about the tearing pain he'd felt in his own abdomen when Andrews had tugged too hard on Maude's pouch. Scientifically it made no sense, but neither did a lot of other things that were going on.

He and Freddy told the others about Dr. Lee and the outrageous price he was offering for bunyip blood. The team showed concern, but pointed out that the country's animal protection laws would automatically cover the bunyips, regardless of whether or not they were officially recognized by the scientific community. Still greater safety was assured as long as no one knew where or how to capture them. Paul and Freddy realized that Andrews would probably use this threat as an excuse to keep them out of the public eye forever, but they wouldn't argue the point if it meant jeopardizing the bunyips. In any case, it was concluded, the CSIRO could always arrange to have state wildlife inspectors patrol the area where the bunyips lived if there was any evidence of poaching. Right now, such a premature move could backfire by drawing attention to the creature's home range.

To avoid attracting notice from the odd passing vehicle, the team stayed crammed inside the field station, dripping sweat on each other by day and sleeping on the floor at night. For the outside observer, about the only thing different at Paul's was the unusual number of meat pies and beers that he and Freddy had been picking up from Newstead's.

The team leader was Clarence Richmond, head of the CSIRO's Division of Wildlife Research. A tall, lean and balding man in his fifties, Clarence had light brown eyes that reflected a certain inherent kindness. Paul and Clarence had taken an instant liking to each other. Clarence had a doctorate in biology himself, and Paul was flattered by the interest he expressed in the progress of Paul's dissertation research.

It was late afternoon on the third day when the team finished its work and began packing its gear.

"Well, I reckon it's time for you to take us back to the plane," said one of them. "Most of us still have to catch connections to Canberra once we get to Sydney."

"Once we get you off, we're taking Maude back home and releasing her," Paul said staunchly. Whether the others concurred or not, Paul and Freddy had already made that decision, and it was not negotiable.

"No way," Andrews responded. "We can't let her go yet. I'm still negotiating with *National Geographic* for a film on—"

"Forget it, Charles," Clarence Richmond interrupted. "Paul's right. Our job is primarily to protect wildlife, not just study it. We've put our little friend here through enough, and it's time to send her home."

Watch what you say, Freddy. Don't taunt Andrews, Paul thought. He fought back a smile of delight that Maude was headed home, and he wouldn't be taking the heat for it.

Freddy cast an understanding glance back, then said coyly, "Well, Dr. Richmond, I reckon yer the boss."

Andrews argued fervently against the decision, insisting that Maude was too valuable to science to be let go so early. Clarence would not be dissuaded. Paul and Freddy were to take Maude back the following day, and Paul would confirm to Clarence by radio as soon as she'd been released.

Andrews was in a surly mood on the way back to the airstrip. The louder he bitched, the harder Paul had to fight back a smile. Finally, the entire crew was loaded and off to Sydney. No sooner had their plane left the ground than a second plane, which had been parked at the end of the airstrip, started warming its engines. Paul had just opened the truck door when the van owned by George Newstead, owner of the hotel and bar, pulled up. Nothing unusual in that. George often ferried people between the airstrip and his hotel. Then Paul's stomach knotted when the passenger door opened and out stepped Dr. Lee.

"Good evening, Mr. McDaniel," Lee called cheerfully. "You'll be happy to know, you shan't be seeing me again. My own work here is finished."

"I doubt you'll be missed," Paul replied as he eased into the truck. The knot in his stomach tightened. What did Lee mean by "my own work is finished?" What was the reason behind his good humor? More importantly, what was in that large cardboard box that George loaded onto the plane along with Lee's suitcase?

Paul returned to the field station to find Freddy pacing the porch in obvious distress.

"It's that bloody Chinaman, ain't it?"

"Yeah, and he seemed pretty goddamn pleased with himself."

"Any idea why?"

"No, but I have a feeling that if we don't—"

"—get Maude home in a hurry, we never will. Right-o."

They decided to leave early the next morning. Although that would mean driving through the heat of the day, it would be easier to avoid being followed. Any moving vehicle would kick up a dust plume that could be sighted for miles in daylight. To be on the safe side, they'd forget about beer this trip and bring only water and soft drinks.

Maude had developed an interest in books of late, or at least in those with pretty pictures of other animals. When she was sober enough, she'd often peruse the bookshelves looking for nature photos. Frauca's *Australian Mammals in the Wild* was one of her favorites, so Paul brought it along for their last ride together.

Dawn came in a brilliant burst of reds upon reds that spilled across the still landscape, starkly illuminating the distant sandstone outcroppings against the hard outlines cast by their fleeting shadows. The Outback always struck Paul as hauntingly beautiful and inviting when seen by first light in the early morning cool. Within hours, the desert would be consumed by a heat of such blinding intensity that the very air itself seemed to melt, dissolving the horizon behind a shimmering veil of ripples. Yet for this one brief moment, heaven and hell seemed united.

Freddy drove, stopping every fifteen or twenty minutes for Paul to stand on top of the cab and scan the horizon with binoculars, looking for any sign of followers. Maude sat in her usual place in the middle, leafing through the book and pointing out pictures to Alex, who sat on her lap. They seemed to find the bats hilarious, pointing those photos out to each other with breathy little laughs that sounded oddly like cat sneezes.

Although neither man mentioned it, they shared a sickening feeling that they were too late, that their previous actions had already destroyed any chance for Maude and Alex to return to their normal lives.

"So tell me some more 'bout Sheila, Perfesser."

Paul figured that Freddy was looking for conversation, any conversation, that would distract his thoughts. So was Paul. "Where'd we leave off?"

"We'd got Sheila an' her mate, Bronwyn, to the University of Kansas. Yer was about to explain how yer and Sheila got together."

"Oh, yeah." Paul's mind drifted back again to his undergraduate days. "I owe it all to my roommate back then, this psychopath named Jacques. If it weren't for his twisted mind, Sheila would never have been more than another classmate to me. But Jacques, you gotta understand, saw life from a *very* unusual perspective . . . "

* * *

Jacques Denis Diderot Desbien had decided on a career in espionage at the age of twelve and worked resolutely at building the many skills his profession would require: languages, electronics, explosives manufacturing, weaponry and almost anything involving destruction. By the time he graduated from high school, he'd built up a thriving business in the black market gun trade and could assemble five different makes of machine gun from a bag of parts while blindfolded.

The son of a retired French military officer and an Arab mother, Jacques grew up fluent in both languages. He was a scrawny kid with dark, deep-set eyes, a hawkish nose, and a brooding intensity vaguely reminiscent of a youthful Ralph Nader. Clearly out of place in his central Kansas home town of Great Bend, Jacques realized that his fascination with death and violence made him suspect to anyone he allowed too close. Although he lived little more than a half-hour's drive from Paul's home town, the farming community of La-Crosse, the two might just as well have been raised on opposite sides of the ocean.

Jacques rejected his early image as a nerd in high school and instead adopted a black leather jacket and tried to come across as a tough—although he was equally out of place with the legitimate toughs. The girls in high school found something at once frightening and alluring about this mysterious young man, and Jacques' social life consisted of occasional brief encounters with a series of young women, each of whom quickly departed without ever saying why.

Jacques and Paul were assigned to the same dormitory room during their freshman year at college. Although he was aghast at Jacques' habit of sleeping with an Uzi under his pillow, Paul never squealed on his roommate for flouting dorm regulations. About the only way Jacques could get him to complain at all was by aiming his deer rifle out the window as if he intended to shoot someone.

Jacques, accustomed to aggravating the shit out of everyone around him, became exasperated with Paul's live-and-let-live tolerance of bizarre behavior. After a month of enduring relentless acceptance, Jacques decided to take action. He was lounging on his bed, toying with a switchblade while Paul sat reading at the desk across the room. Jacques studied the situation carefully, then pitched the knife. His aim was perfect, the blade hitting with a "thock" squarecenter in the oak slat back of Paul's chair. Had the knife landed an inch to either side, it would have embedded itself in Paul's ribcage. Jacques grinned menacingly as Paul turned around.

The attempted provocation didn't work. Paul simply observed the blade, shrugged and replied, "Nice shot," then turned back to his work.

Jacques sensed a sad resignation in the voice, and wondered if Paul even cared whether he lived or died. Painfully shy and quiet, Paul usually kept to himself and seemed almost grateful when anyone went to the effort of saying Hello to him. He generally ate alone at the cafeteria, then returned to the room to read or stare silently out the window. Jacques suddenly became as aware of his roommate's loneliness as he was of his own.

Giving in to his obsessive-compulsive streak, he realized that the time had come to either make friends with Paul or kill him. The decision wasn't easy, but he finally decided that disposing of a body involved an awful lot of fuss.

"You study too much. Let's go the Jayhawk Cafe and have a drink."

Paul seemed startled. "Gosh . . . I'd like to. But I'm only eighteen and—"

"No, you're actually twenty-three." Jacques pulled a Polaroid from a box under his bed. "In a few minutes you'll have the driver's license to prove it. Now smile."

That night at the cafe was the first time the two had exchanged more than a few sentences, and Jacques was surprised by how much he enjoyed Paul's company. Paul not only proved to be a genial conversationalist, but seemed interested in almost everything. He had a knack for asking the very question Jacques wanted to answer next.

That Saturday they went trapshooting together and Paul amazed his new friend with his dead-eye accuracy, not just breaking the clay pigeons but blasting them to powder.

The next weekend they went out drinking again. Two vaguely pretty women caught Jacques' eye, and he introduced himself as an exchange student from Paris who needed to practice his English. He brought them back to the booth where an obviously embarrassed Paul was sitting.

"Thees ees my roommate, Paul. Hee's a good fellow, but rather—how you say?—shy." Then to the short-haired brunette in tight jeans and halter top. "Perhaps, Ramona, you weell seet weeth heem?"

Paul stammered a greeting as the girl slid in next to him until her hip pressed firmly against his.

"Boy, you are bashful, aren't you?" Ramona said with a smile. "That's all right. I like shy guys."

After a couple of scotches, Ramona draped her hand across Paul's thigh and whispered, "I'll bet you're a virgin, aren't you?"

Jacques, who'd read her lips, winked at his roommate. Paul reddened and turned away.

"That's okay," Ramona continued, leaning closer to kiss his ear. "I'm a great teacher."

She must have been. When Paul finally made it back to the dorm the following afternoon, he wore the kind of expression that only comes to one who's been played, splayed, laid, dry cleaned and steam pressed.

Jacques and Paul discovered a surprising mutual benefit in each other's company. Jacques demolished Paul's shell of introversion, finally forcing him to develop some poise in social situations. And with a rational friend like Paul willing to sit up all night talking him through his psychotic episodes, Jacques strengthened his tenuous grasp on reality. They moved to an apartment that summer and remained roommates another two and a half years.

During their junior year, when they were in the same chemistry class as Sheila and Bronwyn, Jacques fixated on Sheila and made up his mind to lay her. Sheila was always polite, but showed no interest in his overtures. Even worse for Jacques was the fact that Bronwyn, who never seemed to leave Sheila's side, did respond and tried to pick up on his deflected flirtations. This intimidated Jacques because Bronwyn was considerably larger and stronger than he. She'd taken an interest in track as a freshman, and was then the

Big Eight Conference women's shot-put champion. In the process, she'd developed a pair of shoulders that were the envy of the football team.

Jacques had heard the rumors that the two women were lesbian lovers, but that didn't seem to ring true. Sheila seemed more shy than cold, and Bronwyn definitely projected a heterosexual interest in him. He figured that Sheila was holding back because she didn't want to compete with Bronwyn for the same guy. If he could divert Bronwyn's interest to someone else—Paul, for example—he could get in closer to Sheila. He devised a scheme.

"Why don't we invite those two girls who sit next to us in chemistry over for a study session?" he asked Paul before class one day.

"Fine with me, but I doubt they'd come. Let's face it. Sheila's out of your league and mine too. And I doubt that Bronwyn's the one you're interested in."

"Actually, the girls are very friendly and outgoing. I talk to them all of the time. The problem is you. You're so standoffish that they think you don't like them. They told me so themselves."

"Huh?"

"It's true, Paul. Bronwyn is convinced that you don't like her. I think Sheila wants to know you better, but she won't come over until you make up with Bronwyn."

"Make up with her? I've hardly even spoken to her!"

"Exactly my point. How can you make friends when you treat people that way?"

"All right, cut the bullshit," Paul said in exasperation. "I know you. You're not going to tell me what's really happening, yet you're gonna drive me crazy until I go along with it. So save us both some time and tell me what to do."

"Be nice to the ladies, Paul, and invite them over. All you have to do is write a quick little note to Bronwyn. Just say, 'Jacques and I would like you and Sheila to join us at our apartment for a study session Thursday night.' Then sign it. I'll even save you the embarrassment of delivering it. I'll give it to Bronwyn myself."

"I'm just curious enough to participate in this idiotic stunt so I can find out what you're *really* up to," Paul conceded as he wrote the note and tore it from his pad.

"Of course you are." Jacques pocketed the note.

Immediately before class, Jacques passed a note to Bronwyn. But this one said: "Dear Bronwyn, I'm really attracted to you, but I'm too shy to tell you in person. Yet I can't keep my feelings for you quiet any longer. I'd like you to come over to my apartment Thursday evening around seven. Unfortunately, my roommate, Jacques, will be there. Why don't you bring your own roommate over to keep him busy while you and I get to know each other better? (signed) Paul McDaniel."

Jacques had correctly assumed that Bronwyn was horny enough to comply. In fact, she and Sheila were about to invite him over for their own little game of bait-and-switch. Jacques' only mistake had been in underestimating Bronwyn's guile.

"I read your note, Paul," Bronwyn said sweetly after class. "We'd love to come over, but you didn't give us an address. Why don't you write it out for me?"

Paul complied, and Bronwyn noted that his handwriting was different from that on her note. Out of the corner of her eye she saw Jacques coming up beside her. She turned quickly and, hitting his shoulder with her own, sent his books flying.

"So sorry," she said as she helped him gather them back up. She picked up Jacques' notebook, opening it to examine his handwriting.

"Now what are we going to do?" Sheila asked as she and Bronwyn walked home.

"We're going over to their apartment. I'm going to find

out exactly what Jacques is up to. I reckon he's trying to pull a fast one on all of us, including Paul."

"That's too bad. I really like Paul. He seems like such a nice person. He's one of the few men I've met who looks me in the eye instead of the chest when he talks to me."

"They're both pretty cute too. Here's what we're gonna do . . ."

The girls arrived promptly at seven that Thursday. After studying half an hour, Sheila went to the kitchen for more coffee and Jacques followed.

"Sheila, do you know the real reason why you and I are here?" Jacques asked.

"I'm sure you'll tell me."

"Paul has the hots for Bronwyn, but he's too shy to just come out and say it. We had to be here to help him break the ice. Now that they're getting along so well, maybe we should give them some privacy. Why don't we go over to your apartment?"

"I have a better idea," Sheila purred as she stroked Jacques' chest. "Let's just go in your bedroom and make ourselves comfortable."

Jacques was astounded that his plan had worked so well so quickly. Sheila followed Jacques, turning out all of the lights as she entered his bedroom. Jacques embraced her, but she pushed him back. "Let's cut the preliminaries and just have sex. I'll go in the bathroom and get ready while you undress here. Meet you in bed!"

Jacques eagerly complied. Minutes later the bathroom door reopened and he felt a warm, bare body ease into bed next to him. It was pitch black, but Jacques preferred to navigate by touch anyway. He moved aggressively onto his bed mate only to discover that the body below him was quite a bit larger than expected. A pair of massive thighs closed around him, and it was too late to ask questions.

Sheila, who'd traded places with Bronwyn in the bathroom that bridged the two bedrooms, returned to the living area. A hollow, popping sound came from Jacques' room.

"What was that?" asked Paul, still sitting at the table.

"Must be Jacques' back." Sheila smiled demurely. "Bronwyn volunteered to work on it for him."

"I didn't know Jacques had back problems."

A muffled scream rose from the bedroom.

"He does now."

* * *

A reminiscent smile tugged at Paul's lips.

"So what happened to Jacques?" Freddy asked.

"Bronwyn nearly tore him in half. Here's the weird part. Even though she'd only been trying to teach him a lesson, they both wound up claiming it was the best sex they'd ever had. They started going together after that."

"Is that when yer started datin' Sheila?"

"Not exactly. Jacques and Bronwyn spent most of the next two years in bed over at her apartment. Sheila couldn't concentrate over all the screaming, so she started coming over to my apartment to study. We talked a lot and, before long, we were hanging around together. Got to be really good friends. Next thing I knew, she was sleeping nights in Jacques' unused room. Just before Christmas our senior year, she moved in with me altogether. It was still platonic almost to the last. She'd told me from the start that the main reason she felt so comfortable around me was that I never tried to come on to her. I just took it for granted that she had no romantic interest in me and put it out of my mind. Little did I know that she was the one who—"

"Yer'll have to tell me the rest later, Perfesser, 'cuz we's comin' up on Maude's billabong pretty quick. Just in case somebody's followin' us, I'm only gonna stop long enough to let Maude out. You get up an' scout around just like yer has been. Then we'll keep goin' straight for a few more miles an' circle the long way 'round. That way, even somebody who's followin' ain't gonna know where we let 'er off. We's gonna cross a bare sandstone bar where we can stop an' not leave no footprints by the road."

Paul looked down at Maude. She'd already tucked Alex out of view, and her expression seemed worried. More than worried—upset. The truck stopped, and she gave each of the men a quick hug, then scampered over Paul's lap and out the door. She seemed to understand about not leaving footprints, since she walked along the bar all the way to the brush, where she quickly disappeared. Paul climbed on top of the cab but still didn't sight anything. After less than a minute, the truck was again underway.

"Maude couldn't wait to get away this time," Freddy said. "S'pose she was upset with us?"

"No, and you don't either. We're both thinking the same thing and—"

"—just don't wanna admit to ourselves that little Maude might be in a hell of a lot of danger, an' she knows it."

They drove around a sandstone pillar, then down into a tree-filled hollow. Suddenly an acrid, rotting stench filled their nostrils.

"No! Bloody Christ, no!" Freddy yelled in horror as he slammed on the brakes.

"Oh, my God, no." Paul said softly.

Ahead of them was a tree, the foot of it strewn loosely with beer cans. Both men got out of the truck, stumbled toward the tree, then stood for a long moment in silent shock. Hanging from the tree's branches, dangling upside down from ropes tied around their ankles, were two small, hairy bodies.

"Unspeakable bastards!" Freddy spat the words out. "Must've hung 'em up like that while they was still alive.

Then they just slit the little bunyips' throats an' let their hearts pump the blood out. Shoulda strangled that bloody Chinaman whilst we had the chance. God knows who that mangy, murderin' bastard's got working for him now."

Sick with guilt and shaking with anger, Paul didn't try to speak. He pulled out his pocket knife, climbed up on Freddy's massive shoulders and cut the bunyips down. Paul knew that, as a scientist, he should save the bodies for dissection. But somehow that idea struck him as obscene.

There was only one shovel in the truck, so the two men took turns digging a grave. A couple of hours later, they laid the bunyips to rest beside each other.

How much like sleeping children they looked, Paul observed. At any second, it seemed, those eyes might flash open and the bunyips would scamper off to play.

Freddy covered them with a blanket and Paul started shoveling the dirt back into the grave. The mid-day heat burned at full intensity by the time they were finished, and both men were soaked with sweat.

"Perfesser, one of us is gonna have to stay behind with the rifle—"

"—and protect Maude and the rest of the bunyips until the other can bring the authorities. Right, Freddy. I'll stand guard here."

"Won't work, mate. Yer don't know yer way around these parts. I'll stay."

They pulled the ice chest out of the truck and set it in the shade. It still contained about a dozen soft drinks and a couple of gallons of melting ice. There were four meat pies left as well as a tin of biscuits. By the time the food ran out, Freddy would be able to shoot a wild pig or something.

"You'd better keep my pack too," Paul offered. He took a lot of ribbing over his ever-present day pack. But his "bag o' tricks," as it was known around Woolly, contained everything from flares to a first aid kit and other gadgets that were forever coming in handy.

"Yeah, I reckon it gots about ever'thing a bloke might need 'cept maybe a machine gun. See yer in a coupla days, Perfesser."

"Right." Paul started back toward the truck. Then he stopped, turned around and hugged Freddy, who returned his embrace.

"Take care of yourself, Freddy."

"You too, Perfesser."

Paul left with the horrible feeling that he'd never see his friend alive again.

5

As Paul sped back to Woolloona, he realized that Freddy had become so adept at complicating their lives that he could get them into trouble doing nothing at all. Take the broken two-way radio in his truck. If he'd fixed the damned thing, as he'd promised six months earlier, they could have stayed together and called for reinforcements. Splitting up only multiplied the dangers ahead. God help them if the truck broke down along the way. Paul had been around Freddy so much of late that doing things the hard way was becoming second nature to him.

It was late when he pulled into Freddy's place. He called the communications base from the house radio, and they patched him into a phone link with the district police.

"If you say a couple of bunyips have been killed, mate, I'll believe you." The tone of the dispatcher's voice indicated he didn't. "But they'd fall under the jurisdiction of the state wildlife inspectors. I can't bloody well send an officer all the way out there unless someone's committed a crime against persons or property."

Clarence Richmond, head of the CSIRO's Division of Wildlife Research, had given Paul his home phone number. Paul called it, and was politely invited by an answering machine to leave a message. Calls to the state wildlife offices weren't answered.

Exasperated and out of ideas, Paul stretched out on his friend's bed and tried to plan his next move. Nature did that for him, and he was soon asleep.

He awoke to the squawk of Freddy's radio. It was already daylight. Travel and exhaustion had left Paul disoriented, but a quick glance at the bookshelves towering over the bed reminded him where he was. He was the only person in Woolloona who knew that Freddy's bedroom housed a remarkably extensive library on Australian wildlife. He was also the only one aware that Freddy's annual holiday in Sydney—which everyone assumed to be a festival of pagan debauchery—was actually spent scrounging through bookstores and libraries.

Stepping over knee-high stacks of notebooks and photocopies, Paul made his way to the radio in the kitchen. The base was calling him. They had a telephone patch-in waiting from Clarence Richmond.

"Paul! All hell has broken loose! Where are you?"

"Over at Freddy's, and I've—"

Clarence's excited voice cut him off. "Listen, Paul, the whole world has gone mad over bunyips. You think pandas and koalas get attention? That's nothing compared with this bunyip craziness. Somehow, the word has leaked out about the MERP project's association with them. Unless I miss my guess, you're about to be deluged with reporters and curiosity seekers."

"That's not the worst of it." Paul cleared his throat and forced the quiver from his voice. "We found two bunyips with their throats slit over at the water hole. I'm sure it was done by locals who sold the blood to that Chinese doctor. Freddy stayed behind to guard the bunyips while I call for reinforcements."

There was a long pause.

"Paul, do you have a gun?"

"There's a .22 rifle over at the field station that I use for—"

"Forget that popgun! Do you have a *weapon*?"

"Freddy has a double-barreled shotgun somewhere, but I don't—"

"Get the shotgun, Paul. Load it and never let it out of your reach. I know what those Outback poachers are like. Some would kill a man for dogmeat. Getting reinforcements to you will be a little tricky since the wildlife inspectors aren't under my direct control. But I should be able to pull some strings and get a couple of them and a Land Cruiser to relieve you."

"How long before they can get here?" Paul asked, anticipating the worst.

"It's a two-day drive at best, I'm afraid. And they'll need time to pack."

Paul fought to control the anxiety in his voice. "We can't wait that long. Freddy and Maude could be killed at any minute."

"I know, Paul. I'll take emergency leave and meet you at the airstrip this afternoon. I reckon the three of us can hold off the poachers for a couple of days."

"I hope so."

"One last thing. Make sure that the truck's two-way radio is in good working order. We'll need it."

Paul found the shotgun, loaded it and stashed it in the truck along with several boxes of shells. He'd never shot anything but clay pigeons before and prayed that he wouldn't have to now.

Next, he needed fuel, provisions, and someone to repair the radio. Fortunately, he could get all three from Newstead's Hotel. He drove there, but noticed a half dozen unfamiliar vehicles parked in front and several strange people milling about. Figuring them for some of the bunyip enthusiasts Clarence had warned him about, Paul passed on by without stopping. He looped the long way around back to Freddy's and called George Newstead on the house radio.

"Perfesser! There's a mob here waitin' to meet yer. And

they'll pay a bloody fortune fer a glimpse at one o' yer bunyips."

"Forget it, George. I'm staying out of sight."

"Aw, be a sport, Perfesser." George cajoled. "Do it as a personal favor to me, anyway. I'm gettin' more business this week than I normally do in three months, and I got a family to support."

"Freddy's life is in danger, George, and we need your help."

"Freddy's in danger?" The wheedling tone disappeared instantly. "Why didn't yer say so? Whattayer need?"

An hour later, George's van drove up behind Freddy's shack with the fuel and groceries Paul had requested.

"Now what about fixing the radio?" Paul asked as soon as they finished loading the truck.

"Wendy's already got her gear waitin' for yer at her house. Y'know, she rather fancies yer, Perfesser. I reckon she'll wanna fix yer radio in exchange for some bedwork," George said with a wink.

Paul felt the hair raise on the back of his neck. George's barmaid, Wendy, the Wild Woman of Woolloona, had taken a distressingly carnal interest in him of late. Tall, blonde, buxom, and rather worn for someone still in her thirties, Wendy was the only unmarried and sexually available woman in Woolloona. Yet there was no forgetting the hunting knife she always kept sheathed to her belt. Nor did one wisely ignore the jagged scar it had left on Freddy's thigh, a souvenir from the time Wendy tried to castrate him as punishment for falling asleep in the middle of foreplay. Freddy had summarized the lesson very neatly: *Don't fuck nobody wearin' a knife longer'n yer dick.*

Bracing himself with a quick beer, Paul headed over to Wendy's. She emerged from the back door as he drove up. She wore no bra under a black tank top so small that the Tasmanian devil tattooed on her left breast was fully exposed.

"I understands y'needs a little help, Perfesser," she said, pressing up against him. "I could use a little help meself, y'know."

Paul tried to back away, but Wendy wrapped her hands around his buttocks and pulled him close, grinding her crotch into his thigh.

Wendy's aggressiveness didn't worry Paul nearly as much as the tender, vulnerable part of her character, the part she shared only with him. He was the only one in Woolloona who knew that Wendy had once been offered a scholarship to the University of Adelaide, or that the locket around her neck contained a ringlet of hair she'd snipped from her baby daughter's head before giving her up for adoption, eighteen years ago. For all anyone else in town knew, Wendy had sprung to life ten years earlier, the day a spat with her biker boyfriend left her stranded alone and unknown in Woolloona.

Wendy had grown accustomed to sex on her own terms, and Paul's polite refusal of her advances drove her crazy. The faster he backed away, the more overt she became. The other bar patrons would look on in envy and disbelief as Wendy rubbed her breasts against Paul and begged him to come home with her after work. He was vaguely aware that half the men in Woolly would gladly have murdered him for the chance to trade places. Little did they know that he would have been just as happy to pay one of them to stand in for him. Especially now.

"C'mon, Wendy, ease off. You know—"

"I ain't askin' yer to bloody marry me," Wendy said angrily. "If I ain't good enough fer yer t' sleep with, then I reckon I ain't good enough to fix yer bloody radio."

Now that he was in need of a favor, Paul would have to play by her rules.

"Look, Wendy, I'm in a big hurry," he sighed. "Just fix the radio, and I'll do whatever you want when I get back."

"It's a deal, mate."

Two hours later, the radio was buzzing and squawking like new.

"That's it, mate." Wendy wiped her hands, then wrapped an arm around Paul's neck and kissed him hard, forcing a thick tongue between his teeth. "We'll pick this up when yer gets back."

Resigned to his fate, Paul made a mental note to check his penicillin supply.

He was waiting for Clarence when the plane arrived at half past one. Clarence had a comfortable desk job and probably never imagined himself in the role of vigilante. But from the way he handled his rifle, he obviously knew how to use it.

They headed directly for the billabong, bypassing the field station which was now overrun with film crews and sight-seers. Paul drove while Clarence took notes on the trail so that he could radio directions to the inspectors. Neither man felt much like talking.

They approached the billabong cautiously. There was no way of getting Freddy's attention without also alerting any poachers who might be about. Paul felt a growing anxiety as he pulled the truck to a stop. Was it just nerves? Or were the bunyips signaling him that disaster awaited?

There was only one way to find out. The two men exchanged worried glances as they pulled their guns from the rack behind their seats. Wordlessly, they headed off toward the place Paul had last seen Freddy.

Paul's pack lay strewn on the ground there. The ice chest had been shattered by the impact of a high-powered rifle bullet. Clarence knelt down to touch some wet stains on the ground.

"Blood," he said. "And it's still fresh."

"Oh, please, God, not Freddy," Paul prayed under his breath.

"Look, Paul. See those marks on the ground? Somebody dragged something heavy and bleeding from here into the trees over there. Let's check it out. Carefully." Clarence pushed the safety on his rifle off.

Trembling, Paul insisted on leading the way. The trail led through trees and into a thicket where dense undergrowth obscured their vision in all directions.

Almost on tiptoe, they pushed quietly ahead.

There was a rustling to one side.

"Something's moving," Paul whispered.

Clarence nodded and motioned toward a tree that they could hide behind. In slow motion, they silently made their way toward it. A twig snapped under Paul's foot, and the undergrowth burst alive with the crunching sounds of many feet charging through the brush.

"Get down," Clarence whispered, instinctively crouching, his rifle at the ready.

Paul dropped to his knees and put the gun butt to his shoulder. Something inside of him balked, refusing to let his finger touch the trigger.

"They're coming this way," Clarence said, voice rising with alarm.

Paul pointed the gun in the right direction, but he could not force his finger to the trigger.

"Now, Paul, shoot!"

Clarence opened fire. The brush parted and several large figures came crashing through.

Paul was struck hard from one side in a blur of motion that knocked the shotgun from his hands and sent him sprawling onto his back. Stunned and barely conscious, he could only close his eyes and pray.

Instead of a gun blast, he heard Clarence laughing. Paul opened his eyes.

"Sorry, Paul," Clarence said, regaining his composure. "It's not every day you see a Yank run over by a 'roo stampede."

"Kangaroos?" Paul asked incredulously.

"Reds, to be exact. Big ones." Clarence pointed to a

crumpled body a few feet away. "The one that hit you weighed a good 200 pounds. Reckon we all gave each other a jolly good fright. Too bad I killed one in the process."

"Jesus," Paul muttered in embarrassment.

"At least you were able to keep your head and not shoot. I was the one who panicked and started blasting away at the poor buggers."

Paul was grateful that Clarence didn't know the real reason he'd held his fire. "We still have to find Freddy." He picked up his gun. "We don't have much daylight left."

They pushed on, this time with Clarence in the lead. The undergrowth ended abruptly, and Clarence stepped out of it. Suddenly, he aimed his rifle and fired. An ear-splitting squeal of agony rose from the distance.

Paul rushed ahead, then stopped short in horror. "Oh my God! Freddy!"

Freddy lay spread-eagled on his back near the water's edge, his shirt caked with blood. Beside him, the large wild boar that Clarence had just shot writhed in its death throes.

Paul rushed to his friend's side. He still had a pulse. "Freddy, can you hear me?"

"They got Maude," Freddy whispered. "Maude and three others."

Fury mingled with the horror in Paul's voice. "Who did this?"

"Nate Townsend an' his mob. Shot me from behind, then drug me here where the wild pigs'd eat me. They made sure I'd be alive and awake when the pigs came, the mangy bastards! I'm just sorry I couldn't save Maudie."

Paul fought back tears. "You did everything you could, Freddy. We'll take care of Nate later. Right now, let's get you outta here."

"Stay here, Paul, while I call for help," Clarence ordered. He headed back to the truck, pushing his way through the tangled undergrowth.

He returned several minutes later carrying blankets and Paul's day pack.

"How's Freddy?"

"Not good. He's drifting in and out of consciousness. But the bleeding doesn't seem too bad now. Is help coming?"

"We should have a Flying Doctor here in about an hour and a half. It'll be dark by then, so I need to mark off a landing strip now. Meanwhile, you clean the pig shit out of Freddy's wounds. I'll have a doctor in tow next time you see me."

Paul didn't speak, but sought reassurance by re-checking the pulse in Freddy's neck. The beat remained steady.

Clarence clasped Paul's shoulder with one hand. "Courage, mate." Then he headed back toward the truck.

Two hours later, the entire party was airborne en route to the hospital. Freddy lay strapped to the plane's gurney and Paul knelt beside him. Crouching nearby, the doctor kept careful watch over Freddy's vital signs.

"Will he make it?" Paul yelled over the deafening drone of propellers.

The doctor pulled his radiophone headset from one ear and leaned toward Paul.

"I asked if he'll make it," Paul repeated louder.

"He seems to be about as tough as these Outback Ockers get," the doctor yelled back. "But he's pretty torn up. We won't know anything until we get him into surgery."

Paul hunched his way to the back of the cramped passenger compartment where Clarence sat. "What about the saving the bunyips?"

"The wildlife inspectors will come through town sometime tomorrow. I'll catch a ride and direct them to the waterhole, then stay with them until we get things straightened out."

"Where are we headed now, anyway?"

"Silver Hill."

Paul's stomach tightened. He returned to Freddy's side. His best friend lay near death, and it was only a matter of time before someone would find Maude's body hanging upside down from a tree. To top it all off, he was going to Silver Hill, the one place in Australia he had never wanted to go. Not since the day he broke off with Sheila had life seemed so futile.

He laid a hand lightly on Freddy's chest. It was comforting to feel him breathe.

"I know you can't hear me, Freddy, but I swear to God that Nate Townsend will pay for this."

Freddy's eyes opened in a sly squint.

"Jist don't mess his hide up, Perfesser, 'cuz I'm gonna nail that ugly pelt to me shed 'fore this is over."

Paul and the doctor exchanged surprised smiles.

"Tell me the story 'bout the first time Sheila parked yer prawn. Did yer sneak in her swag or what?" Freddy asked, straining to be heard.

"Actually, she was the one who crawled in my bed. I'm not sure, though, its a good idea for me to . . . ?" He looked to the doctor.

The doctor nodded. "It's okay, mates. So long as you keep quiet, Freddy, and let your friend do the talking."

Freddy could use a little diversion right now. For that matter, so could Paul. Painful as these remembrances might be, they were a lot more comforting than the present reality.

To make the conversation easier, the doctor pulled off his headset and placed it over Freddy's ears. He pointed to the bulkhead where another set hung.

Paul adjusted the gear to his own head. He felt strange saying this into a microphone, especially with Freddy only inches away. The only alternative would be yelling. "See, it was our senior year, and we'd been living together—platonically—for a little over a month. Sheila, remember, only became my friend because I never tried to come on to her. I'd started seeing another girl, Angela. I had no idea Sheila even cared. Only later did she explain what was *really* going through her mind . . . "

* * *

Sheila herself was surprised by how much she resented Angela Roberts. She tried to tell herself that it was only out of concern that Paul, now her closest friend, was being played for a fool. She knew from earlier conversations with Paul that Angela wouldn't have anything to do with him back when they were in high school together. Never mind that Angela's parents and his were close friends and that they all went to the same church. What mattered was that Paul was shy and skinny and wore thick glasses. Cheerleaders like Angela didn't associate with nerds.

But college had worn well on Paul. Contact lenses had revealed a surprisingly handsome face, and two years of dedicated weight-lifting had produced a broad-shouldered, athletic physique. Although Sheila found Paul attractive even without the improvements, Angela seemed to notice him for the first time.

The last semester of their senior year found Paul, Sheila and Angela together in the same psychology course. Sheila decided that Angela must lie in wait for Paul every day, since she always seemed to intercept him on his way to class. Angela would flash her freshly-lipsticked smile, bat her false eyelashes, and tell Paul things like how well his sweater set off the green in his eyes. Paul would smile back, then tell Angela that her sweater was very becoming too. Meanwhile Sheila, largely ignored during such tail-sniffing, felt like sticking a finger down her throat.

Then one Friday night in late January, when Paul and Sheila were out drinking, Angela and a couple of her friends joined them, uninvited, at their table. One of the friends asked Paul to dance, and he hesitantly went with her.

"So's he your boyfriend?" Angela asked once the music had stopped.

"We live together," Sheila replied, hoping that would end the matter.

"That's not what I meant," Angela responded just as Paul rejoined them. Then in a voice loud enough for all to hear, "I asked if Paul is your boyfriend."

The question caught Sheila off guard. She was well aware of a growing bond with Paul. They'd always been affectionate toward each other, and lately their hugs were getting firmer and lasting longer. Sheila would even sit on his lap during her frequent bouts with depression. Yet, he'd never been overtly romantic toward her. She was unsure of her own feelings, and his.

"We're friends. Very *close* friends," Sheila said.

"But still just friends," Angela reiterated. "Come on, Paul, let's dance."

Sheila wondered what was behind that wistful look Paul cast back at her as Angela pulled him onto the dance floor. At first he was polite but noncommittal. She found his frequent glances back to the table reassuring. After a while, though, Angela's lips were at his ear. Then his hands wrapped around her waist. Whatever that little whore whispered must have worked, because Paul went home with her that night.

Paul spent most of the next two weekends at Angela's and Sheila finally began to confront her feelings. For as long as she'd known him, Paul would occasionally go home with another woman. Sheila never let him know how much she resented it. She tried to tell herself that she was simply disgusted by his cheapness. Yet Bronwyn had slept with dozens of men, including some she wasn't even attracted to. Why didn't that bother her too? It was all very confusing, and distracting from her studies. A pre-med student, she didn't need distractions.

Then, when she was alone with her books one Friday night in mid-February, a telegram came. Her father had suffered a heart attack. He was lying in the hospital in Silver Hill and might not pull through. Even though Sheila was used to being alone, this time she found the isolation unbearable. She picked up the phone and started to call Bronwyn, but stopped in mid-number. She didn't want Bronwyn, she wanted Paul. During the previous two weekends, she'd started to call for him over at Angela's a dozen times, but had always hung up before the phone rang. This time she had a valid excuse for calling. She knew the number by heart.

"Hello?" said the female voice at the other end.

"Angela, it's Sheila, Paul's roommate. I've got to speak to him."

"Why?"

"Never mind why, God damn it, just put him on!" Sheila was surprised at her own abruptness.

"It's that bitch from your apartment," Angela said, not even bothering to cover the mouthpiece. "I'm going to tell her to leave us alone."

"No!" Paul insisted. "And don't *ever* call her a bitch."

Sheila, who could hear every word, was gratified by Paul's firmness.

"Yeah, well, I bet she just wants you over there for herself. And if you leave here, you're never coming back."

"Give me the phone."

Then a bumping sound, indicating that the receiver had been dropped or thrown. Finally, Paul's voice again. "What's up, Sheila?"

"I need you, Paul. It's my dad. I just received—"

"I'm on my way. Tell me the rest when I get there."

Scant minutes later she heard Paul's footfalls on the

stairs, then—God!—how good it felt to have his arms around her.

"Call your mother," Paul said as he read the telegram.

"I can't afford it."

"Well, I can," he insisted. "Call."

Sheila obeyed, knowing that he'd have to wait tables an entire weekend in order to pay for the call. Since leaving Australia, she'd only spoken with her family once a year on Christmas. The conversation was emotional, and hard to end. Paul sat by calmly as the dollars ticked away.

"They say that the worst is over. He's going to live," Sheila said after hanging up. They shared a long hug. "I reckon you'll want to get back to Angela now."

"Nahh. I'll just stay here tonight."

It was after midnight when they went to their respective beds. Sheila stared fitfully at the ceiling for several minutes. She knew that Paul would probably make up with Angela in the morning and spend the night with her again. Sheila would either have to get used to his being with other women or make a move of her own. Finally, she decided. It took a few minutes with a curling iron and brush to get her hair in just the right style, the one Paul had once described as "irresistible." Hopefully he was right. Then a touch of makeup, but no perfume. Paul had complimented her repeatedly on a particular musky-sweet scent she wore. He'd called it seductive and wanted to know the name of it, so he could buy it for "friends." She demurred, not knowing how or whether to tell him that the prized fragrance was simply the natural odor of her body.

Finally ready, she knocked on his door.

"Can I come in?"

"Sure. What's up?" Paul switched on the bedlamp, then did a double-take as she entered. Sheila seldom wore mascara anywhere, let alone to bed.

"I just want to be with you right now," she smiled. "Is that all right?"

"Yeah, okay." His voice showed confusion. "Wanna talk?"

"Not really," she replied in a husky whisper. This was her first attempt at seduction, and she hoped that what she'd learned from the movies would at least cover the essentials.

She wore only an oversized tee-shirt as she slipped under the sheet and slid up next to Paul. He shifted uncomfortably.

"Relax, Paul. I already know that you sleep in the nude."

"How—?"

"Never mind. Right now, I need another hug."

He was lying on his side, so Sheila pushed him onto his back and stretched out on top of him. For a long moment she lay quietly enjoying his warmth. But she'd come for more than that. She shifted her weight from one hip to the other to gauge Paul's reaction. All she felt were his thigh muscles flexing as they held his knees tightly together. Something was missing here.

That's the problem, Sheila thought as she pushed her own knee between his. Paul resisted momentarily but submitted in response to her soft grunt of displeasure. His thighs parted and the erection he'd held locked between immediately bulged upward against her. She suppressed a giggle as Paul's face reddened and turned away from her, his usual response when embarrassed. She thrust her pelvis against him, but he remained as motionless and rigid as a corpse.

"What's wrong, Paul?" Did he not want her? Had she just made a fool out of herself and forced him into rejecting her outright?

"Uh . . . I . . . I guess I'm just a little confused right now."

She pushed herself up so she could face him, making sure that her breasts still rested against his chest.

"Confused about what? Do you love Angela? Is that it?" she demanded.

"No. Of course not."

"Then why do you sleep with her?" She didn't try to hide the strain in her voice.

"What a question. Jeez! I mean, I get the same urges as everybody else. And you don't have to be in love just to sleep with someone."

"Well *I* do. So how do you feel about me, then?"

"You're the closest friend I've ever had."

"That's not what I mean, Paul," she replied in growing exasperation. "How do you *feel* about me? Honestly?"

He hesitated for several moments, then spoke very softly. "I love you."

"Are you sure?"

"Absolutely certain."

"How do you know?"

"Because I can't get you out of my mind. Even when I'm with another woman, I close my eyes and pretend I'm making love to you."

"Well, isn't that dandy! I guess it's easier to fantasize about me than to tell me how you feel."

"Why torture myself? I know damn well the only reason you like me is because I *don't* come on to you, because I'm always there for you even though you have no romantic interest in me."

"Who says I'm not interested? Why haven't you even bothered to ask?"

"But you told me yourself that you—"

"That was a year ago. Things change, Paul, including people's feelings. Including *my* feelings!" She pushed herself up on her knees and was now fighting back tears. Paul's defensiveness just made things worse. How could two people be so close and yet so ignorant of each other?

"Sheila, am I supposed to read your mind? You've never given me any sign that you—"

"A *sign*?" Sheila's voice broke as buried emotions came to the fore. "Night after night I slept alone and miserable while the man I love was off screwing another woman—*while pretending she was me, for Chrissake*! And all because you were waiting for a sign? You want a sign, asshole? How's this?" She jerked off her tee-shirt and slapped Paul's face with it. Angry tears now streamed down her cheeks and onto her breasts.

"Oh, my God, Sheila," Paul whispered. He sat up and put his hands on her shoulders. "I can't believe how stupid I've been. I'm sorry. I really do love you."

He pulled her to him, and Sheila collapsed into his arms, sobbing. Paul didn't speak, but held her close while she cried herself out.

As the tears finally faded, so did the hurt and frustration. Paul might have been incredibly dense, but he was always honest and respectful toward her. If he said he loved her, he meant it.

Sheila's attention gradually shifted back to the physical sensations. Paul's chest was warm and firm and her bare skin felt nice where it touched him. She wrapped her arms around him, sensing the strength of his muscles as they pushed against her with every inhalation. His breath was slow, deep and steady.

She lowered one hand to the small of his back and began caressing him. He responded with a kiss. His lips were moist and full and moved with gentle deliberation. A shiver ran up her spine as he squeezed her tightly against him.

Moaning with delight, she returned his kiss, mouth open and tongue tracing the inside of his lips. His skin grew warmer to her touch.

She welcomed Paul's tongue as it slipped between her lips. Others had tried to kiss her that way, but with them it seemed unclean and foreign. Now Paul's body felt as much a part of her as her own.

She pulled her head back and looked into his eyes. "Are you *sure* you love me, Paul?"

"With all my heart. I've wanted to tell you that for months, but I thought it would only scare you away."

"I'm not afraid, Paul. And if you want me, I'll stay with you forever."

He eased her onto her back as his lips caressed her lightly on the neck. Everything about his touch seemed so very right, and she wanted more, much more.

She guided his attention to her breasts, which he slowly circled with kisses. Then with his tongue he traced delicate arabesques around the hard, prominent nipples. Always self-conscious about the size of her bosom, Sheila had until now tried to hide it behind loose-fitting garments and restrictive bras. Everyone stared, but no one had ever kissed them. Until tonight. Now, for the first time, they brought her pleasure. The touch of flesh was at once scary and liberating. But most of all, consuming. Having suppressed her physical desires all these years, Sheila would tonight find them insatiable.

"Harder, Paul," she whispered . . .

Paul had many, many memories of Sheila. The one that haunted him most was that of awakening the next morning. Sunlight already seeped between the closed blinds, and he lay on his side, facing an unoccupied bed space. Had she really slept with him? Or did he want her so badly that his mind now played tricks on him?

A sleepy "Good morning" came from behind as a hand slipped around his waist. He spun around and—Yes!—there she was, blonde hair swept across a freckled face. Still half asleep, Sheila snuggled closer and pressed once more against him. Her eyes opened half-way.

"I love you, Paul," she said softly. Then she drew his lips back to hers.

* * *

Paul had relived that scene hundreds of times in his mind. It always left him with that same hollow aching.

"So how long was yers lovers?" Freddy asked.

"About three months. We broke up on graduation day. Haven't seen her since."

"Why hasn't yer tried t' find out what became of 'er?"

"After what I did to her, I have no right to interfere with her life ever again."

Freddy didn't follow up on that remark, although Paul could tell that he wanted to. Maybe he saw the tears welling up in Paul's eyes. For whatever reason, Freddy closed his own eyes and drifted back to sleep.

6

Paul awoke after a brief and uncomfortable nap. The couches in the hospital waiting room were already occupied, so he'd stretched out across four of the chrome and vinyl chairs and used his pack for a pillow. Now his entire body felt stiff. He could have accepted the offer to share Clarence's hotel room, but somehow he would have felt as if he'd left Freddy behind again.

It was already daylight, and it took another hour of nervous pacing before one of the doctors, still dressed in his surgical scrubs, escorted Paul into a private office.

"We've done everything we can for your friend. It's out of our hands now," the doctor said.

"Would you kindly tell me just what in hell that means, please?" Doctors wrap everything with gauze, including their speech. And Paul was in no mood for it.

"It means this. Your mate's had the bloody shit blasted out of him. We've put together all the pieces we could find, but he still might die. So if you've got a god, pray to him."

Paul hid his anguish behind a clipped, "Thank you."

"It'll be late afternoon at the earliest before the anesthesia wears off. I suggest you get some rest."

Rest was the last thing he wanted. It was two miles to the Commerce Hotel where Clarence was staying, and Paul needed to walk every step of it. Clarence was just finishing breakfast in the downstairs coffee shop when he arrived.

"Well, I made contact with the inspectors," Clarence said after inquiring about Freddy. "They'll be through here in about five hours. We'll need to round up this Nate Townsend character. Does he live in Woolly?"

Paul shrugged. "I'm not even sure he has a permanent home. From what Freddy's told me, he moves around quite a bit, squatting in abandoned miners' shacks. He's got several men working for him, but none of them talk much. I have no idea where to find any of them."

"Too bad. Our problems are mounting up." Clarence pulled out a series of multicolored maps. "Even if we caught Nate today, I'm not sure we'd be able to save the bunyips. The situation is beginning to appear hopeless."

"Why?"

"Well, Paul, let's assume that the bunyips can only live around water holes. Let's also assume that they won't go out into the desert for more than a two- or three-day walk between water holes."

"Seems reasonable."

"If you look at these water and vegetation maps, then, you can see that there's only a hundred square-mile area that they can live in. They'd have to walk a week or more without water to extend their range beyond that."

Paul glanced at the familiar maps. "Seems to fit with the other observations. That's the only area in Australia where people make serious claims about sighting bunyips."

"It also makes our job of protecting them even more critical, because I doubt that the area has enough food to support more than a few dozen creatures the size of a bunyip."

"If that many," Paul sighed.

Clarence pulled off his reading glasses and rubbed the bridge of his nose. "If we further assume that the males and females pair off like humans, and that some are too young or too old to reproduce, that leaves at most two or three dozen breeding pairs to carry on the species. That, Paul, places the bunyips dangerously close to extinction under the best of circumstances."

Paul's stomach knotted again. The bunyips would probably have done just fine if he and Freddy hadn't "discovered" them. "I see what you mean. Even if some of our guesses are off a bit, it's a safe bet that it won't take long for poachers to wipe out the entire species."

"Here's the worst part," Clarence concurred, his expression growing ever more grim. "The water hole where you found Maude is located in New South Wales, but most of the rest of the likely bunyip habitat falls on the other side of the state boundary, in Queensland. Do you know anything about the Queensland state government?"

Paul's smile held no humor. "I know that the state's premier has about as much concern for environmental issues as Attila the Hun."

"Precisely. Which means we can't count on any help from him. Further, to make a bad situation worse, there's already a dispute going over the use of those waterholes. Because of the unusually dry weather during the last couple of years, the graziers need the water holes more than ever for livestock. At the same time, the area was recently opened up for minerals exploration, and the miners and prospectors want the water, too. So the waterholes are crawling with armed, angry people. It would be nearly impossible to sort out the poachers from the prospectors and graziers. For that matter, there's nothing to stop the prospectors and graziers from poaching a bunyip or two themselves, or even shooting them accidentally."

"Can't we have the federal government declare the area a wildlife refuge or something and get the people out of there?" Paul asked.

"Only if we want a bush uprising on our hands. After

all, these people aren't going to sit by quietly and have their livelihoods taken away from them."

Paul's anxiety sank into despair. "So what do we do?"

"First we capture Nate Townsend's group. I'll be contacting the police for their help in running him down. Then we patrol the rest of the habitat as best we can. In the meantime, let's not forget that the bunyips have been around for many thousands, if not millions, of years. They're bound to have learned a few survival tips along the way."

The wildlife inspectors picked up Clarence shortly after lunch. It would still be a few hours before Freddy woke up—if he ever did. After much deliberation, Paul grabbed the shotgun and his pack and hired a cab to drop him off outside the city limits. He picked up an empty bottle lying by the road and flung it into the air, then blasted it to shards before it reached the ground. He repeated this several times, never missing.

But aim had never been Paul's problem. He had a shelf full of marksmanship trophies back in Kansas to prove it. As he started walking back toward town, he sighted a rabbit about twenty paces away. He took aim. For a long time he stood there with the rabbit in his sights. It was just a stupid rabbit. A pest that wasn't even native to the continent. Paul could do it. He could shoot the rabbit, damn it! Just a gentle squeeze on the trigger would do it.

But instead of firing, he lowered the gun and unloaded it. Killing for food or self-defense was one thing. Shooting a living creature just to prove a point was something entirely different.

He walked back toward town, absorbed in his thoughts.

A faded blue pickup with a crumpled front fender pulled up beside and a broad, friendly face, gap-toothed and unshaven, smiled at him. "Hop in, sport, an' I'll take yer the rest o' the way. Too bloody hot to walk."

Paul hesitated a moment before deciding. "Thanks,

but . . . I guess I'd better walk a while. Appreciate the offer, though."

The driver raised his eyebrows in surprise, shrugged, and drove off.

Gradually the scrub and sandy orange dirt gave way to ragged lawns and sidewalks. Silver Hill was filled with vicarious memories for Paul. The places where Sheila and Bronwyn had spent their adolescence, places he'd learned about from fleeting comments and passing reminiscences, now sprang to life in front of him. It was a bittersweet feeling that left a familiar knot in his stomach. Across the street was the Graziers' Bar. The girls used to sneak in there on Friday nights when they were still under age. They'd sit toward the back in a booth facing the wall, and they never had trouble finding someone to buy them a drink. Paul crossed the street with a sudden longing to go in. He stopped short of the door. He didn't belong in there. He didn't belong in Silver Hill in the first place. He walked the rest of the way to the hospital without looking up.

Freddy woke up briefly that evening, still too groggy to make sense of anything. The next morning he seemed a little better, and Paul was allowed to see him for a few minutes.

Freddy was in no condition to talk, but Paul was allowed to ask one question before leaving. "Freddy, do you have any idea where I can find Nate Townsend?"

Freddy closed his eyes, and Paul thought he'd gone back to sleep. Then his eyes reopened.

"Oklahoma," he whispered. He drifted off again, and Paul was ushered out of the room.

That afternoon, Paul called George Newstead and explained everything. He knew that Freddy's daughter, Melissa, had just turned twelve and that his ex-wife was named Maude. But that was about all he knew. Freddy usually changed the subject whenever asked about his family. Maybe George knew where they were.

"Sorry, Perfesser, but not even Freddy knows. His wife

took Melissa an' just vanished 'bout five years ago. Really tore him up. Y'know, he didn't even drink much before that."

"What about his wife's family?"

"They was from Adelaide, I think. Don't remember what their name was or if they's even alive now. Freddy spent 'bout a year tryin' to find Melissa before he gave up. Rarely talked about her since."

"What about Nate Townsend? Any idea where to find him?"

"No, but I doubt he'll be comin' 'round here. Right after yer left last week, Nate an' one of his mates came to town. They got Wendy drunk an' screwed her. Then, jist fer jollies, they beat the bloody shit out of 'er."

"That sadistic son of a bitch! Is she all right?" Paul had a soft spot for Wendy, even if he wasn't eager to sleep with her.

"Kinda bruised up, but says she feels better'n she looks. In fact, she's already workin' again. She's got a jar of alcohol behind the bar now. If anybody around here knew where to find Nate, his balls'd already be in that jar."

"Do you know if Nate has family in America?" Paul asked. His hatred for the man seemed to grow by the hour, and by now he wouldn't dismiss the idea of chasing him half way across the globe.

"The States? I doubt it. Why?"

"It's probably nothing, but when I asked Freddy if he knew where to find Nate, he said 'Oklahoma.' Guess he was delirious."

"Maybe not," George replied. "There's an abandoned settlement north o' here by that name. Some Yank settled it a long time ago. Named it after his home, I think. Maybe that's what Freddy meant."

"How do I get there?"

"Only one way, mate," came a woman's voice. Wendy must have jerked the microphone out of George's hands.

"That's with me. Nobody touches that bastard till I'm done with 'im."

Freddy seemed a little better the next day when Paul went to say good-bye. He was heavily sedated, and it was hard for him to talk with the tubes running up his nose and down his throat. The telepathic link between them no longer worked. It only seemed to function when a bunyip was around. Paul explained his plan. Freddy seemed to comprehend some of it, but there was no way of knowing how much.

Shortly before noon, Paul caught a northbound bus and asked the driver to let him off at the Darby Trail crossing. Wendy's green Land Cruiser was already waiting there for him. The vehicle was appropriate for her—faded and battered on the outside, but still tough and in perfect running order. Paul threw his shotgun and pack in the back seat, then Wendy handed him a cold beer.

"See this, mate?" She held up a pint jar filled with a clear liquid. "Know what's gonna be in here tomorrow?"

Paul nodded but looked away. This was one conversation he'd rather not continue. The purple marks around Wendy's left eye and right cheek showed that she had plenty of incentive to make good on her threat.

"Now yer drive, an' I'll navigate."

Paul slid into the driver's seat and put the vehicle in gear. Wendy was already under the influence of many beers, and Paul assumed that she needed a nap. His suspicion seemed confirmed when Wendy put her head in his lap. Then he felt a hand on his zipper.

"Wendy, what are you—?"

"Belt up an' drive, mate."

The next twenty miles were, in terms of road conditions, the roughest part of the journey. But Paul was hardly aware that the wheels were touching the ground.

As darkness approached, they pulled over for the night. They built a fire out of dead scrub and heated up tins of bland beef stew. As the fire died down, Wendy, by then violently intoxicated, pushed Paul backward onto the blanket where he sat.

"Awright, mate. You had yer fun earlier. Now it's my turn. And don'tcher ferget—a gen'leman always lets th' lady come firsht." Wendy pulled the knife from her belt and jabbed it into the ground by the blanket.

Paul quickly undid the buttons on his shirt, lest Wendy rip them off, while she removed her own blouse. Moments later her body pressed against his. He became the aggressor in an attempt to gain some control over the situation. For a while, it seemed to work. Wendy let him finish undressing her and welcomed him as he crawled on top. As the action heated up, he began to develop some confidence. Although Wendy's rapid pelvic thrusts were providing a great deal of stimulation, the pain from her fingernails tearing into his back provided just the right distraction to prevent him from climaxing too early.

But then, with a powerful kick, Wendy rolled Paul over and claimed top position for herself. She moved faster than ever, and he found it extremely difficult to hold back. In a desperate attempt to stave off an ill-timed orgasm—which might well become his last—Paul began mentally reviewing integral equations.

"Omigod, Paul, this is wonderful!"

$\int e^x dx = e^x$, Paul thought to himself. It helped, but he'd have to work a lot harder if he was going to block out Wendy's growing momentum.

"Oh, yeah, Paul, yeah."

$$\int xe^{ax} dx = \frac{e^{ax}}{a}$$

"Oh, yeah! This is great!"

$$\int \frac{dx}{1 + e^x} = x - \log(1+e^x) = \log \frac{e^x}{1+e^x}$$

"Oh, yeah! Oh, yeah! Yeah! Can yer feel it?"

$$\int \frac{dx}{ae^{mx} - be^{-mx}} = \frac{1}{m\sqrt{ab}} \tan^{-1} (e^{mx}\frac{\sqrt{a}}{b})$$

"It's coming! Yeah! *It's coming!*"

$$\int e^{ax} \tan^{n} x dx = e^{ax}\frac{\tan^{n-1} x}{n-1} - \frac{a}{n-1} \int e^{ax} \tan^{n-1} x dx - \int e^{ax} \tan^{n-2} x dx$$

"Aaaiiiieeeeeeee!"

Paul breathed a deep sigh of relief. He'd been functioning at the limits of his ability, his masculinity at risk over variables normally consigned to the silicon bowels of dreadnought-class mainframes.

It took Wendy several minutes to catch her breath. "That was great, Paul. I had no idea yer was that good. Now's there anythin' more I can do for yer?"

"Well, you could put some iodine on my back."

"Oh, yeah. Sorry. Reckon I do get a li'l frisky sometimes. By the way, yer seemed kinda . . . well, *distant* toward the end there. What was yer thinkin' about?"

They were underway again by first light. The plan was to arrive at a sandstone bluff overlooking Oklahoma at around noon. George Newstead, who promised to bring several of Wendy's friends along, would meet them there. And if George managed to contact Clarence Richmond's group, they'd probably join the party, too.

A couple of miles from their destination, they cut their speed to a crawl to minimize the tell-tale dust cloud. They parked the Land Cruiser in a gully, then Paul followed Wendy as they crept up onto the bluff. They peered down on a ghost town that seemed part of an Old West movie set. A dozen ramshackle wooden buildings sprawled across a narrow valley framed between two rust-colored sandstone ridges. Sure enough, three pickups, including Nate's, were parked in front of an old store. Four black camp dogs lazed in the shade next to the vehicles.

Paul's attention was drawn to a large shed off to one side of the settlement. Something about it was important, although he couldn't decide what. One of the rusting tin sheets covering the roof had been blown loose and bent back. It now waved lazily in the wind over the rotted shingles below. But the shed really didn't stand out from the rest of the buildings.

Wendy interrupted Paul's thoughts. "Shouldn't be too much longer, mate, 'fore the others get here."

"Yeah. I guess we'll just have to wait and watch till then."

Time passed slowly under the hot sun. No one came in or out of any of the buildings.

"Maybe there ain't nobody down there," Wendy fretted.

Paul's mind was drifting and he hardly heard her. That shed haunted him. *Déjà vu?* Had some long-forgotten memory been jogged? Paul scanned the building with binoculars. Growing up on a farm, he'd seen sheds like that before. In fact, his family's nearest neighbors had one very much like it. It was used as a slaughterhouse.

He thought back to the autumn butcherings. One of his jobs had been to bleed the pigs. Immediately after the hog had been stunned by a hammer between the eyes, he would rush forward with a knife and stab the arteries of its neck. The blood gushed out in a high arched fountain that spurted all the way to the roof. Moments later the carcass would be scalded to remove the bristles, then hauled up by its front legs and disemboweled. In his mind, Paul heard the splattering of pig guts hitting a wet concrete floor.

"Whattayer thinkin' about, Perfesser?"

"I'm not sure myself. It's like I'm trying to remember something, but I don't know what. Whatever it is involves that shed over there."

"Looks like a reg'lar shed to me, 'cept maybe a little more run down than most. Yer been there before or somethin'?"

"No. At least, I don't think so."

Paul tried to shift his attention, but to no avail. As the hours passed, his curiosity grew to obsession.

"Wendy, I'm going down to check out that shed."

"Yer what? I always knew yer was a little odd, Perfesser, but I never thought yer was no bloody lunatic! Look, the others is runnin' late, but they's comin' any time now. Once we settles scores with ol' Nate yer can move into yer damn shed an' bloody well live there!"

"It might be too late then."

"*What* might be too late?"

"I dunno, Wendy, but I've gotta see what's in there. We're already downwind, so if I'm quiet I won't attract the dogs' attention. I'll be in and out before anyone knows I'm there."

Wendy pushed a sweat-soaked strand of hair back behind her ear. "Why's men so bloody full o' brilliant schemes that never fucking work?"

"Do you want to stay behind and stand guard?"

"Shit! Look what happened when yer an' Freddy split up!"

"Then keep down and follow me," Paul said, picking up his shotgun and pack.

"Fer gawd's sake, mate, yer gonna carry yer bag o' tricks along?"

"Yeah. You'd be surprised how often it comes in handy."

Paul headed out, followed by Wendy carrying a carbine, her ever-present knife still sheathed to her belt. Slowly they edged their way around the bluff and down the escarpment, darting behind trees and bushes whenever possible. The sandstone was soft and eroded, crumbling to the touch. Even ledges that looked solid turned slippery as their boots loosened sand particles that rolled beneath their feet. Then they passed over a long stretch of loose gravel, where every step seemed to unleash a minor avalanche.

The last obstacle before level ground was a ledge with about a ten-foot drop. It would be too risky to jump straight off, so Paul decided to hang over feet first and lower himself part-way before dropping to the bottom. He'd just begun easing himself down when his handhold suddenly broke loose.

"Shit!" he whispered as he slid backward, trying to dig his fingers into the bare rock.

He found no purchase as the rock slipped out from under him. An instant later found him clawing the air.

He landed on his back with a thud. A moment of blackness, then a crushing ache in his chest. Desperately, Paul sucked for breath. It would not come. An invisible band seemed to squeeze his ribs inward.

He forced away the panic. *I've just had my wind knocked out. I've lived through it before.*

He couldn't control the loud, wheezing gasps of his lungs fighting to reinflate.

Wendy froze in place, unable to help.

A long, sick pause ticked away as they waited for the dogs to start barking.

No alarm sounded.

Once he could breathe again, Paul motioned Wendy to slide down where he could catch her and break her fall. Less than a minute later, they were at the back door of the shed.

He checked the door. The knob turned easily, but the corroded hinges would surely squeak. Since a brief noise would attract less attention than a long one, he opened the door with a hard jerk. An ear-piercing squeal was followed by a blast of hot, fetid air.

"Gawd!" Wendy whispered. She held her nose against the stench.

Paul used a stick to prop the door open, then led the way inside. The windows had been boarded shut, and their eyes needed a while to adjust to the low light. Even then, it was still too dim to make out any details. The heat was as suffocating as the smell, and they tied bandanas around their faces to keep the buzzing swarms of flies out of their nostrils.

Saturated with sweat, their clothing clung to their bodies.

"This way," Paul whispered, pulling the flashlight from his pack. The beam traced something in the far corner. As they approached he made out the shape of a bloated figure lying face down. He couldn't tell if it was Maude or not.

Shaking with anxiety, he used a loose board to roll it over. The belly split open to reveal a writhing cauldron of maggots. Paul swallowed hard several times to force back the vomit before he was able to look at the face.

"Is it yers. The one yer call Maude?"

"No."

"Let's git outta here, then."

"Not until we've checked out everything." He trained the flashlight on the doors of two storage rooms on the other side of the shed. One door was slightly ajar. Paul pulled it open to find a small table covered with glass bottles and clear plastic tubing. All contained blood residue. He picked up a piece of tubing and stared for a long moment at the hypodermic needle dangling from the end of it.

"The other bunyips must still be alive."

"Huh?"

"Look, if you're going to get all the blood out of something at once, you don't use hypodermic needles. The only reason Nate would be using this type of equipment would be to bleed them a little bit at a time. Which means he's probably keeping them alive somewhere."

Paul charged for the other door. It was padlocked.

"The bunyips are in there."

"How d'yer know?"

"Instinct."

How to get past this door without attracting attention?

He studied it for several seconds, then rummaged through his pack. He pulled out his Swiss Army knife.

"Yer'll never break the lock with that, Perfesser."

"That's not the idea." He put the screwdriver blade of his knife against the head of the pin connecting the top hinge and tapped the other end using the flashlight as a hammer. Within seconds he'd removed the pins from both hinges. He pulled the door back and trained the light inside.

"God damn it!" He surveyed a room that was totally empty.

"You an' yer bloody instincts. Now let's git our arses outta here 'fore Nate fills 'em with lead."

He started out, but something was nagging him. Why would anybody padlock an empty room? And how could the bunyips survive for long in the heat of an unventilated building in the first place? After all, the only livable temperatures in there would be found . . . *underground*! Paul bolted back to the storage room.

"*Now* what?" Wendy moaned in exasperation.

On his hands and knees, he inspected the plank flooring. There were no obvious trap doors, but one seam in the floor was somewhat wider than the others. He stuck his knife blade into it and pried. The plank moved a little.

He repositioned the blade for better leverage and tried again. This time, a cleverly-disguised section of planking, about two foot by three, popped loose. He pulled it away to reveal the top of a ladder leading down into a large hole. The flashlight revealed only the hole's dirt bottom about ten feet below, and a tunnel going off to one side.

"Think yer bunyips is down there?"

"Gotta be, although I doubt the hole was dug just for them." Whatever force had drawn him to the shed now beckoned him into the tunnel. "More likely, it's some kind of hideaway or storage pit that's been here a long time. But it'd be a good place to keep the bunyips alive and out of sight."

He eased himself onto the ladder. As he approached the bottom, his hand touched something wet and sticky on the rung. Half-dried blood. He forced himself to shut out any emotional reaction. There was a job to do, regardless of the consequences.

Wendy lowered the guns and stepped onto the ladder. "The bloke's not gonna be happy 'til he get us all killed," she muttered.

The air was cool and damp.

"Smells like a shithouse," Wendy said.

"Yeah . . . which means there's gotta be something alive down here."

He played the light along the walls of the tunnel. It was long, with no end in sight, and several alcoves carved into the sides. The passage was only about five feet high, so he and Wendy had to stoop as they made their way along. The first opening appeared to be a storage chamber. Boxes of everything from booze to small appliances were piled there. Probably stolen, Paul thought.

The next opening led to another chamber. Three large wooden crates, ventilation holes drilled in the sides, squatted there like turtles hiding in the shade.

"They've gotta be in here!" He rushed ahead. The boxes were hinged on one side. He flipped the latch on the first one, jerked the door open, and shone the light inside.

A small, hairy form covered its face with its hands against the blinding beam.

"Maude?" Paul quickly surveyed the bunyip. It was male. "Shit. Please, Lord, let her be in one of these."

He flung the door of the second box open. Again, a bunyip shielded itself from his light. Another male.

"Damn!" Paul's hands shook as he turned to the last box. "C'mon, Maude, *please* be in here.

The door, off-center, opened only a couple of inches before the far corner jammed against the ground.

A burst of putrid air.

Paul grabbed the top of the door and yanked hard, wrenching it off the hinges.

A tiny figure rolled out, sprawling limply on the ground like a discarded rag doll.

His heart dropped. "Oh Jesus! It's Maude."

Wendy touched his shoulder. "Sorry, mate."

It dawned on Paul that such a strong odor could only come from a bloated, rotting carcass, like the one upstairs. Maude was not only limp, but warm. He felt her pouch. With a mixture of joy and crushing sadness, he realized what had happened. He extracted the decomposing body of Alex.

"Maude? Can you hear me?"

She opened her eyes a little.

"Maude, it's me, Paul. I've come to get you out of here."

Her eyes narrowed, then her head nodded slightly in recognition.

"She's really weak. They've bled her almost to death, but I think she'll make it. Now let's get the hell outta here."

"Best idea yer've had all bloody day!"

They wasted no time. He carried Maude while the other two bunyips, holding onto Wendy's belt for support, rushed toward the exit. Seconds later they were topside.

Paul led the way out of the storage room and toward the back door. Suddenly, he froze. "Sssshhhhh. Don't make a sound."

"*Now* what?"

Outside, the wind howled about the shed like a wolf pack closing in for the kill.

Paul stood silent, listening. Nothing but the wind and the ragged hiss of his own labored breathing. Still, his blood ran cold. Danger awaited, lurking just beyond some sensory threshhold.

Wendy clenched her teeth and grimaced in silent frustration.

She was about to speak when a man coughed just outside the front door.

"Someone's coming," Paul whispered.

She nodded and raised her gun. He waved her back, laid Maude down, and rushed to the front door quietly.

Seconds later, the door swung open. It was one of Nate's henchmen, the one they called Big Al. He took a couple of steps into the darkness of the shed, then stopped and stared at the open back door.

"What's goin' on in—?"

Paul lunged forward, jamming the shotgun like a battering ram into the man's solar plexus. Al hit the floor with a thud.

"Okay, Wendy, get moving."

"He's the bludger what held me down whilst Nate stomped me," she hissed, raising her gun. "I outta blow his fuckin' head off."

"No! A gunshot would just bring the others down on us. Besides, you wouldn't kill somebody in cold blood. We'll catch up with him again later. Right now, we've gotta save our own asses."

She lowered her gun. "Yeah, reckon yer right. I'll stand guard here fer a few minutes whilst yer gits the bunyips to safety."

This was no time to argue, so Paul draped Maude over one shoulder and headed out. The other two bunyips seemed a little stronger but still clung to his belt for support.

Blinding sunlight seared his eyes as they burst from the shadows. Paul groped forward, unable to block the light except by squinting. He struggled to keep his eyelids from jamming shut altogether.

The wind hitting his sweat-drenched clothing created a slight but welcome cooling.

Paul judged the pace as best he could. He'd be running uphill, into the wind, carrying a heavy load. Going too fast could mean heat stroke and death. Going too slow could prove just as deadly.

His mind and body dissociated. Thoughts darted and ricocheted madly through his skull, while physical movements seemed only to come in tortured slow motion. Time itself seemed to falter, the seconds dragging.

Would Wendy be all right? Secretly, Paul would have enjoyed letting her wreak vengeance on Big Al. Paul hated that sadistic moron even worse than Nate. After a 'roo shoot, Al liked to pull the live joeys out of their mothers' pouches and throw them to Nate's dogs. The joeys would make three or four leaps before they were snatched by the neck and ripped to pieces.

Paul would try to ignore these scenes, aware that the others barely tolerated his presence even when he kept his mouth shut. Besides, wild dogs and dingoes killed joeys all the time. It was a part of nature. But it was Al's laugh that made his skin crawl, that hard-edged cackle of delight at watching something suffer.

Paul recoiled at these thoughts, surprised that his mind could wander under such stress.

He'd paced himself too fast, and was already panting. His lungs ached as he fought for every scorching breath that the wind seemed to suck away. His ears buzzed and his head floated loose. He felt dangerously close to passing out.

There was no way up the ledge that he and Wendy had slid down earlier. They'd have to take the long way back to the Land Cruiser, and that meant going upwind where the dogs would catch their scent. They forged ahead, Paul fighting to reconnect brain with body.

A dog barked, and the others quickly joined in. Then Big Al began yelling—screaming, actually—for help. Four men with rifles exploded from the old store and headed for the shed.

Paul turned back to help Wendy, and felt relief to see

her already bounding toward him. She even carried his pack over one shoulder.

An eternity seemed to pass in the ten minutes it took for the five of them to reach the Land Cruiser and head out.

Paul drove full throttle as Wendy screamed into the radio. "George! Where the bloody hell are yer, yer stupid son of a bitch? Yer was supposed to be here two bloody hours ago!"

Newstead sheepishly explained that his van had a mechanical problem. But he promised to make Oklahoma with five other men first thing in the morning. Wendy proceeded to describe for George his entire sexual anatomy in explicit—and hopefully inaccurate—detail. It took her many minutes to yell herself out. Paul's ears were ringing by the time she finally hung up the microphone.

He stopped the vehicle just long enough to scan the horizon. "We're not being followed," he reported, relieved. "Of course, that just means that Nate and Al and the rest are packing up and heading out. And it's my fault that they're getting away." The thought weighed heavily.

"Yeah, but yer did the right thing, Perfesser. The bunyips is safe now, and that's what's really important. We'll catch up with ol' Nate someday. An' leastwise I got to settle scores with Al."

"Knocking the wind out of him hardly counts. After all, he did get away in one piece."

"Not exactly." Wendy smiled proudly as she held up her jar of alcohol.

Paul looked over in disbelief and horror.

Inside the jar floated two fleshy objects the shape and size of small hen's eggs.

7

Paul kept driving while Wendy worked at raising Clarence and the inspectors on the radio. After several minutes of nerve-grating static she finally made contact. Wendy explained that they had three bunyips with them in need of medical attention. Clarence suggested a rendezvous point. His group arrived first and already had an RFDS doctor and plane waiting as Paul and Wendy drove up. Clarence rushed to the Land Cruiser ahead of the others.

"Listen, Paul, this is a little irregular. The RFDS wouldn't have come had they known that the patients aren't human. So let me do the talking."

"No problem."

Seconds later the doctor, a gangling scarecrow of a man about Paul's age, caught up with them. "Where are these children I'm supposed to be treating?"

Paul pointed to the back seat. The two healthier bunyips sat upright with Maude spread across their laps. All three responded with wan but pleasant smiles.

The doctor stared in slack-jawed bewilderment for some time. Then he took Clarence aside.

"Did you say that these three . . . uh . . . patients . . . are your children?"

"Yes, that's correct. Maude, Anthony and Clarence, Jr."

"Uh . . . yeah. Listen, do they have some . . . uh . . . uh

. . . genetic irregularity . . . or something . . . that I should know about?"

"If I tell you the truth will you promise to keep it a secret?"

"Of course."

Clarence dropped his voice to a whisper. "Their mother and I are cousins."

"Ah!" The doctor nodded his understanding.

Still bewildered, the doctor opted to fly his patients to the hospital in Silver Hill. "We have many specialists there. One of them undoubtedly knows the best therapy for children with this . . . condition."

Paul and Clarence rode along, leaving Wendy and the inspectors to their own affairs. The doctor had just checked the bunyips into the emergency room when he was recalled to the airstrip. He seemed relieved at being able to move on to more familiar crises.

The three bunyips now lay together on a gurney, curtained off from the rest of the room. Maude wore a pink stretch tank top donated by Wendy, and the males wore khaki shirts borrowed from the inspectors. The oversized clothing made the three a little less obvious, Paul concluded, but the overall effect remained unavoidably strange.

He paced a narrow strip alongside the gurney, wondering how much longer Clarence would be able to fast-talk them through. Clarence paced the opposite side of the gurney, polishing his glasses. The curtain parted as a nurse backed in, pulling with her an IV stand and a cart loaded with saline bags and tubing.

"What are you doing?" Clarence asked.

"Starting an IV drip. The poor kids are so dehydrated that the doctor—"

"No, absolutely not. Their blood chemistries are completely different from anything—"

"Look, mister, if you don't mind—"

"It's *doctor.* Doctor Clarence Richmond. I'm a board-certified taurocoprologist with the CSIRO in Canberra." His voice carried a sudden air of urgency, and left no doubt of his authority. "We have an emergency here, so let's move quickly. I need for you to draw 3 cc's of blood, no more, from each of these children and run, not walk, the samples to the lab for stat chemistries. I assume that there's a hematologist on staff?"

"Well, yes, but—"

"Call him *now* and tell him he's needed immediately. We've got to have those blood chemistries waiting when he gets here. Then he can order the proper infusions."

"But I don't—"

"I'll handle anything else that comes up."

"Doctor, I was told to—"

"Yes, I'm aware of that." He ushered her out with a reassuring pat on the arm. "You know how suddenly these things change, though. I'll explain everything to your supervisor later, and see that you're commended for your prompt assistance."

"Yes, sir," the nurse sighed in exasperation, then muttered, "And they wonder why there's a nursing shortage."

Paul whispered, "By the way, what's a torco—"

"Taurocoprologist? Like the word? I made it up myself. It's from the Greek stems 'tauro' for bull and 'copro' for shit."

"I had a feeling. What are you gonna tell the hematologist?"

Clarence wrinkled his brow and shrugged. "Whatever works."

An hour later, an angry male voice rose from the other side of the curtain. "Would somebody kindly run up to the lab and shoot the bloody technician? Just look at these chemistries! A sodium of 750 milligrams?" A middle-aged man in a white coat came through the curtain, continuing to address someone behind him. "The only kids with profiles like this would be a bunch of bloody—" He turned to his patients and froze, voice dropping to a whisper. "—*bunyips*!"

"Yes, indeed." Clarence stepped forward and clasped the doctor's hand with both his own. "You've obviously been following the news reports, so you're aware that our little friends here were en route for treatment at St. Luke's in Sydney. With all the recent publicity, though, it's tough getting them around without being mobbed. So the head of hematology at St. Luke's sent us here. He insisted that if," Clarence quickly scanned the doctor's name tag, "*David Kaplan* couldn't take care of them, nobody could. You come highly recommended, you know."

"Well, thank you. But I don't—"

"No one else knows anything about treating bunyips, either. That's why we so desperately need a physician of your stature. You, my friend, are about to make medical history . . . "

Not only did Kaplan agree to take care of the bunyips, but the medical staff director even allowed them to be hospitalized on condition that they remain isolated on the top floor of the five-story building, the old polio ward which had gone unused for many years. Clarence had no trouble convincing the chief veterinarian of Sydney's Taronga Zoo, who specialized in treating marsupials, to catch the next plane to Silver Hill.

With the immediate crisis behind him, Paul paid a visit on Freddy.

"You're eating on your own already?"

"Too right! Been a long time since I got dinkum tucker like this, mate!" Freddy replied happily. He seemed oblivious of the IV lines still plugged into his left arm. He polished the last residue of custard from his dish with a bread crust and ate with obvious relish, pointing eagerly to the bed table. There a second meal tray awaited.

Paul exchanged the trays. "I guess even hospital food would be a treat to someone used to eating straight out of the tin. I can't believe how fast you're recovering."

"It's the women, mate. Gawd almighty! Ever' five minutes there's a bird in here fluffin' me pillow or takin' me temperature or rubbin' me somewheres. They's got me circulation goin' to parts o' me anatomy that ain't been serviced in years! I made naughty suggestions to a couple of 'em, an' they says to ask again soon's I'm well enough to live up to me promises. That's enough incentive to heal the dead, mate!" He cut a slice from what looked oddly like boiled steak and popped it in his mouth. "So tell me about yer chasin' Nate."

Paul related the events of the past few days, and Freddy had to struggle not to burst several dozen stitches when he learned about the twin trophies in Wendy's jar. It was the last light-hearted moment. Next came the news of Alex's death, and the conversation turned serious. There was a long pause at the end, and Paul knew that something was bothering his friend.

"Come on, Freddy, out with it. What's on your mind?"

"Perfesser, I learnt somethin' the other day that yer just ain't gonna believe."

Paul stiffened. Freddy normally just blurted whatever he had to say, and seemed to enjoy catching Paul off guard. Why would he now try to soften the blow?

"It's about yer Sheila. 'Fore I tells yer, though, I want yer to explain t'me how yers broke up."

"My God, Freddy, you're asking me—"

"—about the worst time o' yer whole bloody life. I knows. But yer've gotta trust me, mate. I wouldn't ask if it weren't important."

Paul took a deep breath. What was Freddy hiding from him? But then again, maybe Freddy wasn't holding back. He seemed pretty confused too. Not surprising. Sheila herself didn't know the whole story. It was a private agony that he'd carried alone for seven long years. But if he couldn't trust Freddy, well . . .

"It was graduation day." Paul spoke in a monotone to mask the hurt and shame. "My folks had ridden up with Angela's to attend the ceremonies . . . "

* * *

Paul and Sheila had been engaged for about a month by then, and he was looking forward to telling his parents about the wedding plans. His family had already met Sheila, back when she and Paul were still just friends and he'd taken her home for Christmas. They'd been thoroughly charmed by her and had heartily congratulated Paul on coming to his senses before she got away.

Sheila had agreed to marry Paul on the condition that, instead of buying her a diamond, they'd combine their savings and go to Australia for two months. She was not only homesick, but she'd set her mind on getting married in the same little church in Silver Hill where her parents had said their vows twenty-five years before.

The first few years of marriage would be hectic. Sheila had been accepted to the University of Kansas Medical School in Kansas City. He would begin his graduate studies at KU. They planned to move into an apartment in Kansas City, and Paul would commute the 45-minute drive to Lawrence. Money might be tight, but Sheila had won a full scholarship, and he had a graduate assistantship lined up. Somehow they'd make it work.

As Paul sat waiting for his parents to call, he felt relief that they were going to Angela's apartment instead of his. They were warm, loving people but also very traditional. If confronted, they'd probably accept the fact that Paul and Sheila were already living together, but why cause them unnecessary pain?

The phone rang and he answered. It was his dad. They'd arrived at Angela's.

"We'll be right over," Paul said cheerfully.

"Come over by yourself, son." His dad's voice sounded grave. "We've got something important to talk over."

Worried, he told Sheila he'd be back for her soon and then headed over. Angela was waiting for him in the hallway outside her apartment door. Her arms were folded against her chest, her expression tight-lipped. She'd obviously been crying.

"I'm pregnant, thanks to you!" Her eyes burned into his. "And if we don't get married now, my folks will disown me."

Neither abortion nor adoption would even be considered. Both families regarded marriage as the only morally acceptable solution. A long conversation with Angela and both sets of parents followed. Paul was in too much shock at the time to absorb a lot of what was said.

There was no forgetting the implacable resolve in his dad's sun-weathered face as he grasped Paul by both shoulders, his steel-gray eyes anchored like a rock into Paul's soul. "You have to marry Angela."

It would have been far easier to stand up to the devil himself. Paul didn't owe the devil for raising him. "No way, Dad! Sheila and I—"

"Tell me that my only son is a responsible Christian who's man enough to own up to his mistakes."

The devil never appealed to your basic decency. "Of course I am, Dad. But it doesn't—"

"Tell me that you'd never disgrace your family."

The devil never showed anguish when you disappointed him. "You know I wouldn't. But Angela herself—"

"Tell me that my own flesh and blood isn't going to leave his child behind to run away with another woman."

The devil never made you feel like a son of a bitch. "No, Dad, I won't run away."

Nowadays, when that scene came back to haunt him, Paul pictured himself stopping the confrontation by grabbing his father's face and squeezing it into a shapeless mass like so much bread dough. Back then, he was still the obedient son.

He couldn't even remember the words he used to tell Sheila that he had to marry Angela. But he clearly remembered her reaction—that hard, silent stare that to this day seared into him from his dreams. Then she turned around and walked into the bedroom, closing the door behind her.

Paul bought a quart of tequila and drove to his favorite spot in the woodlands south of Lawrence. He wasn't among his black-robed classmates that evening as they paraded proudly down KU's Mount Oread into the stadium to have their degrees conferred upon them. By then he'd already passed out in the back seat of his car.

The next day, still reeling from a dry-heave hangover, he drove back to the apartment to beg Sheila's forgiveness. She was already gone. She'd packed all her belongings, the contents of two suitcases, and taken a bus to the West Coast. He never even had a chance to say good-bye.

Three days later, Paul and Angela were wed in a private ceremony in the same red brick church in LaCrosse, Kansas, where both sets of their parents had married.

The cruelest blow of all, though, came two months later when Angela's doctor discovered that her "pregnancy" was actually a tumor in her uterus. She nearly died during the surgery to remove it. As Paul sat in Angela's hospital room, he struggled to avoid blaming her. After all, she hadn't wanted to get married, either. She'd fallen victim to the same parental expectations that Paul himself had succumbed to. No matter how sorry he felt for his wife, he couldn't help feeling that he'd been cheated.

He forced himself to be compassionate and supportive of Angela during her recovery, but their relationship began showing strain shortly thereafter. The marriage was dissolved in less than a year . . .

* * *

"So why didn't yer go back to Sheila an' explain what happened?"

"I started to, right after Angela and I split. The registrar at the medical school told me that Sheila had gotten married and transferred to a school back in Australia."

Freddy remained silent as Paul paused a moment to keep his voice from breaking. Even after seven years, the memories still ripped him apart.

"Do you realize that this is the first time I've ever said out loud that she's married? It's like I couldn't admit it to myself. It didn't seem like something she'd do. I was the only man she'd ever had a relationship with. As weak and stupid as I'd been, I thought it'd take years for her to love anyone again. Yet just a few months later, she got married. And today's the first time I've even been able to say it: Sheila married another man."

"D'yer know her husband's name?" It was obvious from Freddy's tone that he already had the answer.

"No, and I never tried to find out. It hurt too much just knowing I'd lost her. I didn't want to learn anything about the lucky bastard she wound up with. In fact, I still don't want to hear about him . . . unless maybe she's divorced." Paul felt a powerful mixture of hope and dread rising from within.

"I gots news 'bout her husband, all right, an' she ain't divorced."

Paul's last hope now lay crushed.

Deep down, though, he knew that his grief over Sheila was an infection that would fester until drained. No matter how much Freddy's news would hurt, he had to face it.

"Okay," Paul sighed. "Out with it. What have you learned?"

"I ain't sure meself. Even with all yer've told me, this still don't make sense. I thought the sister who tol' me was havin' a joke. It's the dinkum truth, though! Seems that yer Sheila—"

"Paul!" Clarence Richmond exploded into the room. "Grab your shotgun! Let's go. We've got *real* problems."

"Just a second. Freddy here was about to tell me—"

"No time. The plane I've hired is ready to take off the second we get to the airport. Let's go!" Clarence grabbed Paul's arm and dragged him out the door. Minutes later they were airborne again.

A full-scale range war had broken out in the bunyips' habitat, Clarence explained. Someone had been setting fires in the brush and grasslands around the waterholes, and the graziers and miners were blaming each other. There were reports that gunfire had been exchanged.

"More than likely, Nate Townsend's gang has been setting the fires to flush out the bunyips," Paul commented.

"Exactly." Clarence Richmond's face was a mask of exhaustion. Only a month ago he'd complained that his desk job in Canberra was too boring. Right now, he'd probably be delighted to spend an uneventful day at that desk.

He closed his eyes for a brief rest while Paul stared out the window. They were flying over one of the drier parts of what the Aussies called the Red Centre. Below, the ground was barren and scarred, with orange pockmarks standing out against the red soil. How much like the surface of Mars it looked, Paul thought. Occasionally they'd fly over the flat, grayish-white expanse of a lake bed. The water had been long since burned away by the sun, leaving only a ghostly residue of salt.

The desert gave way to grass and occasional trees. They were approaching the bunyips' habitat. As the plane began its descent, the pungent odor of burning wood filled the cabin. On the horizon, smoke the color of steel wool belched from behind an orange curtain of flames.

"If you blokes want to turn back, better say so now," the pilot advised. "We're landing too close to the fire for my liking already, and I'm not waitin' around for you to change your minds. We touch down, you hop out, and I'm gone."

"I don't blame you," Clarence replied. "Just stay tuned to the radio. We'll be in contact, although I have no idea when."

Moments later, Paul and Clarence were on the ground. The two wildlife inspectors, Roger and Jay, were waiting for them. Rugged, good-looking bachelors about Paul's age, both projected the cockiness of mercenary warriors.

"We've been trailing the poachers since early this morning," Jay explained. "They seem to be movin' just ahead of the flames, where they can pick off anything fleeing for safety. I caught a glimpse of their truck a couple of hours ago. It's a green utility. Three men. There might be four. They didn't see me, though. Our scheme is to come up from behind and surprise them. If we can corner them between ourselves and the flames, they're not likely to put up much of a fight."

They boarded the Land Cruiser, Roger at the wheel, and drove toward the billowing wall of smoke. Capturing the poachers would be a risky affair. Not only would they be chasing armed men, but they'd have to keep constant watch on the position and direction of the flames to avoid being trapped themselves.

Paul's cheeks already burned from the heat radiating off the inferno beyond a stone's throw away. Jay picked up fresh tire tracks through the dry grass. They followed them for a half mile or so. The path ahead turned rocky and treacherous, leading into scrub that stood taller than a man's head.

Roger pulled to a stop. "It's too dangerous to go any

further. No idea what's beyond, and we'd be in a bad way if we had to back out in a hurry."

Clarence concurred. Roger was just about to put the Land Cruiser in reverse when a man's shout rose from the distance. "I got one!"

"What d'yer reckon?" Jay asked. "They're two, maybe three hundred feet away?"

Roger nodded. "Yeah. But it could be an ambush, too." He paused a moment, thinking, then turned to Clarence. "How about you wait here with the vehicle, Dr. Richmond, in case they try to come back this way? The rest of us will sneak in on foot. That'll give us the upper hand even if it is a trick."

Clarence shook his head. "I don't want you men taking that kind of risk. This isn't come kind of game that—"

"We'll be fine," Jay insisted. He turned to Paul. "Yer comin' with us?"

"Yeah. You'll need cover, and I'm a pretty decent shot." He stuck a handful of shotgun shells into the pocket of his bush vest. The adrenaline was flowing. He wouldn't have trouble using the gun this time. At least, he didn't think he would.

"Right, then. Paul, yer stay to me left, and Roger, to me right. We'll have to spread out. Be careful. Let's not go shootin' each other."

They pushed forward into the brush. For the first hundred feet or so, Paul could still see Jay off to the right. Paul crouched down, passed under the canopy of a ten-foot witchity bush, then tried to re-establish Jay's position. His heart surged as he realized that he'd lost sight of his companion.

He didn't dare yell. He began edging to the right, hoping to resume contact.

Then, for no apparent reason, he felt a peculiar urge to head left, on a course that would take him farther away from the others. The idea made no sense. Paul pushed it aside and continued right.

The urge grew stronger with every step, until he could no longer ignore it. Something more important than his own safety beckoned him.

He paused to wipe the sweat from his face and, during the brief moment his eyes closed, saw an image of a large gum tree. The smooth white trunk shot upward in a single shaft for about twenty feet, then split off in a thick lower branch and three smaller, upright branches, the whole effect resembling a hand with the thumb and three fingers extended.

He surveyed his surroundings. Off to the left, about 500 feet away, towered the gum tree he'd just envisioned. Against all common sense, he walked toward it.

About half way there, he noticed a movement in one of the shrubs ahead and crouched for cover.

One of Nate's gang, the dumb-looking youth from the field station, walked past with a tied-up bunyip in his arms. Paul sprang from behind and smacked the side of his gun butt against the kid's left temple, dropping him instantly.

Paul untied the bunyip and used the same ropes to hog-tie the youth. The flames were moving away, so he decided to leave the hostage to be picked up later.

He expected the bunyip, a female with a bulging pouch, to run away. Instead, she sat in place rubbing her head groggily. Paul pulled the bunyip's hand back to observe an egg-sized lump where she'd been clubbed.

"I don't know how much of this you understand, but I'm going to carry you to safety." He pointed in the direction of the Land Cruiser. "I won't keep you, though. You can leave anytime you want."

Maybe it was just the reassuring tone of his voice, but the bunyip seemed to understand. He picked her up and made toward the Land Cruiser.

The wind shifted and thick clouds of black smoke

seemed to blow in every direction. The situation had turned even more dangerous. Not only was visibility obstructed, but the fire was now headed this way. Paul pushed himself faster.

Roger's voice rose from downwind. "Jay! Paul! Where the bloody hell are yers? Let's get our arses outta here!"

The blare of the Land Cruiser's horn pierced the air, providing both a warning and a beacon for their return.

A shotgun boomed from somewhere ahead. Paul hoped it was only a signal for attention.

His blood ran cold when Jay yelled, "Roger! Bloody Christ! They got Roger!"

Paul's breath came in ragged gasps as he raced toward Jay's voice with a sixty-pound bunyip in his arms. No easy task. Adrenaline kept him going.

The blasts of the horn grew urgent.

Paul nearly ran past the men. Only a glimpse of red off to one side caught his eye.

He turned in horror to find Roger sprawled face down in a pool of blood. The shotgun blast had caught him in the neck, nearly blowing his head off. Jay knelt beside him in disbelief.

Paul looked behind. Orange flames were gaining on them. "Jay! Let's go! In another minute, we'll all be cremated!"

Jay started to pick up the body.

"Leave him, Jay! He's dead. If we try and take the body with us, we're all gonna be caught in the fire."

"Belt up, Yank! I ain't leavin' me mate behind!"

Another boom, and Jay's head exploded in front of Paul as the full charge of a shotgun ripped through his skull.

Paul dove for cover. A thick cloud of black smoke obscured everything for several seconds. There was a brief clearing of the air, and he looked up to see Nate's face peering down the barrel of a shotgun that was now leveled at his own head.

Paul sprang forward, landing belly first on top of the bunyip just as Nate's shot split the air. Another cloud of smoke obscured everything, and Paul aimed in Nate's direction.

He had only two shots without reloading and didn't dare fire without a clear target.

The smoke choked him, but he fought the reflex to cough. Any noise would bring a hail of gunfire.

"Didja git 'im?" asked a voice from somewhere behind the smoke.

"Reckon so," Nate replied. "I'm just goin' in to make sure."

Paul steadied himself, trigger finger at the ready. For once, there were no doubts, no worries about balking at the last moment. He stood ready to fight.

Nate would die the second he revealed himself.

Paul listened for movement, but heard nothing over the crackling of flames and the persistent beep of the horn. Sight alone would guide his shot.

He scanned the brush, senses prickling.

Nothing moved.

Where was Nate? Circling in from behind?

Paul eased himself up to a crouching position, weight balanced on the balls of his feet, ready to wheel about and fire in any direction.

The seconds ticked away in cruel countdown.

Still nothing. The flames crept ever closer.

C'mon, fucker. Show yourself, he thought.

No movement.

The fire scorched his face.

Deciding he'd rather risk being shot than burned to death, he lifted the bunyip onto his left hip and stood up, shotgun still ready in his right hand.

Clarence continued to blast away on the horn, and Paul had to reach him before Nate did.

The wind picked up, driving the flames faster. Both

Paul and the bunyip were gagging on the smoke, but somehow he pushed ahead.

A crackling came from ahead. He looked up.

"Shit!"

The wall of flames was now directly to the left of him, and closing in rapidly. He headed right. The bunyip seemed more alert, so he put her down where she could provide at least some of her own power while he pulled her by the arm.

She seemed to know where she was going, soon taking the lead. The passageway through the brush narrowed. He let go of the bunyip and began following her.

She quickened the pace, easily gliding under and around the branches that snagged Paul's every step.

"Slow down! I can't keep up!"

The passageway seemed to disappear.

So did the bunyip.

"Wait! Where'd you go? Don't just leave me here!"

There was no time to search for her. He pushed on in the same direction she'd been leading him. He made another twenty feet and stopped cold.

"God damn it!" The flames were now straight ahead. He was completely surrounded. Of all the ways to die, being burned alive horrified him most. It had happened to him before, in his nightmares. He'd watch helplessly as the flames crept toward him. Then his clothes would catch fire, burning away to reveal blackened, peeling skin below. This time, there'd be no waking up.

An agonized scream rose, then faded in the distance. The man he'd left tied up back there would have his revenge when Paul met the same fate. Already, the heat stung his face.

"If you die saying a prayer, you get to finish it in heaven," Grandma McDaniel had always told him.

"All I ask, God, is that You please get it over with quickly."

Something tugged his ankle. He looked down to see a

small, hairy arm coming out of a bush. He lifted the branches with both hands, revealing a tunnel about two feet in diameter. It led down at a diagonal for several feet and opened into a den.

Paul squeezed in feet first. A hatch made of woven twigs and dried mud leaned by the opening, and Paul secured it in place before easing backward into the den. It was cool and moist inside, and the only sensation of the inferno above came from the muffled crackling of flames.

Four adult bunyips sat tightly packed around him, the ceiling too low for Paul to sit comfortably. He scrunched down until his chin rested almost on his knees. Surprisingly, the air was fresh; two holes leading out from the ceiling seemed to provide ventilation. Where the holes went remained a mystery, since no light entered the den from either.

Paul settled in as the others watched him in quiet anticipation.

Now what? he wondered.

None of the bunyips moved or showed any sign of emotion. They just stared at him. He studied their faces. The female he'd rescued sat directly across from him, her toes resting against his boots. She looked a little older than Maude, with small wrinkles around her eyes and touches of gray sweeping back from the temples. Although she didn't show pain or touch the lump where she'd been clubbed, Paul knew that her head must hurt horribly. Next to her sat another, slightly younger-looking female with a joey in her pouch. She was plumper than the other, with wide-set eyes and a maternal calm to her expression that belied the terrible danger they were all in.

Immediately beside Paul sat a male, larger than the females, muscular and apparently in the prime of youth. He had a sturdy face with a broad nose and strong chin. Paul detected an inherent suspicion behind the deep-set eyes that glared back from only a few inches away. And finally, against the far wall, sat a smaller male whose gray hair framed a timeworn face. His eyes, almost obscured by folds of skin at the corners, stared into Paul's with fixed intensity. He seemed to understand Paul's reason for being there.

Paul suddenly realized that he'd been observing all these details in pitch darkness. The hatch had completely sealed the den's entrance, blocking out all outside light.

Sweat poured down his forehead and stung his eyes. He pulled the bandana from his hip pocket and wiped his face. As he did, Paul noticed something very unusual.

"I can still see you," he whispered in awe. Sure enough, whether his eyes were open or closed, Paul saw with the same clarity.

The old male nodded, as if to acknowledge Paul's glimmer of understanding. Then Paul saw a vision of Maude, hog-tied, being carried toward a truck by one of Nate's henchmen.

"You want to know what happened to her, is that it? Don't worry. She's okay, and so are two of the males that were with her."

Paul felt an eagerness he knew the bunyips must have shared. They were so close . . . so close . . . to comprehending each other.

The old one leaned forward anxiously but didn't change his expression.

"I guess you can't follow human speech, can you?"

What *would* they understand? Obviously, the bunyips used some kind of telepathy involving mental pictures. Yet with all the time he and Freddy had spent around Maude, the only messages they'd exchanged with her had been in the form of gestures. The passing images they'd received from her here and there really couldn't be considered any kind of dialogue. Then again, neither man had ever attempted to enter directly into Maude's thoughts. Perhaps the bunyips would understand if he sent them a picture. He'd last seen Maude and the two males alive and well, lying on a hospital bed. He concentrated on the scene, trying to visualize it.

He could see it now.

Paul felt a prickling up the back of his neck. Almost there.

He forced his mind clear of all else. The vision grew clearer.

He sensed the old one pulling the thoughts forward, drawing Paul's mind into his. All Paul had to do was concentrate . . . concentrate . . .

A burst of blue light streaked through Paul's mind like a lightening bolt arcing the midnight sky.

Contact!

The next morning, Paul headed out alone. The grasslands around the waterhole had been reduced to smoldering black ash, and the heat from the ground still scorched his feet through his boots. Eventually he sighted the unscathed Land Cruiser that Clarence had been driving. Paul already knew from the bunyips that Clarence had escaped the fire and poachers and had now returned to look for him. But he remained wary. A lot of things had gone wrong lately, and he still couldn't see Clarence. He moved cautiously, one eye scanning the horizon, his shotgun loaded and ready.

There was still no sign of Clarence when he reached the Land Cruiser. He looked inside. Still nothing. Walking around to the driver's side, Paul saw footprints in the ashes leading off into the distance. Smoke from a smoldering patch of trees obscured his view. He followed the trail into the smoke, covering nose and mouth with his bandana.

When he reached clear air again, he saw Clarence Richmond on his knees, staring silently at the charred remains of Jay and Roger.

"Dr. Richmond?"

"Paul! You're alive!" Clarence sprang to his feet and embraced him.

Clarence's sallow face showed all its years and more as Paul explained how Jay and Roger had been murdered.

"We'll have to let the police take over from here." Clarence was resigned. "How did you escape the flames yourself?"

Paul took a deep breath and concentrated on sounding rational. "The bunyips saved me. I spent the night with four of them in one of their underground dens. I can't begin to explain what an experience it was."

"I don't doubt it. I just hope you learnt something that will help us put an end to the killing."

"Unfortunately, what I learned is that we'll have to evacuate the bunyips entirely. Even if we were to round up Nate's gang immediately, they've already destroyed most of the bunyip's food base and ground cover. They'll starve and be easy targets for other poachers if we don't get them out. Also, several of them need treatment for burns."

Clarence lifted a shaggy eyebrow.

"Just how do you propose we round them up?"

"We don't have to. They're ready to come on their own. There's plenty of room for them on the fifth floor of the Silver Hill hospital. We can keep them there until we find them a safe haven. They've agreed to—"

"Wait a minute, Paul. What do you mean, 'they're ready to come?' What did you do? Sit around the campfire discussing strategy? Do they speak English or is bunyip that easy to pick up?"

"They don't speak. In fact, they don't even have vocal chords. They communicate with thoughts."

"Say that again?"

"It's true, Clarence." Although Paul had never addressed him by first name before, it now came easily. "How could any creature as intelligent as the bunyips exist without some means of sharing knowledge and experience? Yet the bunyips have no obvious form of communication. At least, not one we understand."

"Are you suggesting that—"

"—the bunyips communicate by mental telepathy. Yes! Not using words, exactly, but by sharing images and sensations."

"And humans can understand them?"

"Sometimes, anyway. The messages seem to get clearer with practice. Even then, they're hard to interpret. Some are like movies on fast rewind. Others appear as premonitions, where they see you doing something in the future. I think it's their way of telling you what they *want* you to do. Still other messages are simple relays, transmitting one person's thoughts to another. That explains why some of us had the weird feeling that we were reading each other's minds back at the field station. There are other forms too, but I don't even know how to describe them. I'm just beginning to sort things out, and the bunyips are trying to learn how human minds work."

Clarence paused a moment, eyes widening. "As scientists, Paul, you and I both know that this makes no sense. On another level, I think I do understand. I remember back at the field station when I first met Maude. I kept having these crazy . . . sort of . . . daydreams. They weren't my own daydreams, though. More like . . . *other people's* daydreams." He smiled slightly. "The one I remember most clearly was about this naked blonde girl with big tits who kept saying 'I love you, Paul.'"

Paul turned away, his cheeks burning. Would he ever have privacy again?

"So how did the bunyips tell you that they're ready to be evacuated?"

"In my own mind I pictured Maude and the other two in the hospital. I was trying to show that they were safe. Later, I got back a very clear picture of the bunyips joining Maude and the others on the fifth floor. They were showing me that's where they want to go. I'm sure of it."

"So where are they, then?"

"Rounding up the others. The entire population is only about three or four dozen. I explained to them, as best I could, that we'd bring in a plane big enough to hold them all. They'll meet me wherever the plane lands. They hooked me into your mind back when you were radioing for a plane to pick up the bodies. Why don't you fly back to Silver Hill and get things ready for us at the hospital?"

"You realize that we're both going to look like bloody fools if the bunyips don't show up. But at this stage—"

"—who cares? You're right."

Clarence was a specialist at getting things done. Less than six hours after he called the airbase, the bunyips were boarding the aging twin-engine Beechcraft he'd chartered. It was a commuter plane designed to hold twenty passengers. Since bunyips were only a bit more than half the size of their human counterparts, they could all crowd in together. There were only 33 adults and adolescents plus four children, too large for the pouch. Six of the adult females had bulging pouches that probably contained infants. Add in Maude and the two males back at the hospital, and the world bunyip population came to only 46, not counting embryos.

Paul ached as he watched the tiny figures, many with oozing burns on their arms and legs, help each other up the steps to the plane. One older male, badly burned, was carried by two others. Although his carriers tried to be gentle, the old one's burns were so extensive that it was impossible to move him without inflicting further pain. He could only grimace in silent agony, and Paul realized that there was very little likelihood he'd survive.

Those too young to make it up the steps were lifted on board. Paul noted that two young adult males, including the one from the den, had taken charge of the juveniles. Paul stepped forward to assist, but the males immediately placed themselves between him and the children. The bunyips didn't seem aggressive or hostile. In fact, they avoided even looking in Paul's direction. Nevertheless, the message was unmistakable.

He raised his hands slightly and backed off. "Sorry. I only meant to help."

Among young and old, the facial expressions were uniformly somber. None of them looked forward to what was about to happen, and all were afraid. But they had no choice. A series of human deeds, starting with Paul's decision to use Maude to further his own career instead of releasing her immediately, had destroyed the only way of life the bunyips had ever known.

An invisible boundary separated professional responsibility from avarice, and Paul realized that he'd stepped over it. As a result, the bunyips were reduced to this pathetic collection of refugees forced to entrust their destiny to the very species that might well destroy them.

Paul could not conceive of a less comfortable ride than the flight back to Silver Hill. He was tempted to sit up front, in the vacant copilot's seat where he'd be at least partially isolated from the bunyips. But he couldn't fly and wouldn't be of much use even if the pilot dropped dead on them. Besides, honor dictated that he stay with his charges. Sitting in the front row of the passenger compartment, Paul was fully aware of the dozens of tiny eyes burning into the back of his head. He felt lonely, conspicuous, and very much ashamed.

Hundreds of scattered, incomprehensible images darted through his brain. He tried in vain to make sense of a few, but the barrage overwhelmed him. Focusing on his own thoughts proved even more worrisome.

The plane jumped and heaved through a seemingly endless stretch of turbulence, and the odor of vomit soon permeated the cabin. Paul fought to control his own nausea, not knowing whether he was clinically sick or sharing the reaction of those around him. In either case, there was nothing to be done since the plane had no lavatory. The airsickness proved almost a relief from the other things occupying his consciousness. The ride dragged on.

Finally they touched down. True to form, Clarence already had a bus waiting. As the ragged little band made its way off the plane and onto the bus, Paul observed that Clarence's expression betrayed the heartache the man surely felt. At last the bunyips were loaded.

Paul hesitated before boarding the bus himself.

Clarence seemed to understand without asking. "You've been at this too long, Paul. You haven't slept in a couple of days, I'm sure. I want you to take a break and let me manage things a while."

Paul sighed. "Yeah. I guess I do need to clear my brain a little. The bunyips already understand that they're to follow you. So if it's all right, I'll walk from here. I should make the hospital in an hour or so."

"Yeah . . . good idea . . . take your time."

The door closed, and the bus departed in a cloud of dust and diesel fumes.

Paul walked slowly, totally absorbed in his thoughts. He didn't even notice the young woman he passed on the downtown sidewalk, and was startled when she spoke.

"Balloon, mate?"

"Huh? Sorry. What did you say?"

"Care to buy one of these, mate?" She giggled as she pointed up to the cluster of helium-filled balloons she held in her other hand.

"Yeah . . . yeah . . . I would. How many y'got there?" Paul reached for his wallet.

"About two dozen, I reckon. How many d'yer want?"

"All of them." He pressed three bank notes into the startled girl's free hand. "Keep the change."

Paul took the cluster and followed the signs to the city park. There he found an empty bench and, for a long time, sat and stared at the balloons. He'd tug down on the strings and watch as the fragile rubber globes floated back up, straining against their leashes. Helium balloons had always delighted Paul. They reminded him of happier times, of birds, and free spirits.

He tied the strings to a leg of the bench and pulled out his pocket knife. He took a balloon—a bright red one—and detached the string. Then he carefully trimmed off the excess rubber below the knot. After every bit of unnecessary weight had been removed, he released the balloon and watched it float effortlessly away.

In a day or two it would be earthbound. Already helium was seeping from invisible pores in its latex skin. When enough had leaked out, the flight would be over. The balloon would sink slowly back to ground, where it would blow loosely about until it brushed against a thorn and burst. The relentless sun would dry the rubber until it shriveled and cracked and fell apart. Within weeks it would disintegrate into the dusts of the Outback. But for now—for this one brief moment—it flew above the thorns and the dust.

As the balloon faded to a distant speck Paul reached for another and, one by one, liberated them all.

When the last had disappeared from view, he sat down again and buried his face in his hands. He tried to hold back at first, to dam the salty stream trickling through his fingers. But even his well-practiced stoicism could not mute the impact of recent events.

What started as a faint quivering in his shoulders grew to a wracking sob. And for the first time in many years, Paul McDaniel allowed himself to cry.

8

Paul arrived at the hospital after dark. He boarded the elevator and used the special key he'd been given to access the closed-off fifth floor. Clarence was waiting for him.

"How's Maude?" Paul asked.

"Still pretty weak, but otherwise okay. I'll take you to her in a minute. First, I want to show you where the healthy ones are staying." Clarence directed him through a double door and into the old polio ward. It was a scene out of the 1950s, with huge iron lungs lined up like boilers on a steamship. Amid it all, the bunyips wandered about, exploring their new surroundings like curious children, fascinated by the simplest detail.

"We offered them beds," Clarence continued, "but they seem to prefer these old iron lungs."

Paul smiled with wry understanding.

"Makes sense, I guess. They normally sleep in underground dens not much bigger than that. They probably feel safer in the iron lungs than laid out on a bed."

The double doors swung open. A burly man of about forty sporting a thick black mustache stepped into the ward.

"Paul, meet Bruce Wilson, chief veterinarian of Sydney's Taronga Zoo."

"My pleasure," said Bruce with a hearty smile and a bone-crushing handshake.

"How are your patients doing?" Paul asked.

"I'm in over my head," Bruce confessed. "I haven't much experience with burns. They're pretty rare in zoos. With the medical doctors helping out, though, I'll give it a try."

He led them back out of the ward and down the opposite hall where the private rooms were located.

Maude's room was the first stop. She was laid out on the same bed with the two males from the shed.

"They don't seem to like sleeping by themselves," Bruce explained.

Each bunyip had an IV line dripping fluid and nutrients into one arm. Maude sat up and hugged Paul weakly with her free arm. The other two smiled as they rubbed his cheek with the knuckles of one hand, a gesture he now recognized as the standard bunyip greeting.

Paul looked into Maude's eyes and concentrated his thoughts.

There was a flash of blue light that only the two of them could see.

Maude blinked with surprise, then smiled approvingly.

"We could have transfused them with blood from the others," Bruce explained, unaware that he'd interrupted. "but I thought there'd be less risk of complications if we stuck with IV fluids and let them grow their own blood."

"They seem to be responding just fine," Paul noted.

"Yeah, but they're the easy job," Bruce sighed as he led them to the next room. "This is the hard one."

Inside the room, the old male with the horrible burns lay stretched out on the bed. Long tubes connected him with transparent bags of fluid hanging from an IV stand. His eyes stared blankly at the ceiling.

"A burn specialist is coming in from Sydney tomorrow," Bruce continued. "Until then, all I can do is keep the poor fellow covered with moist dressings and pump him full of antibiotics."

Bruce paused a moment, as if he himself didn't believe what he was about to say. "Y'know, an odd thing happened earlier. The other bunyips tried to come in this room—to see him, I guess. I was going to herd them out. But before I could even stand up, they nodded at me sorta sad-like, then turned around and walked out. I mean, they weren't scared of me. They seemed to understand that I was just trying to protect the old fellow. It was as if they knew what I was thinking."

Paul and Clarence exchanged glances, then the older man turned to Bruce. "We have a lot to tell you about bunyips. Let's save it for tomorrow."

Paul noticed a bottle of rubbing alcohol on one of the shelves. He picked it up and emptied it into the sink. "We have to keep all alcohol and anything even containing it off this floor. The bunyips, from what I've seen, are born alcoholics with no resistance to the stuff. If it weren't for Maude finding Freddy's beer, she'd still be just another mythical creature living free and safe in the Outback."

Next, they visited the bunyips who were being treated with serious but not life-threatening burns. At the end of the tour, Paul suggested that Clarence get some rest.

"Shouldn't we see the bunyips to bed first?" Clarence asked.

"Too early. They're nocturnal, and as much excitement as they've had, they'll have a hard enough time getting to sleep at their normal bedtime."

Clarence left a few minutes later. Bruce showed fatigue too.

Paul agreed to babysit the bunyips overnight so Bruce could go to bed. The veterinarian needed to be well-rested and ready to assist the burn specialist the next day, but he decided to check on his patients one last time before leaving.

Paul excused himself to go to the men's room. Although he felt the need to use the toilet, his body wouldn't cooperate. The urge was still there, and getting painfully stronger.

He tried again.

Still nothing.

"Uh-oh." He pulled his pants back up and returned to the hallway.

"Bruce, have any of the bunyips relieved themselves since they've been here?"

"Not that I know of. I haven't seen any piles or puddles yet. Why?"

"Well, several of them have to go. Very badly."

"So why don't they?"

"I'm glad you asked. Bruce, I need a very important favor before you leave."

"What is it?"

"Use the toilet and let the bunyips watch."

"Eh?"

"They don't understand where or how they're supposed to relieve themselves around here. One of us has to give them a demonstration on how to use the toilet. I'd do it myself, but I don't have to go yet."

"Let me get this straight. You want me to sit on the dunny in front of three dozen hairy-assed, lizard-eating alcoholics and enrich their little minds by letting them *watch me take a crap? Bloody hell!*"

"I *knew* you'd understand. I'll go round them up while you make yourself comfortable."

Paul had picked up Freddy's art of persuasion by relentless enthusiasm, and soon had a bare-bottomed, muttering Bruce demonstrating his expertise in the use of indoor plumbing. While Bruce sat in place, the wide-eyed bunyips gathered around him in the black-and-white tiled chamber. As the lesson proceeded, the bunyips' initial curiosity quickly degenerated into hilarity, and the room echoed with the breathy little sneezing sounds of bunyip laughter. His modesty and dignity shattered, Bruce buried his increasingly crimson face in his hands and headed down the stairwell the instant class was over.

Bruce's reluctant demonstration served its purpose. The bunyips were enthralled by the workings of the porcelain fixtures, and for the next several hours the late night hush of the hospital was broken by the ceaseless flushing of toilets, more often out of curiosity than necessity.

As Paul had anticipated, the bunyips were too excited to sleep and spent the entire night exploring the novelties of their new environment. When the rising sun heralded their normally-appointed bedtime, they were finally ready. One by one, they disappeared into their iron lung "dens."

As they did in nature, the bunyips gathered in tightly-packed groups of five to eight per den and went to sleep. Paul observed that they contorted themselves until each of them was physically touching at least two of the others.

He was much in need of sleep himself, but Clarence had already scheduled an early morning joint strategy session. Paul was too tired to be attentive and dozed off several times. Finally, about lunch time, Clarence told him to get some sleep. They could update him later.

Paul accepted the offer without argument. He'd been offered the use of one of the old private patient rooms on the fifth floor, and was undressed, showered and asleep within the space of fifteen minutes.

He dreamed of Kansas, of being six years old again and watching the hot summer wind rippling across the fields of ripening wheat. An old cast-iron bell, which had once summoned his mother to a one-room schoolhouse, rang from the back porch. Dinnertime. The wheat tickled his bare chest as he ran home, and his only worry was whether or not there'd be enough dessert for seconds.

Other dreams unfolded and were quickly lost to memory. Then Sheila appeared. Her image was vivid, but different than he remembered. Her face was a little older now, with the faint traces of laugh lines at the corners of her mouth. Her hair was pulled back into a bun, and her bearing reflected authority and self confidence. The woman in his dream was approaching thirty, as was the real Sheila, and the retouches of maturity made her all the more desirable. Was this how she looked now, or just how he wanted her to look? Kindness and concern were written into the friendly smile she gave as she stood up to leave.

There was no wedding ring on her left hand.

She turned back to say good-bye.

Then she spoke. "It was nice talking to you, too, Freddy."

Freddy? *Freddy*?

"Freddy!" Paul yelled as he awoke with a jolt and jumped out of bed. In his haste, he misjudged the distance to the floor and went sprawling across the room, knocking over the bed table with a crash. With single-minded intensity, he lunged for his clothes, only to trip over the steel water pitcher that had been knocked off its tray. Another crash and thud.

The door opened. "Paul? Are you all right?" Clarence stuck his head in. "My God, Paul, I thought Nate Townsend had gotten hold of you!"

Too excited to speak, Paul could only smile and shrug while dressing as fast as he could. There could be little doubt that he was about to learn exactly what had become of Sheila. His anxiety was almost painful, yet he dared not get his hopes up too high. He ran down the stairs and crashed into Freddy's room.

"Freddy! What in hell is going on?"

Freddy was staring at his watch. "Five minutes an' 32 seconds, Perfesser. That's almost twice as long as it shoulda taken yer. Now we can't have yer dawdling about like that." He was in his "Uncle Freddy the Omniscient" mode.

"I repeat: Freddy, what in hell is going on?"

"I'm doin' good, thanks. An' how's life on the fifth floor?"

Sometimes Freddy's coyness could be entertaining. Right now, it had Paul looking around for a large blunt instrument.

"Cut the crap, Freddy. Tell me what you know about Sheila."

"Really, now, Perfesser, we's gonna have t' discuss yer manners."

"We'll discuss them at your funeral, you sadistic moron!" He grabbed the stool by Freddy's bed and jerked it overhead in an obvious threat.

"Tch, tch, tch." Freddy clucked. "You know better'n to assassinate a bloke with a piece o' furniture. We'd *never* get the mess cleaned up. Jist put the stool back, calm down, an' let Uncle Freddy unravel the sweet mysteries o' life for yer. First, I want'cher t' meet someone." He turned toward the door and yelled. "Rosie! Come 'ere a minute."

A tall, big-boned woman of about thirty stormed into the room. Almost pretty, she had a round face and a cheerful but crusty demeanor. She wore her nurse's cap with the authority of sergeant's stripes.

"I told yer before, Freddy, this ain't no pub," she scolded. "Don't go hollerin' down the hall whenever yer fancies yerself in need of attention."

"G'day, sister. Good t' see yer. Like yer to meet me mate here. He went to the University of Kansas—with Sheila Mayor."

"Did yer, now? She's certainly one woman that few men forget, if y'know what I mean." She winked at Paul and cupped her hands in front of her breasts.

Freddy picked up the phone receiver, dialed a number, muttered a couple of words and hung up. He was obviously up to something.

"So you knew Sheila too?" Paul replied awkwardly as he turned his attention back to Rosie. He tried to mask the tension in his voice.

"*Knew* her? Hell, she ain't dead yet, mate," Rosie

laughed. "Yeah, I know her. Have since we was in high school together. 'Cept her name's McDaniel now."

So she'd married someone with the same last name as Paul. The irony made the hurt even worse. No matter how many more surprises awaited him, no matter how much pain they'd bring, he'd already accepted that it was time to face reality. Only then could he finally get Sheila out of his mind.

"Tell me about her husband. Don't think I ever met him." Paul's stomach knotted. Her husband was probably rich, handsome, and famous—the kind of person to be envied even if he weren't married to Sheila. God, this conversation was going to be pure torture.

"I never met the poor bugger neither. He was a biologist or somethin' like that."

"Come again?" Paul braced for a practical joke. Freddy and Rosie had better enjoy themselves now, he decided, because this kind of cruelty demanded retaliation. He looked at Freddy accusingly.

"It ain't no joke, Perfesser, an' it gets a *lot* more interestin'."

"Anyway, he was a Yank," Rosie continued. "Got himself eaten by crocodiles somewhere in South America. Think his name was Paul. That's it—Paul. Paul McDaniel. Poor bugger."

Several seconds of silence elapsed as the blood drained from Paul's face.

"Yer all right, mate?" The nurse reached for a vomit pan.

"I'm okay. Too much sun I guess." Paul shook his head violently. "Please, keep talking."

"Not much more to say, I reckon. Sheila started medical school in the States, but transferred to the University of Sydney right after her husband's death. She's *Doctor* McDaniel now. Finished her residency a few months ago an' joined the staff here as a house medical officer."

"You mean she's here . . . in this hospital . . . right now?"

"Right-o. And she'll be glad to see the likes of you, I'm sure. By the way, mate, me name's Rosie Simmons. What's yers?"

"Uh . . . Paul . . . I mean . . . Mac . . . no . . . I . . . it's Daniel . . . that's it . . . Daniel . . . Daniel McPaul. Friends call me Dan."

"Yer *have* been out in the sun too long, Dan, but welcome to Silver Hill, anyway."

"Thanks. You did say that Sheila works right here . . . in this hospital?"

"Aye. Started back in January. 'Course yer know, she's got a—"

The door opened behind Paul, and a woman's voice addressed Rosie. "Someone just asked me to check back on Freddy before I left for the day."

"Well, look who's here! Dr. McDaniel, say hello to yer ol' mate, Dan."

Paul spun around so quickly that he had to grab the bed to keep from falling over.

He tried to speak, but his voice choked to a coarse whisper. His heart pounded so hard he could hear it. "Sheila!"

Sheila froze. Her eyes widened, but she didn't speak.

"Remember me?" Paul said deliberately. "I'm Dan McPaul. We went to the University of Kansas together."

"Of course I remember you. What are you doing here?" She spoke in flat, measured tones that concealed whatever emotion she was feeling.

"I had to see you again," he replied, using the same flat tones. "I'm divorced now." Just maybe it would make a difference.

"Rosie, would you and Freddy please excuse us? I have something to discuss with Paul."

"Dan," he corrected.

"Whatever!" she snarled between clenched teeth as she

grabbed his arm and jerked him out the door. She dragged him around a corner and into a vacant room.

"What the bloody hell are you doing here?"

"Now is that any way for a grieving widow to talk to her dear, departed husband?"

She drove her fist full-force into his solar plexus, doubling him over.

"You bastard! Couldn't leave well enough alone, could you? Well, if you think you're gonna fuck my life up again, here's what I have to say to you!"

Her foot made a swift and amazingly powerful connection with his groin. He hit the floor like a dropped brick.

It took Paul several minutes to catch his breath and right himself. Sheila stood in place, hands defiantly on her hips.

"I still love you," he said, forcing the strain from his voice. "You're the only one I've ever loved. I just needed to see you again."

"Stuff it! I've already seen what your 'everlasting love' is all about. What about Angela? How many kids did she get stuck with when you dumped her?"

"Angela was never pregnant. It turned out to be a uterine tumor. And for the record, she was the one who left me, although I gave her plenty of reasons for doing so. I tried to contact you after the divorce, but they told me you'd already married someone else. After all the hurt I'd caused you, I wasn't about to interfere with your marriage. Anyway, I'm not asking you to forgive and forget. All I'm saying is that I had to see you again."

"All right. You've seen me. Now push off."

She turned and reached for the doorknob.

"*Sheila*!" Seven years of anguish overflowed his voice.

She grasped the knob but didn't turn it.

"Sheila, the stupidest thing I ever did was to let you go. I've regretted it every day of my life since. I want you to know how sorry I am."

She hesitated, then turned back around. Paul looked into her eyes. She held his gaze.

"I've never lied to you, Sheila. You know that."

"After all this time, you think I'll just—"

"I don't expect anything from you. I just need to set the record straight. You must feel something for me too. Why else would you be posing as my widow?"

She lowered her head, eyes closed. A tear trickled down one cheek.

"Please, Sheila," he reached out and lightly touched her shoulder. "Talk to me. That's all I ask."

She sighed deeply, then blinked back the tears.

"All right. For a little while, anyway. Let's go to my house. I have something to show you."

Back in Freddy's room, Rosie peeked through the closed blinds and reported that Paul had just left with Sheila in her car.

"Good on yer, Perfesser!" Freddy replied with a grin.

Rosie had intentionally forgotten to remove the "Physician in attendance—Do not disturb" sign from the door. Her shift was already over, but she was checking Freddy's vital signs anyway. As she bent over him she knew he wouldn't fail to note the cleavage exposed by her half-unbuttoned blouse.

"Any idea what Dr. McDaniel and yer mate, Dan, will be doin' tonight?" she teased.

A huge left hand slipped behind Rosie's knee and slid up her skirt until it grasped a plump buttock. "I know what *I'd* like to do tonight."

"Men! Yer've only got one thing on yer minds!" Rosie protested. She didn't move away, though. Nor did she push back his other hand as it slipped inside her blouse.

"Yer supposed to comfort the sick, Rosie. All I'm askin' for is a little comfort."

Rosie sighed in mock exasperation as she pulled off her panties. "How do I let meself get talked into these things?"

Paul, riding in Sheila's car, felt a growing erotic surge. It was totally inappropriate. Sheila had done nothing to promote such expectations. He closed his eyes and, sure enough, saw an image of Rosie kneeling on Freddy's bed. Her top was unbuttoned and her skirt had been pulled up around her waist . . .

"What are you thinking about, Paul?"

"Just wondering what Freddy and Rosie are up to right now."

"Not much, I'm sure. After all, it is a hospital."

Paul didn't reply. Instead his thoughts shifted to the bunyips. Were they transmitting stronger messages now or had he simply become more receptive to them? For that matter, who might be peering into his own mind right now? The mental images faded as the car took him farther from the hospital. Hopefully, that meant that he and the bunyips were now out of each other's range.

Sheila rented a furnished two-bedroom cottage sheathed entirely in that ubiquitous Outback construction material, corrugated tin. Once inside, Paul was directed to a brown velour sofa with armrests rubbed shiny from use. An ancient window-mounted air conditioner across the room vibrated fitfully as it dripped water into a blue plastic bucket.

Sheila slipped into the kitchen and returned with a cold beer in each hand. She handed one to Paul and placed herself in the easy chair across from him.

"So tell me what you've been doing with yourself for the last seven years."

Paul described life in Woolloona. Sheila got them another beer, then told him about medical school. By the third beer they were reminiscing over their undergraduate years together. Finally, after two hours and four beers, they were laughing. Sheila had a husky laugh that seemed to come from innocent delight one moment and sensuous abandon the next. Hearing it again made Paul want to reach out and touch her, but he knew that the present magic would burst like a soap bubble the moment he tried. Instead, he stretched one arm across the back of the sofa in hopes that she might eventually accept the silent invitation.

Out of sight, the back door creaked open, then slammed shut with a rattle.

Sheila smiled knowingly. "You wanted to know why I'm posing as your widow? Well, I reckon your explanation just arrived."

Running footsteps thundered down a wooden hall, then a blonde-haired boy about six years old burst into the room.

"Mummy, I'm home!" he yelled happily. Surprised by the presence of a stranger, he stopped short.

The boy's face seemed oddly familiar. Bright green eyes, high forehead and broad smile with full lips—all these features were known to Paul. Many years ago he'd seen a face very much like that. In a mirror. Could this be . . . ?

"Dan, I'd like you to meet my son, Paul McDaniel, Jr. P.J., this is my friend, Dan."

"G'day, Dan. Nice to meetcha." The boy offered a cheerful handshake.

A stunned Paul could only return the handshake with a stiff, "Nice to meet you too, P.J. I . . . uh . . . I went to college with your mother . . . in Kansas."

The boy's face lit up. "You're from Kansas? My dad was from Kansas too. Did you know him?"

Paul, caught completely off guard, looked to Sheila in bewilderment. She offered no help, instead turning away with one hand over her mouth to suppress her laughter. He looked back at his son. For every minute of the past seven years Paul had been painfully aware that he'd made a very big mistake with his life. Only now could he begin to appreciate the enormity of it.

"No, P.J., I'm sorry to say that I didn't know your dad. At least, not very well."

Supper was a thrown-together affair of leftovers and awkward conversation. Paul tried not to stare at P.J., but he could hardly disguise his wonderment. There was no denying the boy's paternity: the posture, the shy half-smile, the sharp-eyed intensity while speaking. All these had come from Paul.

There was much to talk about, so Sheila sent P.J. to bed early. Once they were alone again, Paul was finally able to ask, "So how did you become my widow?"

"What else could I be? Angela might not have been pregnant when you broke off with me, but I was."

Paul's cheeks burned from shame and embarrassment.

Sheila took a deep breath. "I found out right after graduation. You'd married Angela by then and I was left, as we say here, up a gum tree. My parents were already planning our wedding and I couldn't very well disguise my condition for long. So I bought myself a gold ring and told everyone that we'd eloped, and that our plans for a second wedding in Australia had been spoilt when your professor sent you on a six-month expedition up the Amazon. After that, it was simply a matter of killing you off so I could get on with my own life. Until today, no one questioned the story."

"And after all these years you still use my name?"

"Yeah, but don't get the idea I've been pining away for you," she warned. "The only reason I haven't married yet is that, between medical school and P.J., I haven't had time for a permanent relationship. And your name is the *only* part of you I've kept."

They talked into the night. At one point Sheila came back from the kitchen and, instead of returning to her chair, sat on the couch next to Paul. He started to move closer but was stopped short by the stern command of, "Back off!"

The fact that he so richly deserved the rebuke made it that much harder to bear. But Sheila was hurting too. They drank and talked until alcohol and exhaustion suffocated the pain.

Paul's watch said 4 a.m. when he awakened. The beer had worn off, and he was wide awake as he sat up. The room was half-lit by the full moon beaming through open windows. He was alone, wrapped in a sheet on Sheila's sofa. She had let him sleep over on condition that he leave in the morning. His head throbbed.

Aspirin! he thought. He wore only undershorts as he stumbled to the bathroom in the pale light. Locating the box by touch, he gulped down two headache powders with warm water tasting heavily of chlorine.

He turned to leave. Sheila stood naked in the doorway directly in front of him. Her blond hair, previously tied into a bun, now streamed across her shoulders. The fresh tracks of many tears still glistened on her cheeks.

She didn't move or speak. How many times had he dreamt of her, only to awaken alone or in the arms of another woman? Now she stood almost within his grasp. Reality is far more fragile than dreams. Paul had started yesterday alone, and he would probably end tomorrow the same way.

"I've never stopped loving you," he said softly. "And I never will."

As if in slow motion, Sheila stretched out her arms. Paul stepped forward and embraced her. Her kiss was stiff and unfamiliar, her body tense. Gradually, she softened. Her lips parted, inviting his tongue to enter.

Her breath came in husky, rhythmic gasps when he kissed her neck. When his lips reached her ear, he held her tightly and kissed her earlobe, a move that had always been one of her favorite parts of lovemaking. This time she groaned loudly and pushed him back, breaking the embrace.

"I'm sorry, Paul," she whispered. "It took me too long

to get over you the first time. I just can't go through that again."

All of a sudden it seemed to Paul that he'd been a spectator in his own life, that he'd allowed too many important decisions to be made by others. But if he let anyone else—even Sheila herself—make this decision for him, then he deserved the heartache that had tortured him. His passion overwhelmed him. Even if he'd wanted to hold back, he couldn't.

"I'm not letting you go," he said firmly. "Not now or ever again. You're a part of me, and my life has been hell without you."

With a fluid sweep of his arms, she was off her feet and cradled against his chest. She kissed him hard on the lips.

"Just for tonight, and no promises," she whispered as he carried her to the bed.

People change a lot in seven years, and it would take much more than fond memories to rebuild a relationship. Maybe the magic could be revived, maybe not.

But the future lay somewhere over the horizon. This moment would be lived for the present.

9

Paul awoke alone in a bedroom bathed with sunlight. Had it all been a dream? No, Sheila had been there, all right. There could be no mistaking the slightly sweet, slightly musky aroma on the sheets. She never wore perfume. That seductive scent was her own. Mingled with it were the odors of sweat and lovemaking.

He pulled back the faded blue spread and slid out of bed. The bare wood floor creaked beneath his feet as he walked across the room. His clothes were neatly folded on the rocking chair by the door. A handwritten note lay on top of them:

Paul,

I didn't wake you because you seemed so incredibly tired. Also, I don't want P.J. knowing that you spent the night. He's in school now, and I rode to the hospital with a friend so you'd have my car to drive back. The keys are on the kitchen table. Just leave the car in the doctor's parking lot and put the keys under the floor mat.

Thanks for keeping our little secret from P.J. and the hospital staff. Let's just leave things the way they are, at least for now.

You've changed, Paul, and I think for the better. Your boldness last night was refreshing, but also scary. My own

boldness was, well, not typical of me or my real feelings. As I said then, no promises. Right now, I don't know what I feel about all the recent surprises. So I want you to respect me enough to stay away while I think things over. I'll let you know when I'm ready to talk. Please understand that I may well decide to just say good-bye once and for all.
Sheila

PS. Sorry, but there's not much for breakfast. I left a jar of instant coffee on the kitchen counter and there's some bread and Vegemite in the fridge. Help yourself.

Paul was disappointed but not surprised by the reserved tone of the message. She needed breathing room, and he'd give it to her. But say good-bye forever? Not with P.J. involved.

He dressed quickly and headed to the kitchen where he filled the electric jug with water and opened the refrigerator.

"Yechh," he whispered, observing the large jar of Vegemite sitting prominently on the top shelf. Paul had concluded that the Aussies had an inborn contempt for the natural order of the universe in general and culinary propriety in particular. And nothing spoke more eloquently of the fact than Vegemite. A bitter, salty ooze the color of dung and allegedly extracted from yeast, Vegemite appears at first acquaintance to be the kind of noxious sludge that accumulates in the meat drawers of refrigerators that go uncleaned for months on end. And the taste does little to dissuade one of that opinion. Yet the Aussies, probably out of spite, had learned not only to eat but actually enjoy—verily, crave!—the malodorous goo. Even little P.J., his own flesh and blood, doubtless had a Vegemite sandwich tucked away in his schoolbag for an after-school snack. The thought sent a chill down Paul's spine.

He was half through a breakfast of dry toast and instant

coffee when the phone rang. He ignored it at first, but it kept ringing. And ringing. Finally he picked up the receiver.

"Paul, it's Sheila. I'm in Freddy's room. You'd better come in a hurry. He seems to think there's something wrong up on—"

"Perfesser!" Freddy had apparently pulled the receiver from her. "Get yer arse up here, mate. We gots problems."

"What going on?"

"The bunyips is about to riot. I dunno why. I can't get a clear picture of what's happening up there, an' I can't get outta bed to see fer meself. But they's plenty upset. I can feel it."

"I'm on my way."

Paul gulped his coffee and headed out the door. Despite the urgency, he resolved to drive with care. The new Holden sitting in the driveway was surely the first and only major purchase that Sheila had ever made. He couldn't fathom what sacrifices she must have made in order to support herself and P.J. through all her years of training. The car was an obvious triumph for her and would be respected as such.

He felt a growing tension as he neared the hospital. By the time he pulled into the parking lot, he was fighting to control the panic that had become very real to him, even though he knew it was transmitted. He bolted up the stairs and found Clarence waiting just outside the door to the fifth floor.

"Paul! So glad to see you. The bunyips are going mad. They practically attacked me."

"Any idea why?"

"No. All I get from them are a few mental pictures that make no sense to me. And I doubt that anyone else around here is getting even that much. Aside from Freddy, you're the only one who seems to understand them."

"I'll see what I can find out."

Paul unlocked the door and stepped in. The bunyips quickly crowded around him, and he felt the anxious touch of many small hands. He struggled in vain to make sense of their multiple and simultaneous messages. Finally an old male, the one Paul had first met in the den where they escaped the fire, stepped forward and rubbed his knuckles against Paul's cheek. Paul returned the greeting. He'd dubbed the old one Moses, since he seemed to be the closest the bunyips had to a leader.

Instantly, Paul's mind cleared of the commotion of messages as if a hush had come over the room. It was the cue that Moses would now explain the situation to him. To improve his concentration, Paul sat down on the floor and shut his eyes as Moses did likewise.

A burst of blue light.

Then came a vision of the old male with the horrible burns. He was lying on an operating table with green-clad humans all around. The vision zoomed to a close-up of the burned one's head. Then came a blur of motion, like a movie being rewound at high speed. The motion stopped at what appeared to be a freeze-frame of Moses walking through the desert. Standing next to him was an adolescent male. Then another fast-rewind jerked by, followed with another still image of the same two bunyips. The process was repeated many times. Gradually, the adolescent became a child, then was replaced by a female with a bulging pouch. The female herself became an adolescent, then a child. Moses changed back from gray to reddish brown as his wrinkled face became once again smooth and youthful.

The vision shifted back to the old one on the operating table, again zooming to a close-up of his head. Then it shifted to another male, a young adult now on the fifth floor. A zoom to his head followed.

I don't follow, Paul thought. Moses wouldn't understand the words, of course, but he could surely sense Paul's confusion.

Moses continued. Another bunyip's life was run backward in stop-motion. Then a series of geographical scenes, each followed by a freeze-frame of bunyips drinking water. Then a series of moon phases interspersed with more geographical scenes. Each vision began with a zoom to the burned one's head and ended with a zoom to the younger male's head.

Paul wondered if he was even beginning to comprehend. He pictured himself popping the burned one's head off like a plastic doll's and using it to replace the younger's. Was that what they wanted Paul to do?

Moses gave him a sardonic smile as if to say, "Well . . . sort of."

It took the rest of the morning and many, many repeats of the messages before Paul was able to patch together a working comprehension. At long last, Paul and Moses rubbed each other's cheeks to signal the end of their meeting.

A note taped to the stairwell door informed Paul that Clarence would be waiting for him in the hospital cafeteria. There he found Clarence sitting alone drinking tea and tending to the paperwork that overflowed his briefcase. He looked up as Paul approached.

"So . . . what's their problem?"

"It's about the old fellow with the burns. He was taken off the floor. They need to get to him—immediately."

"Can't you explain that we had to take him away to save his life? In fact, he's in the operating room right now getting skin grafts. We've even got Neville Peterson, a burn specialist from Sydney, up there running the show. You have no idea what kind of arm-twisting I had to do to get the hospital to allow a non-human in the OR. Frankly, Paul, the only chance the old boy has of making it is by staying put."

"He's dying, Clarence, and the bunyips are afraid he'll go before he's transferred his knowledge."

"What knowledge?"

"The bunyips keep mental archives. They're like the oral history that some human tribal societies keep, where one elder spends years memorizing the tribe's history, birth records, and so on. Then the historian turns around and trains a younger tribesman to memorize the information. Without writing, it's the only way they can keep track of their history from one generation to the next. Well, the bunyips do something like that. Except their records are a lot more extensive and are stored in the form of mental images. I told you about them earlier, the images that look like movies rewinding at high speed. I didn't know what they meant until now."

Paul broke off the conversation long enough to get himself a cup of coffee.

"Anyway, those archives are a lot more important to the bunyips than any one individual. They need them to survive. Imagine how difficult our own lives would be if we were suddenly stripped of all recorded knowledge. Their archives contain not only history but maps, survival strategies, locations of hidden food and water supplies, and a lot of other things that I still don't comprehend. Without that knowledge, they can't return to the wild. The bunyips are already scared and demoralized. Losing those archives would be an utter catastrophe for them."

"I see your point. So what do they want us to do? Haul the old fellow up to the fifth floor, then sit around watching him die while he reels off the bunyip archives?"

"Not exactly. The burned one—let's call him Plato—has been training another bunyip to take over the archives for a long time. They just want us to make sure that his pupil gets the archives before Plato dies."

"And Plato's pupil should obviously be named Aristotle. How much of the archives has Aristotle mastered so far?"

"Aristotle is like a librarian in charge of the card catalog. He knows how to use the information, but the library itself is still in Plato's head."

"And our job is to help the two of them transfer the books?"

"Exactly. All we have to do is bring Aristotle physically close enough to Plato to set up a good, clear communication link. We don't have much time, though. Plato's getting weaker by the minute."

"This won't be easy, Paul. You, Freddy, and I are the only ones who know about the bunyip's psychic abilities. Bruce Wilson is vaguely aware, but I haven't had a chance to discuss it with him. The others will think we're a bunch of bloody lunatics if we try to tell them. And just imagine their reaction if we told them to risk their patient's life so he can do a psychic transfer of the sum total of the species' cumulative knowledge. Come to think of it, it sounds a little mad to me, too."

"If there's one thing we can rely on, Clarence, it's your ability to convince the right people to go along with your ideas."

Paul went to fetch Aristotle while Clarence headed to the operating room. Minutes later Paul entered the third-floor operating suite with Aristotle in tow. He'd forgotten to ask which room the others would be in, so he went down the hall peeking in the tiny windows on the swinging doors.

"Just what the bloody hell do you think you're doing, mister?" came a stern voice from behind.

Paul turned around to observe a stocky, sour-faced woman of about fifty. She was dressed in surgical scrubs, and he deduced that she was probably the head nurse. She had a commanding voice well-cured by many years of heavy smoking.

"I'm looking for the room where the bunyip is being cared for."

"Not dressed in street clothes, you're not. This is a sterile area, and I'm certainly not about to let your little monkey here wander about. Who gave you permission to come here in the first place?"

"I don't have time to explain. I've got to get to the—"

"You've got to get your little arse out of the OR, mister, that's what you've got to get." She dug her fingers into his shoulder with a grip worthy of a large bird of prey.

"Get away, damn it! I don't have time to screw with you." Paul broke loose and headed down the hall with the nurse in hot pursuit.

Aristotle seemed to grasp the situation. He darted ahead and led Paul straight into the appropriate OR.

"Would someone kindly call off the Wicked Witch of the West?" Paul asked with annoyance.

The door burst open, and the nurse entered the room with the authority of a predator about to dispatch its evening meal.

"It's all right," said one of the green-clad and masked figures at the table. "He can stay, sister."

Paul still hadn't adjusted to the Australian custom of addressing nurses as "sister." To him, the title still referred to those mysterious, hard-eyed penguins who spent their lives whacking away at small hands. This nurse was at least as formidable as the crustiest black-and-white.

"And just who are you to grant others the run of this place? I don't know you."

"I'm Neville Peterson, professor of surgery at the University of Sydney," the man replied patiently.

"Well, I've never heard of you. We'll see if Dr. Coburn knows anything about this." With that, the nurse wheeled around and stormed out the door.

"Too bad we don't have a live intern or medical student we could throw her," Peterson dead-panned. "I'll bet she calms down once she's been fed." Then to Paul, "I understand that our patient has to have an important discussion with your little friend there."

"Something like that. How soon can you get him conscious?"

"Actually, he's awake now. Since we don't know very

much about bunyip physiology, we were afraid to use anesthesia. Too great a risk that he wouldn't wake up. Instead, we're keeping him awake and just killing the pain with intravenous morphine." Peterson pointed to the clear bag of fluid suspended from an IV stand. "That's a solution of saline and morphine. The syringe attached to the line contains a drug called naloxone, an antidote for narcotics. That way, if the little fellow gets too much morphine, we just inject the naloxone into the line and undo the damage almost instantly. It's the safest way to keep him out of pain."

Paul and Aristotle stepped up to the operating table. Aristotle was too short to see over the table, so Clarence found a stool for him. Plato looked up with resignation. Despite the euphoria of morphine, he knew the end was near. Paul could see the sadness in Aristotle's eyes. More than his teacher, Aristotle was losing both a father and a very close friend.

Plato closed his eyes and Aristotle did the same.

"We need to be as quiet as possible," Paul said. "They both have to concentrate for this. It may take a while, so anyone who isn't essential at the moment might want to leave for a break. I can call you when they're done."

Peterson worried. "Look, the old boy's touch and go. We can't just walk away and—"

"He's dying. He knows it and so does everyone in this room. Please, just leave the two of them in peace for a while."

Peterson must have sensed the gravity of the occasion. "Actually, I think we could all use a break. We just need one person to remain here and monitor the vital signs."

Bruce Wilson volunteered and Peterson quickly ushered the rest of the team out the double doors. Paul and Clarence stepped back from the operating table to wait and watch. Only the beep of the heart monitor broke the silence. The signal was weak but steady.

Several minutes elapsed as Aristotle stood motionless at the table. Then he looked at Paul and shook his head sadly.

"What's wrong?" Clarence asked.

"It's the morphine. Plato's too doped up to concentrate. Bruce, didn't Dr. Peterson say that the stuff in that syringe would counteract the morphine?"

"The naloxone? Yeah, in less than a minute," Bruce replied. "Of course, that'll leave the poor bloke suffering horribly. The shock might well kill him."

"It's the only way. We'll have to do it."

Bruce shrugged, then pushed the plunger of the syringe home. Seconds later, Plato stiffened as the veil of morphine dissolved to unmask the agony behind it. Paul's own skin began to ache as if it too had been charred. He trembled with pain and fought the urge to cry out.

"Can you feel it?" he whispered to Clarence between clenched teeth.

"The burning? A little bit."

The beeps from the monitor came less regularly. Paul looked at the screen, where the white dot traced a series of jagged, irregular lines.

Hurry! Not much time left! Paul warned through his own thoughts. He could sense that the transfer was about to take place. If only Plato could hang on a few more minutes.

The alarm on the monitor went off.

"Hurry!" he said out loud, no longer able to contain his anxiety. Tension welled up within his mind, like a dam about to burst. This was it. The archives were ready to come.

"He's starting to fibrillate," Bruce whispered. "Get Peterson."

The double doors burst open. That damned nurse was back!

"Look at this, Dr. Coburn. Not only does the man barge in here in street clothes, but he puts that filthy monkey right up there by the operating table."

"Get out of here!" Paul yelled, pushing the nurse back toward the door. "You're gonna screw everything up."

"Now see here," said the balding man with thick glasses and white coat who followed the nurse in. "I'm chief of staff at this hospital, and I won't have you assaulting our employees. And if anyone's leaving this room, it's going to be the likes of you. Now I want that animal out of here this instant."

Coburn headed straight for Aristotle.

Paul angrily shoved the nurse out the door and ran to stop Coburn. "Get away, you fucking idiot!"

But the doctor had already grabbed the younger bunyip, who sank his teeth into the man's forearm. Coburn screamed.

Bruce managed to keep his attention trained on Plato. "Get Peterson! The old boy's about to arrest."

Clarence tried unsuccessfully to pull Aristotle away from Coburn. In full fury, Paul wrapped his arms around Coburn's ample midsection, yanked the man off his feet, and began carrying him toward the door.

"Wait, Paul!" Clarence yelled over Coburn's screams. "I can't get Aristotle's jaws loose. He's still locked to the bloke's arm."

"Then cut the fucking arm off!"

Paul felt a strong tug.

"I still can't pull Aristotle loose. Now, Paul, you've got to calm down before somebody gets—"

"Calm down my ass!"

The double door behind Paul opened and someone rushed by in a blur. Paul and Clarence were too distracted to notice that the head nurse had returned with a steel surgical tray in hand.

Before either man could yell No!, the nurse brought the tray down on Aristotle's skull with a sickening crunch. The bunyip crumpled.

Paul dropped Coburn and started toward the nurse. All

of a sudden, he stiffened—paralyzed, as if by an electric current. His eyes closed involuntarily in response to a blinding flash of blue light that only he could see. Then his mind exploded into a blur of color and motion.

Now it was Clarence's turn to yell.

"You idiots!" He shoved Coburn out of the room, smacking the man's head against the door in the process. Then he turned toward the nurse. Aghast at the rage overflowing Clarence's face, the woman ran screaming out the door.

"He's fading fast," Bruce yelled. "Get Peterson, quick!"

Paul stood frozen in place like a statue. Clarence ran out the door and moments later had Peterson back at the table helping Bruce resuscitate Plato. Meanwhile, Clarence rushed Aristotle down to the emergency room with the assistance of another doctor and a nurse.

Peterson put the defibrillation paddles on Plato's chest and pressed the discharge button. Plato heaved in spasm as the electricity surged through him. Peterson looked up at Bruce.

"Slight heartbeat," Bruce advised.

"Okay, let's give him some atropine and epinephrine."

"Damn it! We've lost the heartbeat again."

"Shock him again. Clear."

Bruce jerked his hands back to avoid getting shocked himself. Plato heaved once more under the paddles.

"We've got a pulse, Neville."

"Good. I'll incubate him and get him on the respirator."

Peterson carefully guided the tube into Plato's trachea. Minutes later, the respirator began wheezing away. No sooner did the two men sigh with relief, than the dancing white dot again traced a flat line.

They shocked the bunyip over and over. The white dot yielded nothing but a lifeless horizontal line.

Finally, they had no choice but to cover Plato's body with a sheet.

"Well, that's it, Bruce. Buy you a beer?"

"I'll need a lot more than one, mate." Bruce followed Peterson out the door.

They didn't seem to notice Paul, who now sat on the floor in the far corner. He'd drawn knees up to his chest, and stared silently into space.

Some time later the doors swung open again as Clarence returned.

"Paul? Are you all right?" He leaned over to touch Paul lightly on the shoulder.

"Shit, Clarence. I don't even know how to answer that."

"I'm sorry. I know how you must feel."

"I doubt it. How's Aristotle?"

"In a coma. She cracked his skull, and he may never wake up. Do you know if he got the archives?"

"He didn't."

"Damn. Then they're lost forever?"

"Maybe, maybe not."

"I don't follow."

"The archives—I've got them. They're in *my* head!"

"Great."

"It's not great, Clarence, it's a goddamn travesty. I don't know what anything means. It's like I'm suddenly in charge of the central library in Beijing. I don't know how to find anything, and even if I did, I wouldn't know what to do with it. I don't even know how to transfer it to one of the others."

The men looked at each other in quiet desperation. Everything they'd done to help the bunyips so far had backfired, bringing the species yet another step closer to extinction.

The air in the bar was blue from cigarette smoke, and beer in their schooners quivered with every bass note thumping out of the jukebox across the room. Clarence seemed out of place, but Paul felt oddly comfortable in this environment. Change the accents of the people around him, and he could be in any of the small-town pool halls in central Kansas where he'd whiled away the boring stretches of late adolescence. They'd come here directly from the operating room because Paul wasn't ready to face the bunyips after the recent catastrophe.

What the hell am I doing? Paul wondered over and over. He was supposed to be in Woolloona, of course, finishing his dissertation. A few months ago, getting his doctorate was the only important objective in his life. Now, it was his biggest obstacle. He could hardly expect Sheila and P.J. to wait for him. For that matter, how could he leave them behind in the first place? Even if they were willing to wait, he wasn't. Yet what was the alternative? He hadn't spent seven years in graduate school to sell used cars in Silver Hill.

Paul drained his beer and ordered another round. Clarence continued to stare wordlessly into his glass.

Paul's mind wandered back to his senior year at college. He remembered a picnic he and Sheila had that weekend in late April. They'd gone to the woods several miles south of town and spread a blanket under a huge walnut tree that was just beginning to green. They'd only planned to eat lunch, but wound up making love in the warm sunshine. As evening came they rolled up together in the blanket and talked about what a wonderful life the two of them would share. He was happy then.

In fact, the only time in his life he'd ever been happy was with Sheila.

Somehow, he'd have to figure out a way to stay in Silver Hill, at least for now. An idea struck. All he needed was the approval of Jim Knox, his dissertation advisor. He checked his watch. Knox would still be in bed now, but this was worth the risk of annoying him. All Paul needed was a pocket full of change and directions to a pay phone. He started to motion for the bartender when Clarence spoke.

"I have to go back to Canberra before things there get any further behind. I'll be leaving in a few days."

Paul could sense relief in his voice. Who wouldn't want to leave this madness behind and go back to a family and a stable job?

Paul seized the opening. "Won't you need someone to watch after the bunyips?"

"Exactly my thoughts. Obviously, we'll repatriate them to their home range as soon as possible. But there's no telling how long that will take. I'd like for you to stay with them until then."

"Great. The only problem is that my salary runs out in May, and I still have to dispense with my dissertation project back in Woolloona."

"Something tells me, though, that you'd rather stay here. I know you feel responsible for the bunyips. But I'll wager that a certain blonde-haired doctor and little boy named Paul, Jr., also figure into the equation."

Clarence chuckled as Paul looked away, cheeks burning.

"How did you . . . ?"

"I picked up on some of it, and Freddy filled me in on the rest. He's wonderfully devious, you know. I could learn a few pointers from him myself."

"You're right about my wanting to stay." Paul leaned forward with excitement. The pieces of his life finally seemed to fall in place. "In fact, I was just getting ready to call Jim Knox, my advisor back in Kansas, to discuss it. See, I think I might just—"

"—have enough data already to complete your dissertation. Freddy told me that you'd mentioned something along those lines once before. So I took the liberty of calling Kansas to speak with Knox. I hope you don't mind, but I do have a little more leverage than you at this point. Anyway,

Knox said that as cautious and meticulous as you are, your comment probably meant that you had enough information in hand to write two dissertations. So I suggested that we close down the Woolloona field station and find a nice, quiet place—say, a fifth-floor hospital room—for you to write. He said that it was *basically* a good idea . . . " His voice trailed off.

"I can tell that there's a very large 'But' coming."

"*But* he wants you to remain under the direct supervision of Charles Andrews while you write."

Paul cringed.

"Yeah, I know, Paul. I feel the same way about Andrews myself. But he is, after all, the director of your grant. I need him here anyway. Even a born conniver like myself has to play by certain rules. One of those rules is that you don't leave an entire species, let alone one as remarkable as the bunyips, in the hands of a graduate student."

"I understand. I just have some differences of opinion with Andrews."

"Very tactful. I know what you'd *like* to say. Look, I've known Charles for twenty years or more. He's really not a bad sort. He just gets a little obsessed with his studies sometimes and forgets that there are more important things. While he can be, as you Yanks say, a pain in the ass, all of us, including the bunyips, will benefit from his presence in the long run."

"Is this conversation supposed to cheer me up?"

"I'll settle for a healthy display of caustic cynicism."

Paul and Clarence returned to the hospital shortly after midnight. An overwhelming sorrow enveloped Paul as the elevator approached the fifth floor.

"We need to be really quiet," he whispered. "The bunyips are in mourning."

"Yeah, I feel it too."

The elevator opened, and the men stepped wordlessly into the lobby. Clarence returned to his own room, but Paul felt drawn to the bunyips. He pushed silently through the double doors to the polio ward.

The bunyips sat motionless on the floor, packed together in a tight circle with their arms around each other. At the center, with her head bowed and arms stretched outward to envelope the others, sat an old female. A long, hard life had been etched into her face. Only a tattered stub remained of her left ear, and her right eye, probably blind, was covered with a milky membrane. Yet strength and wisdom were unmistakable behind the scars and wrinkles. This was a face that had learned from adversity rather than just struggled against it. Paul had named her Minerva, after the Roman goddess of wisdom. Although he hadn't figured out exactly what role she played in bunyip society, he'd observed that only Moses would ever sit or eat in her presence without first attending to her.

Minerva looked up. Her cheeks were streaked with tears, but her expression bore the calm resolve of Mother Nature herself.

He saw a flash of blue light, then a vision of Plato and Minerva embracing, smiling at each other.

Paul bowed his head respectfully.

The outer circle of mourners opened, and Paul took his place among them.

10

A frantic tugging on his arm awakened Paul.

"Who's there?" He reached overhead and flicked on the bedlamp.

"Maude! Are you strong enough to be wandering around?"

Something obviously worried her. Paul helped her up on the bed, then closed his eyes and opened his mind to her.

A blue flash.

Paul stood alone under the stars of the Outback, wrapped in his blanket. The sand tickled his bare feet as he turned to survey the mulga scrub surroundings. He felt oddly at peace.

In the distance he made out three small figures coming toward him, single file. They moved in slow, solemn procession. As they approached, Paul made out the face of Minerva. She walked in front, forearms crossed against her chest.

Behind her came the large, muscular male that Paul had met the day of the fire and, following him, the smaller young male who also guarded the juvenile bunyips. These two seemed to take almost studious disinterest in people. Yet they invariably positioned themselves between their charges and any humans in the vicinity. Paul had named the big one Crockett and the other Travis, after two defenders of the Alamo.

None of the three bunyips acknowledged Paul's presence as they passed by. Crockett and Travis carried Plato's body between them.

The vision evaporated.

"You need to dispose of Plato's body? Is that it?"

Maude smiled at him.

"Oh, Lord! And you'll need my help, won't you?"

She nodded.

"I *can't*. I'll be fired if I so much as touch that body without permission."

Maude's smile faded to a glare of contempt that made Paul's blood run cold. Would he now betray another friend?

"All right! I'll do it. Anything. Just don't look at me like that."

He hadn't drawn any mental pictures, but Maude smiled again. She obviously knew that he'd agreed to her request. Maybe it was just the tone of his voice. But something told him that she was beginning to pick up on the spoken words too.

The three bunyips from the vision now filed into the room.

Paul started to get out of bed but stopped short when he noticed that all four were staring directly at him. He was bare-assed naked under the sheets.

"Turn around, please." He deliberately avoided any gestures or mental images, wondering if they'd understand just the words.

Travis sniggered, then shot out an image of Paul getting out of bed to discover that he'd become a bunyip from the waist down. The other bunyips seemed to find the thought quite amusing.

"Okay, okay. I get the point." Paul pushed himself out of bed and dressed. Modesty was totally out of place among bunyips in the first place. After what he'd put Bruce through, Paul realized that he deserved a little ridicule.

Then Crockett shot out an image of Paul as a bunyip from the waist *up*. The others must have found this exceedingly funny and fought to restrain their laughter. Were they not on a funeral mission, Paul guessed, they'd probably erupt into hysterics.

Once the bunyips were back in control, the burial party headed down the stairs to the basement morgue which, luckily, had been left unlocked. Then Plato's body was carried out the back freight entrance by Crockett and Travis. Paul had an extra set of keys to Clarence's rental car and soon had the entire party loaded up and headed out of town.

Exactly where to go was a problem, since none of them was at all familiar with the area. He followed the highway for several miles out of town before Maude pointed off to one side. There was a dirt trail, and he drove along it for about four miles. Finally Maude motioned him to stop near a large rock outcropping.

As he turned off the ignition, Paul made a surprising realization. He'd driven all this way without headlights. Thanks to the bunyip's nocturnal vision and mind link, he hadn't needed them.

Paul started to get out of the car when a mental image told him to stay put. Disposal of the dead was a private affair among bunyips, and Minerva now took charge. Travis and Crockett, who seemed to have come along only to provide muscle, carried Plato's body as Minerva led them behind the outcropping. Maude herself had no place in whatever rites were to be carried out. She stayed behind in the car with Paul.

If there were any mental images being generated from the ceremony, assuming that's what it was, Paul wasn't picking up on them. Maude had grown very quiet, and he did pick up an image of a younger-looking Plato holding Maude on his lap when she was still a child. She laughed as he tickled her and regaled her with stories of generations past.

A single tear slid down her cheek and dripped onto her hands, now folded in her lap. Paul reached over and placed his hand on hers. Gently she rubbed it against her cheek, then held it for a long, long time.

Lightness approached by the time Crockett and Travis returned. They sat quietly in the back seat until Minerva finally rejoined them, just as the sun came into full bloom. Whatever had been done with Plato's body, the survivors were content that he was now at rest.

Paul headed back to Silver Hill, wondering if he and Freddy had done the right thing when they buried the two bunyips back at the water hole. Minerva answered him with a reassuring pat on the shoulder.

The bunyips ducked out of sight onto the floorboards as the car entered Silver Hill. He drove up to the hospital's rear loading dock. The bunyips stole out of the car and slipped through the door unnoticed. Paul parked the car and headed through the back door himself. The bunyips sat on the fifth floor landing, waiting to be let in.

Clarence's room was next door to Paul's, and he stepped out the door as Paul headed to his own room.

"Good Lord, Paul. Look at the bags under your eyes! You need to get more sleep."

"Good idea. In fact, I think I'll just—"

"I've set up a meeting for us with Bruce Wilson in fifteen minutes. We need to discuss what's to become of our little charges after I leave. But first, you and I have to decide whether or not to bring up the bunyips' psychic abilities. What are your feelings?"

"Well, obviously we don't want to come across any crazier than we already have. Nothing's going to destroy our credibility faster than ranting on about mental telepathy. Bruce, however, seems to be picking up on some of it. I think he'll listen. As for the others, I think we should—"

"—answer their questions and let it go at that. Yeah, you're right. Besides, most of these scientific-types would insist that it was some trick, no matter what kind of proof we—"

The double doors burst open and Bruce marched triumphantly toward them. "I *knew* I wasn't going crazy!" came a hearty baritone. "I knew there was something going on here that you weren't telling me about."

"I take it you overheard us?" Clarence asked blandly.

"Yeah, right up here." Bruce tapped his temple with a forefinger. "Yesterday I asked ol' Peterson if he was picking up on the bunyip's thoughts too, and he told me I was bonkers to even suggest such a thing. I was starting to believe him."

Paul felt both relief and dread. It was good to have a knowing ally in Bruce. But on the other hand, it was now patently clear that there was no way of knowing, let alone controlling, who was getting what information through the bunyips. His concern about watching over his own thoughts would now have to become an obsession.

Paul's heart pounded in his throat as the hospital operator connected his call. He felt like a lovesick schoolboy.

"Dr. McDaniel speaking."

"Hi, Sheila."

She sighed impatiently. "Paul, I thought I told you—"

"—to leave you alone for a while, and I will. It's P.J. I wanna talk about. He's my son too, even if I did just discover the fact. I want to see him again. I wouldn't bother you if it weren't in his best interests as well."

There was a long pause. "So what are you suggesting?"

Paul spoke slowly as he fought to control his anxiety. "How about I take him up to the fifth floor and introduce him to the bunyips? I'll bet that'd be a real treat for him."

"Yeah, I reckon it would. And P.J. could benefit from a

little male company too. So long as you remember what *not* to discuss with him."

"Just call me 'Dan.'"

"Okay. I'll have someone drop him off by Freddy's room after school. Have him back at the house around seven."

Although Paul had wanted to project himself as relaxed, he'd clearly failed. He desperately wanted to build bridges to both Sheila and P.J. Was this the right way to do it? Everything he did these days led to more worry.

Now that the last of his tubes had been disconnected, Freddy was finally allowed out of bed. He sat in a chair by the window and Paul stood, leaning his elbows against the bed table. The door behind Paul opened, and P.J. came running into the room.

"G'day, Dan!" P.J. still wore his school uniform of brown shorts with a khaki shirt. His cheeks were flushed with excitement.

"Hello, P.J. I'd like you to meet my friend, Freddy."

"G'day, Freddy. Nice to meet'cha. And this is my Auntie Bronwyn."

"Bronwyn?" Paul lurched upright in surprise. "You mean the one who—?"

As he turned, Paul was jerked off his feet in a crushing bear hug. "Yeah, mate, he means *that* Bronwyn!" said a jubilant voice.

Paul tried to defend himself by returning the embrace, but his exuberance was no match for hers. His back popped in a couple of places before he was standing on his own again.

"Bronwyn! Let's have look at you." He pushed himself backward to safety in the guise of seeking a better view. "My God, I hardly recognize you."

Although still a hefty woman, she had trimmed down considerably since college. If one squinted hard enough,

Paul surmised, she might even be considered . . . well, almost . . . pretty.

"Boy, have you benefited from the hand of time."

"Actually, mate, the hand belonged to a plastic surgeon."

That would have been Paul's second guess.

"But I'm wilder than ever. An' after two divorces, I'm a lot more assertive in getting what I want from a man."

Paul paused a moment at the thought of a "wilder and more assertive" Bronwyn. "So what are you doing these days?"

"Just looking after me dad's properties. He died a few years back, leavin' me with more hoot than I'll spend in three lifetimes."

After several minutes of catching up on Bronwyn's life, Paul felt P.J. tugging his arm. "Listen, Bronwyn, would you mind keeping Freddy company for a while? See, I promised P.J.—"

"I know all about it, Dan," she said with a wink. "You and P.J. get going. I'll be happy to stay here and get better acquainted with your handsome friend." She turned a knowing face to Freddy. "I dunno what you've heard about me, mate, but it's the dinkie-die truth. Every word of it."

"I was hopin' yer'd say that." Freddy grinned.

Ye gods! What have I started? Paul shuddered as he ushered P.J. out of the room.

The bunyips and P.J. developed an immediate mutual fascination. Maude and the others crowded around the boy, eager to touch the first human their own size they'd ever seen.

P.J. immediately caught on to the basics of bunyip communication. "They're dreaming inside my head!" he'd blurted in happy wonderment within five minutes of setting foot among them.

How did he learn so fast? Paul wondered. Perhaps P.J. had picked up on the telepathy so quickly because he simply didn't know that it was supposed to be impossible.

Maude took P.J. by the hand and led him around the ward, introducing him—if that's the right term—to the others and showing him their iron lung dens. Even Crockett and Travis dropped their guard, allowing the boy to join the bunyip children they normally herded away from humans. P.J. seemed utterly enchanted as he sat on the floor and allowed the younger bunyips to explore the first human they'd been allowed to touch. He pulled a package of chocolate drops out of his school bag and shared them around, instantly becoming the most popular person ever to grace the hospital's fifth floor.

Bruce called Paul aside to talk for a few minutes, then it was time to take P.J. home. As the two of them were getting ready to leave, Paul noticed that his son had suddenly become quiet and withdrawn.

"Did you have a good time, P.J.?"

"Mmmmpph."

"We still have a few minutes. Like to go by the milk bar and get some ice cream?"

"I just wanna go home." The boy's eyes were fixed on the floor.

"Are you all right?"

"I wanna go home!" he shouted, tears welling up in his eyes.

As they drove back to Sheila's, Paul tried in vain to think of anything that might have upset P.J. He could either force the issue now or ignore it and hope it would pass. Paul was too much of a worrier to opt for the latter.

"Please tell me what's wrong."

"Just take me home!" Tears now streamed down the boy's cheeks.

Once more, Paul experienced that sick feeling of helplessness. Obviously, he'd screwed up again. But how?

Sheila sat in the rocking chair on her front porch as they drove up. She must have been waiting to talk, since it was still too hot to be comfortable outside. Sure enough, she walked over to the car.

"P.J., have you been crying?" she asked, opening the passenger door.

The boy shrugged noncommittally and headed for the house.

"What happened, Paul?"

"I can't figure it out myself. One minute he was happy and laughing, the next he started acting like that."

"Perhaps he doesn't feel well. Why don't you come in and have a beer? Maybe we can get to the bottom of this."

Paul didn't need further prompting to follow her inside. They both sat in the living room and Sheila called P.J., who'd gone to his own room. The boy obeyed, but stood silent, staring at his shoes with his hands jammed into his pockets.

"Are you all right, darling? Do you feel sick?" She reached to touch his forehead, but the boy recoiled from her.

"I'm okay. Can I go back to my room now?"

"Well, I reckon. But first, why don't you fetch Dan and me a beer from the fridge?"

P.J. glared at her. In that instant, Paul saw the expression of betrayal that Sheila had herself shown seven years earlier.

When the boy finally spoke, his voice brimmed with contempt. "His name's not Dan! It's Paul. He's my dad. You lied to me. You said my dad was dead. Now you're both lying to me. You don't want me to have a father, either of you."

Sheila shot an angry look at Paul. "You bastard! You promised not to tell."

Paul's heart sank as he desperately floundered for a response.

"He didn't tell me!" P.J. shouted back, voice breaking.

"The bunyips told me. The bunyips told me everything. I hate both of you!" P.J. stood a moment longer, staring at his parents in hurt and anger. Then his face crinkled up in a sob, and he turned and ran back to his room, slamming the door behind him.

Sheila sighed. "Well, Paul, I don't know what he means by talking bunyips, but it looks like you and I have a lot of explaining to do."

Paul nodded but didn't speak. No matter how difficult the conversation with P.J. would prove, they'd just taken their first step toward becoming a family.

Even at ten in the morning the tarmac of the Silver Hill airport was sweltering.

"I'm going to miss everyone," Clarence said. But from the way he held his bags, he obviously couldn't wait to board the plane that was taxiing toward them.

"Oh, I almost forgot to tell you. You'll be needing a computer for your dissertation work, so I've ordered one sent to you."

Paul had to yell to be heard over the approaching roar from the propellers. "Great. I don't know what to say. A simple 'thank-you' hardly seems enough."

"Just keep the madness under control so I don't have to come back here, and I'll consider the debt more than repaid."

Minutes later, Clarence was airborne, and Paul was loading the baggage of Andrews and his colleague, Lawrence Pike, into the rental car. They'd arrived on the same plane that was now flying Clarence back to Canberra, and Paul had taken an instant dislike to Pike. A pale, pudgy and balding man in his late fifties, Pike was a professor of genetics and physiology at the University of Sydney. Although he seemed pleasant enough, there was something about him that bothered Paul. Maybe it was the hardness in those ice-blue eyes.

Not a single bunyip was visible on the fifth floor when Paul escorted the two scholars to their rooms. Whether they were simply echoing his reservations or had developed a set of their own remained to be seen.

Paul escorted the men to their rooms, then headed back to Freddy's room.

"We gots problems, mate," Freddy said the moment Paul entered. Never mind that Freddy and Maude hadn't seen each other since the day he was shot. The two of them stayed in close contact.

"Yeah. I thought Andrews was bad enough. But something tells me this Pike fellow is going to cause us some real grief. I wonder why?"

" 'Cuz the whole bloody thing stinks! Why did Andrews bring a laboratory-type scientist here in the first place, 'stead o' someone like an ethologist to study bunyip behavior? Because he's more interested in publishin' a bunch o' bloody monographs on bunyip anatomy than he is in doin' somethin' to help 'em survive! That's why we's both worried shitless."

"Once again, you've hit the nail on the head." Paul poured himself a glass of ice water from Freddy's bedside pitcher. "Whatever happened to the drunken buffoon I could always ignore when I wanted to?"

"Right here, mate. I'll unleash him the minute we gets our bunyip friends to safety."

"Promise?"

Paul sat in his room reading later that afternoon when Andrews, clearly agitated, burst in without knocking.

"Do you have any idea what happened to the dead bunyip? I just got back from the morgue, and they told me that the body is missing."

Here we go, Paul thought as he stood up from the oak table he used for a desk.

"Yesterday I helped the bunyips remove the body. Two of them carried it out to the car, and I drove them several miles out of town so they could do whatever it is that they do with their dead."

"What the bloody hell are you talking about? No, don't answer. I already have more than enough doubts about your sanity. This is a direct order, Paul: Bring that body back to us, and do it now."

"With all due respect, No." Paul braced himself for the fury about to be unleashed. He spoke softly, hoping not to provoke Andrews to the point of firing him. "I can't. The bunyips have a special way of taking care of their dead. Anything else would be a desecration, too offensive for them to even consider."

"Offensive?" Andrews was already red-faced. "Where do you get this 'offensive' shit from? I suppose next you'll be telling me that they had you over for tea and you all had a lovely conversation about bunyip sensitivities, after which they had a little poetry reading in your honor. We're sitting on top of the most remarkable find of the century, and you're babbling some nonsense about *offending* them? Now I demand that you . . . "

So it went for the next hour. When Andrews became hoarse from yelling, Pike came in and took over. Yet through all the threats and verbal abuse heaped upon him, Paul somehow managed to hold his ground and his job.

He hardly felt relieved after they left his room. There was little doubt that he and the professors would butt heads again in the future. How much longer would he be able to protect the bunyips?

Paul had taken to his bed to recuperate mentally from his confrontation with Andrews and Pike.

"C'mon in, Maude," he said in response to a mental cue that she stood outside the door.

Maude entered and, with a hand from Paul, pulled herself up on his bed. He could use some cheering up, and Maude knew just the thing. She pulled her pouch open to show him the joey that he'd last seen in its dormant stage when it still looked like an embryo.

"That's great, Maude. I can't believe that he's grown that much."

She responded with a quick mental image.

"Sorry—that *she's* grown that much."

Maude beamed with pride. The joey, still fused to her teat, had already developed tiny, distinct hands that wrapped themselves around the finger Maude offered her.

"Let's call her Alexis."

Maude smiled. Personal names were a foreign concept to bunyips. If it made Paul happy to call her Alexis, then Alexis she'd be.

Paul's mind couldn't keep from wandering back to what was really worrying him. "Maude, do you know anything at all about the archives?"

Maude gently pushed him back until he was lying down again. She slid her hand down across his eyes, closing them.

He saw a blue flash.

Then Plato, kindly, gray old Plato, stood beside Paul's bed. He showed no sign of the burns that had killed him, and looked the way he must have right before the fire. Was this a dream or a vision? Maude wasn't there to answer. Plato handed Paul a wad of faded pink cloth and gestured for him to unfold it. It was a tee-shirt picturing a koala bear on a surfboard riding a tornado. The caption read "An Aussie in Oz."

I've seen this shirt before, but I don't remember where.

He suddenly found himself in his old apartment in college. He was lying in bed, with Sheila kneeling beside him, wearing that same pink tee-shirt. She was starting to cry.

"*A sign*?" she yelled, her voice breaking. "Night after night I slept alone and miserable while the man I love was off screwing another woman—*while pretending she was me, for Chrissake*! And all because you were waiting for a sign? You want a sign, asshole? How's this?" Then she tore off the tee-shirt and slapped Paul's face with it.

That memory stood out very clearly. What did it have to do with the bunyips? Moments later, he found himself standing beside Plato in the apartment's kitchen. Plato pointed to the old calendar that Sheila had taped to the refrigerator. From the questioning look in Plato's eyes, he apparently wanted to know the date. Why? Bunyips didn't seem to even mark time, let alone worry about dates. What *was* the date, anyway? Paul wasn't very good at these things, but he should certainly remember the first day he and Sheila made love. Yet, try as he might, he couldn't remember. Plato walked over to the kitchen table and picked up the newspaper lying on it, then held the paper up with his index finger pointing to the date: Friday, February the 18th. Then he reached over and tapped Paul's forehead with the same finger, turned and walked out of the room.

Paul's mind went blank, and he assumed the message was over. Then Plato returned, tapped Paul's forehead again, and vanished.

When Paul opened his eyes, he was surprised to find that it was already morning. Had he been asleep? Apparently, but it seemed like only a few minutes since Maude had pushed him back and closed his eyes.

He still lay exactly as Maude had left him. Paul sat up, finding himself alone. Maude had started sleeping in one of the iron lung dens, and he went to check on her. Through the Plexiglas window he observed her curled up with her eyes closed.

He headed down to visit Freddy, who was just finishing the second of three breakfast trays.

"Do you have any idea what's going on, Freddy? I just had the craziest dream or vision or whatever about Plato."

"Sorry, mate, but I reckon I ain't been invited to the party. If Plato has a message for yer, he ain't sharin' it with me."

Just to make sure it wasn't some crazy dream of his own, Paul needed to check on the date Plato had given him. Was it the same day that Sheila's father had his heart attack? Since the hospital personnel were growing used to his comings and goings, he had no problem sneaking into the room where patient records were kept. Sure enough, a seven-year-old logbook showed that one Stephen Mayor had been brought to the hospital on the morning of February 19th. Calculate the time difference and date change, and that would make it the afternoon of the 18th, a Friday, back in Kansas.

So Plato had given him the right date. Why? What did it matter to the bunyips in the first place? What was the point of the tee-shirt? Try as he might, he couldn't come up with even the most far-fetched hypothesis to explain what was going on. He'd have to wait for a better clue, he decided, heading back to the fifth floor. He still had a job there, and it wouldn't be wise to antagonize the professors further by neglecting it.

Back on the fifth floor, Paul helped Andrews and Pike unload their equipment. One of the old patient rooms was being set up as the laboratory, and several more cases of equipment were being freighted in from Sydney.

"We'll need an emergency shower in here," Pike explained to Pete, the handyman who was in charge of these things. "I'll be working with some potent preservatives, and I'll need to wash them off in a hurry if there's an accident."

"Gettin' runnin' water inta this room is gonna cost yer a lotta bucks, mate." Pete spoke with the slow, measured pace of a man who didn't experience very many emotions. He pulled his hat off, wiped the sweat from his bald head with a red bandana and shifted his pipe to the other side of his mouth.

"No worries. We don't need plumbing. I have a 50-liter plastic drum coming. I want you to figure out a way to attach a shower head to it using a lever valve. We fill it with water and hang it from the ceiling. In an accident, I can just step under the drum, pull the lever, and there's my shower."

"Aye. That I can do for cheap."

Potent preservatives? Paul thought. You don't use preservatives on living tissue. The other materials he unpacked were equally unsettling: biopsy needles, scalpels, specimen jars, dissecting equipment. Everything seemed to involve pain or death in its use.

Paul was hardly on firm enough ground to risk challenging the professors. The bunyips stood to lose most of all if he got himself fired.

As he lay on his bed and stared at the ceiling that night, he had a very bad feeling about the bunyips' future. A very bad feeling, indeed.

11

By midnight Paul still hadn't fallen asleep. He sat up in response to a mental image of Maude standing just outside his door.

"C'mon in. If you've brought me another vision, I hope this one makes sense."

Maude walked in and stepped up on the stool beside his bed. She smiled as she pushed his head back onto the pillow. She closed his eyes.

A blue flash, then Plato returned. This time Plato stood beside him in the hospital room. He reached over to the pants folded across the chair and pulled out Paul's wallet. He removed a ten-dollar bank note, folded it in half and held it up to Paul's face. Plato's index finger stretched across the lower left corner of the note, covering up the serial number.

I don't understand. Do bunyips care about money?

Plato shook his head No, then pulled his finger back a little, revealing the first letter—K—of the serial number. Then he tapped Paul's forehead with his other index finger.

I still don't understand. Do you want to learn about money?

Plato shook his head impatiently.

Another letter—N—and Plato tapped him again on the forehead. Another letter—D—then 9—2—3.

You want me to remember the rest of the serial number? Is that it?

Plato smiled at him.

Why would anyone remember something like that?

Plato shook his head and was gone. Then he was back, holding the same ten-dollar note up. The first six digits—KND 923—were exposed again.

I still don't remember the rest.

Plato tapped him on the forehead. Paul looked at the note again, and this time he noticed a dime-sized brown spot about an inch above the serial number. He remembered being handed that note at the drug store. He'd bought a magazine that morning and given the clerk a twenty. She'd counted out his change, handed him the coins first, then laid that ten-dollar note on top of them. Paul had noticed the spot at the time, and wondered if it might be dried blood. He mentally replayed the drug store scene. This time, he looked at the serial number. *And there it was!* KND 923 . . .

"Six—five—two!" Paul yelled as he exploded out of bed. "I remember now—KND 923652."

"Eeeeaaaaiiiggghhh!" came a frightened scream from behind.

He turned around to see a startled cleaning woman, now standing wide-eyed in the corner, holding her mop overhead like a club.

"Don't come near me, yer bloody pervert, 'r yer'll be eatin' me mop fer breakfast!"

Paul realized from the sunlight streaming through his window that it was already morning. And he'd just jumped screaming out of bed, stark naked.

"Sorry!" He jerked the sheet off the bed and hastily wrapped it around his waist.

The old woman was shaking her mop at him. "I mean it, mister. Not one step closer."

"I'm really sorry. I didn't mean to startle you." He stepped over to his pants, pulled out his wallet, and searched through the ten-dollar notes. "I was trying to remember this one particular serial number. There it is—KND 923652. Here, see for yourself."

"Get back, yer bloody pervert. I always knowed yers Yanks was mad about money." The woman edged sideways toward the door, mop poised at the ready. "But I never thought yers was such bloody lunatics yers'd scare an old woman to death over the bloody serial numbers!" She eased herself out, never once lowering her mop.

What did the serial number have to do with the first time he made love to Sheila? What did either have to do with the bunyips? Paul had more than enough problems already. The last thing he needed was to worry about was some riddle.

The fifth-floor store room was locked, and Pete the handyman had been brought up to open it.

"They don't make these kinda locks no more," Pete said as he unlatched his tool box. "I don't have no keys to 'em, neither. I'll hav'ta pick it open an' change out the bloody tumbler."

"That's fine," Paul replied. "The professors just need some place to store their crates and supplies."

The handyman pulled out his picks and set to work. Paul noticed that Maude watched Pete's hands intently, and was almost certainly tapping into his brain.

She's learning how to pick locks, he thought. Maude gave him a conspiratorial wink.

Later that afternoon, he sat at his desk. The computer Clarence promised had arrived, and he was learning how to use it.

A mental image interrupted his concentration. "C'mon in Maude. I've been expecting you."

She slipped inside and sat on the chair beside the desk.

"I already know what you're after. You want me to give you some tools so you can learn to pick locks yourself."

She smiled broadly. Her comprehension of spoken English seemed to be increasing at a phenomenal rate.

"Look, Maude, you know I'll do whatever's in your best interests. I'm not sure this is it. You can get in a lot of trouble by going places you've been locked out of."

Maude sent him an image of Pike chasing her down the hall with a butcher knife in hand. She ran to the stairwell door, but found it still locked. She pounded helplessly on the door as Pike closed in, raising the knife over his head . . .

"Stop it! I get the point. I'll do it, but only if you promise not to try anything unless it's an emergency and I'm not there."

Maude smiled and nodded.

Paul fished the utility pliers out of his pack and pulled a large paper clip from his desk drawer.

"You can straighten out a paper clip like this, then use the pliers to bend the end into a hook. I've never tried to pick a lock with something like this, but I imagine you can teach yourself how with practice and a little patience. You got a better look than I did at the different sizes of picks that Pete had in his kit, so I'll let you figure out what size to make your own. There's also a wire cutter on this thing. It works like this."

Paul clipped the stretched-out paper clip in half, and Maude nodded her understanding. She rubbed his cheek with her knuckles, then took the pliers and a handful of paper clips and scurried off.

Paul could only hope that, for once, he'd done the right thing.

* * *

Two weeks later, Paul was well underway rewriting the literature review section of his dissertation. He'd already written most of the review before coming to Australia, since it had to be submitted with the proposal for his research grant. Mostly, the section just needed updating.

Meanwhile, Maude had become an expert at picking locks. She seemed to handle her knowledge responsibly. Or, at least, there'd been no reports of bunyips turning up in places they didn't belong.

Bruce, the veterinarian, and Neville Peterson, the burn expert, had returned to their jobs in Sydney. Medical care for the bunyips was provided by the regular hospital staff. Freddy had recovered enough that he could help watch over the bunyips, so he'd moved into the room next door to Paul's. Andrews and Pike had agreed to let Paul and Freddy serve as intermediaries between them and the bunyips, much to Paul's relief. He was finally beginning to feel a little more at ease about life on the fifth floor. A good thing too, since Pike and Andrews now had their laboratory in working order.

Andrews had developed the annoying habit of walking into Paul's room without knocking. "Paul, we need a couple cc's of bunyip blood to do some preliminary tests."

Paul kept his irritation to himself. Butting heads over petty issues would make him look like a "whinger" and erode what limited authority he had. He'd save his objections for the important issues.

"No problem," Paul answered. "I've already lined up two male volunteers, and the lab says that if I take them down there, they'll draw the blood for us."

"Yeah, but what if some passer-by recognizes the bunyips? It's only by a miracle that we've managed to avoid public attention so far. I'd hate to spoil it now."

"I've already thought of that. Wait here." Paul pulled a shopping bag containing several articles of clothing from his closet and headed out the door. Minutes later he returned with Maude, Crockett, and the male Clarence had dubbed "Clarence, Jr." They wore footed children's pajamas and, if you didn't stare too closely at the places where bunyips have hair and kids don't, they looked like reasonably authentic children.

He escorted Crockett and Junior to the second-floor laboratory and Maude, who was more adept than the others at understanding human speech, went along in case a translator was needed. The blood was drawn, and they were heading back to the elevator when they heard a voice from behind.

"Hey! I recognize those kids."

The speaker was a tall, lanky man about Paul's age.

"Remember me?" the man said with a friendly smile that revealed a desperate need for orthodonture. "I'm the Flying Doctor who brought the kids here last month."

"Sure, I remember you. But I don't think I ever caught your name. Mine's Paul McDaniel."

"I'm Ned, Ned Cochran," he responded as they shook hands. "I'm surprised the kids are still here. I thought they'd have been sent home by now. Where's their dad, by the way?"

Paul did a double-take. "Huh?"

"Their dad. Oh, I reckon he's probably working back at his station, right?" Ned dropped his voice to just above a whisper. "Y'know, when the kids have their clothing on, you'd hardly notice their . . . uh . . . condition."

Was Ned putting him on? Did he still believe the line that these were Clarence's children? Then again, Ned seemed like the smart-but-goofy sort who went through life with full academic honors and his fly unzipped. Paul remembered that Ned had dropped the bunyips off at the hospital, then turned right around and headed back to the airport for another emergency run. Apparently he'd never learned his patients' true identity.

"Yeah. Clarence is back at work. I'm looking after the . . . kids . . . while they undergo some . . . uh . . . tests."

"Let's see if I remember now. The little one here is Maude. Clarence, Jr., is . . . ?"

"The one who looks like his dad."

"Right-o!" Ned tousled the smaller male's hair. "Good t'see yer, Junior. Your big brother, of course, would be Anthony. How y'doin', mates?"

"Anthony"—who was really "Crockett," and not even one of the three bunyips Ned had originally treated—looked at Paul in utter bewilderment. Paul replied with a shrug. It dawned on him that the doctor could be a blessing in disguise.

"Say, Ned, I just happened to think of something. I need a lift to Woolloona. Does Mike Berg still do the monthly RFDS clinic there?"

"Why, no. I've taken his place. The next Woolloona clinic is scheduled this Monday."

"Great. Can I ride along? I'll be driving a truck back, so I just need a one-way lift."

"Fine with me. We're not supposed to bring passengers along, though, unless there's some medical justification. Can you think of one?"

"As a matter of fact, yes." Paul lowered his voice to a whisper. "I'm not supposed to tell, but I'm a medical epidemiologist from the University of Kansas, here with a special research team that's studying kids with this . . . uh . . . disorder. To keep from causing a panic, we're working in secret until we find out what's causing it. I thought I might update you, confidentially, of course, on our findings during the flight."

"You mean there are more of them?"

"We've already identified nearly fifty cases in this area."

"My word! What's the name of this disorder, anyway?"

"Fulminating bunyiposis, also known as the Frederick-Brennan Syndrome. Heard of it?"

"Not since medical school."

"Frederick-Brennan Syndrome, me arse!" Freddy Brennan sat on Paul's bed, roaring with laughter. "I dunno who's been the worse influence on yer, mate, me or Clarence."

Freddy was right, Paul realized. Only a few weeks ago he couldn't have faked any kind of story with a straight face. "Hey, great teachers bring out the best in their students. I'll tell Ned the truth once we're airborne for Woolloona. I can't do any more on my dissertation without the data still at the field station. I'll bring all my stuff back in your truck, along with whatever you need from your place. I've been needing to make this trip all month, but I put it off until you could take over for me up here. God knows what those two idiot professors might pull if one of us weren't around."

Freddy frowned in disgust. "Let's hope we never finds out, mate."

"Right. Did I tell you that Pike threw a fit when I brought the bunyips back from having their blood drawn? He said that from now on, *he and he alone* would do all the blood drawing."

Freddy leaned forward, putting his hands on his knees. "Sounds odd. Why should it matter?"

Paul shrugged. "I dunno. The worst part is, he won't use anything smaller than a 15 cc collection tube with a 16-gauge needle."

"Ow! That's not a needle, that's a bloody nail."

"Yeah, and he's none too gentle with it, either. The bunyips haven't figured him out yet, but they hate him even worse than they hate Andrews."

"What I don't understands, mate, is how come them two

perfessers don't seem to be gettin' none of the bunyips' messages."

"I wonder about that too. As best I can tell, it's like talking over a shortwave radio; it only works if both parties are on the same frequency and speak the same language. I don't think either condition is being met here. The bunyips are learning fast, though. God knows where all this is headed."

Paul checked himself in the mirror. He wore new khaki slacks and a freshly-starched plaid shirt. "I'll let you worry about it for a while, though. Right now I've got a very busy weekend to take care of. Tonight, I'm taking P.J. and Sheila to a movie. Saturday it's a cricket game with P.J., and Sunday it's church and dinner with both of them."

Freddy winked, his smile returning. "Any chance yer'll be gettin' lucky?"

"I'd settle for a hot, sweaty goodnight kiss. She's warming up to me, but she's the last woman on earth to be rushed into these things. P.J., on the other hand, is as eager as I am to spend more time together. It took him all of two days to forgive me for being gone all these years. If he happens to be pressuring his mother into tagging along with us, well . . . "

Paul sensed that Freddy shared his happiness. That accounted in part for the smile beaming through that thick, red beard. The rest of it could be attributed to the fact that Bronwyn would be coming over in about an hour to spend the night. With Bronwyn, you didn't worry about "getting lucky." You worried about collapsing from exhaustion or spraining something.

"Okay, P.J., off to bed with you," Sheila said as she unlocked the front door.

"Please, Mum, can't I just stay up and . . . ?"

"No, darling. Dad's spending all day tomorrow with you. Now it's late and you've had a long day."

P.J. sighed, hugged Paul, then headed inside.

"What are you smiling about, Paul?"

"I'm not—"

"Yes, you are. Stop trying to hide it."

"Well, when you were talking to P.J. just now, you called me 'Dad.'"

"So?"

"When P.J. first called me that last week you sorta wrinkled your nose and—"

Sheila interrupted him by wrapping an arm around his neck and placing her lips firmly across his. With her other arm, she hugged him tightly against her. Then, just as abruptly, she broke off the kiss.

"You're too analytical, Paul. The most important decisions in life aren't the ones you figure out. They're the ones you make with your heart. If you ever learn that, we just might have a future together."

She slipped inside and closed the door, leaving a slightly stunned and confused Paul behind to ponder her words.

As Paul lay in his bed alone that night, he hoped that Maude wouldn't be back with another one of Plato's memory games tonight. She'd brought him eight messages over the past two weeks. He could now recite passages of books he'd read twenty years ago, the serial number of the bicycle he'd gotten for his twelfth birthday, the scientific name of every known species of marsupial, extinct as well as living, and the phone number of every person with the last name Schneider living in Rush County, Kansas in January, 1982. He still had no idea why the bunyips were so obsessed with such trivia.

Maude didn't visit him that night, and Paul eventually drifted off to sleep. As he turned over, a tongue slipped into his mouth and a warm, bare body embraced him. Paul opened his eyes in surprise. Bronwyn! In bed with him!

Paul jerked his head back. Before he could yell at her to

get away Bronwyn moaned, “Oh, God! This is wonderful, Freddy.”

Freddy? Paul rolled away from her so forcefully that he spun entirely out of bed. His bare buttocks hit the tiles with a smack. As he sat up, awake at last, he found himself on the floor alone. From the room next door came the muffled squeakings of a bed being put to its optimal use.

“Ohhh, this is great, Freddy.”

Paul shuddered. Mind-linkage definitely had some drawbacks.

The weekend ended all to soon, and Paul returned to Woolloona. George Newstead had previously recovered Freddy’s pickup, and Paul had dropped by the bar for the keys and a quick drink.

George wiped the ice off of the beer he’d just opened and placed it in front of Paul. “So how’s ol’ Freddy doin’?”

“Depends on your point of view. If you enjoy being raped by Amazons, he couldn’t possibly be any better off.”

“Sounds like he’s in heaven to me, mate.” Wild Wendy had slipped up behind Paul and now rubbed a breast against his shoulder.

“Nice to see you again, Wendy.” Paul was pleasant but noncommittal.

“It’ll be even nicer tonight. I’ll come by for yer soon’s I gets off work.”

“Listen, Wendy, I have a girlfriend now and—”

“—an’ what she don’t know won’t hurt ’er.” She pulled him backwards from his stool until he was off balance and had to grab her to avoid falling on his head. Embracing him tightly, she planted a wet kiss on his lips, then pulled him back to safety.

“See yer ’round midnight,” she said with a wink. She headed back to the tables with a tray-load of drinks.

Fortunately, Paul kept a sleeping bag at the field station.

He enjoyed sleeping alone out in the desert sometimes, and tonight would be the perfect occasion.

He spent the rest of the day loading the truck. As evening approached he drove through the desert looking for a place to camp. Feeling adventurous, he headed off in a direction he'd never gone before.

Several miles from town he noticed a boulder off to one side of the trail. It had a large crack in it, which seemed to form an arrow pointing off to one side. Paul stared at the rock with an odd sensation of . . . *déjà vu*? No . . . more than that. Not just a feeling that he'd been here before. It was more like *he'd always known* about that arrow-shaped crack. He'd learned by now not to fight his instincts, so he followed the path that led off in the direction the arrow pointed.

After about 200 yards, the path dead-ended into an overhanging rock outcrop. Shaded from the western sun, it proved by far the coolest place around. With no further urges to explore, Paul made camp. He ate a meat pie he'd picked up from Newstead's, drank a couple of beers and was asleep by dark. Then Plato returned.

I thought all the bunyips were back in Silver Hill.

Plato nodded.

Can Maude's thoughts reach me from this far away?

Plato shook his head No.

Wait a minute. There wasn't a blue flash, was there?

Plato smiled a little as he shook his head.

Then I'm not linked in with any of the bunyips, am I?

Plato's smile broadened as he shook his head again.

Where are you coming from?

He leaned forward and tapped Paul's forehead with his index finger.

You're coming from inside my head?

Plato smiled again and nodded.

My God! I get it now! You're part of the archives. The archives themselves are teaching me how to use them.

The bunyip took a courtly bow. Then he motioned for

Paul to follow him, and they walked the desert by starlight. Six other bunyips trod ahead of them. Except for Plato, none paid particular attention to Paul. He realized he was reliving a memory from the archives. Through callused soles he felt the remnants of the day's heat in the sands that crunched underfoot.

They flushed an emu from her nest, and the enormous eggs were gathered and carried along. Next they came to a waterhole where they rested and ate. With a thorn they poked a hole in the eggs, then carefully sucked the contents out without breaking the shells.

Paul noticed the battered left ear of one of the females. Minerva! She was a young adult in this memory, and had a large child in her pouch. After the meal, the eggs were filled with water and sealed with wads of chewed grass. They walked again, carrying the eggshell "canteens" along with them.

They topped a hill, and Paul paused a moment to observe the stars, which flickered like countless campfires set out as beacons to welcome the weary travelers. It seemed that they were wandering, not this tiny planet, but the entire universe.

He wasn't surprised to learn that they were walking along the same trail he'd just driven. When they came to the boulder, Plato pointed to the arrow-shaped crack, then tapped Paul on the forehead.

For once, I understand, he thought. *The crack is some kind of index sign—the key that unlocked this memory, and that brought you back to me.*

Plato smiled. The group came to the outcropping where Paul now—how many years later?—slept. Plato and another male pulled away a large rock at the foot of the outcropping to reveal the opening of a den. Paul followed the others inside. The eggshell canteens, which carried the next day's water supply, were placed in a special recess at the far end of the den.

Soon it would be time to sleep, but first came the most important part of the night. Minerva and the other adult females stroked their full pouches, inviting their offspring to join the group. The children, full of those breathy little sounds of bunyip laughter, were passed from hand to hand, objects of delight to be admired and shared by all. Paul already realized that parenting was a communal responsibility among bunyips. Biological motherhood was a happy accident of nature. On a social level, every adult served equally as father or mother to every child.

He couldn't keep from smiling while he observed the delight on everyone's faces. Minerva handed her daughter to him and he happily accepted. She was a pretty child, even by human standards, and also a lively one. She gave an impish little grin as she wrapped her fingers around Paul's ears and pulled.

That face is familiar, he thought, cuddling the child and tickling her. *In fact, she looks just like . . . oh, my God . . . it's Maude!* Paul, who'd passed through life a loner and outcast, now felt an intensely powerful sense of belonging.

Only now could he fully comprehend. For bunyips, all happiness came from within, and physical possessions were irrelevant. Nothing could improve on the joy of being at one with nature and family. Bunyips were certainly intelligent enough to develop a civilization—and wise enough not to bother.

Paul awoke to daylight with a sense of wonderment. He eased himself out of the sleeping bag, pulled on his jeans and boots and went to the foot of the outcropping. He rolled back the rock and, sure enough, there was the den. He looked inside, and found it exactly the way he'd just seen it. He started to crawl in and explore but found himself overtaken by a sick feeling of guilt. Thanks to him, bunyips would probably never come here again. He pushed the stone back in place, carefully concealing the entrance.

He stuffed his sleeping bag back in the truck, popped the top of the lukewarm beer that would serve as breakfast and drove back to town. There he loaded the things Freddy had requested, mostly clothes and textbooks, and left Woolloona for good at just after two in the afternoon.

* * *

"Okay, Charles. Now's our chance. Let's go."

"What are you talking about?"

"Drawing blood from the juveniles. That red-headed buffoon is downstairs getting a medical progress evaluation of some kind. He'll be out of our hair for at least a couple of hours."

"Look, Larry, we agreed to leave the little ones alone."

"Only to keep the peace with Clarence Richmond and the others. If we act quickly, we can get the samples and no one will be the wiser until after our results are published."

"That's crazy! For one thing, the bunyips won't let us anywhere near the juveniles."

"They won't have a choice." Pike pulled a dart pistol from the pocket of his lab coat. "We just sedate the two males who guard the young, take the samples, and we're done."

"Don't be an idiot. Even if you get past those two, there's no telling how the others will react."

"We're wasting time."

Pike loaded a tranquilizer dart into the pistol and headed for the polio ward with Andrews in pursuit. As they passed through the double doors, Travis and Crockett instantly took up their positions, with Travis gathering the smallest charges in his arms and herding the larger ones together while Crockett moved forward to intercept the humans.

From a range of about ten feet, Pike aimed his pistol at Crockett's thigh.

"Stop, Larry! There's no telling what might happen."

Crockett lunged forward. In an eyeblink, he slapped Pike's hand so hard that the pistol spun across the room and hit the wall, gouging a chunk of plaster.

Stunned, Pike stared at his trigger finger, now dislocated and bent backwards.

"Don't move a muscle, Larry," Andrews said with deliberation. "Just look up . . . slowly."

Two dozen or so angry adults now encircled the two men. Pike turned and bolted. He made three strides before his legs were jerked out from under him. Then all hell broke loose.

* * *

Paul found it slow going over the dirt trails and camped out again overnight. He didn't make Silver Hill until late Wednesday afternoon.

As he entered the city limits, he could sense that something had gone horribly wrong. Stopping for a red light, he closed his eyes and tried to make contact with Freddy or Maude. No luck. All he could pick up was a growing sense of alarm. He raced to the hospital, pulled the pickup to a screeching halt by the hospital emergency entrance and ran past the startled nurse who tried to stop him. He shot up the stairs, taking them three at a time. He bounded onto the fifth-floor landing and jammed his key into the lock. It didn't work. He checked the key. It was the right one, all right. He tried it again, but it still didn't work.

"Open up! It's me, Paul!" he yelled, pounding on the door. No response. He ran back down the stairs to Sheila's office. "Sheila! Do you know what the hell's going on up on five? Where's Freddy, anyway?"

"Sit down, Paul. I'm afraid I have some bad news." She stepped around in front of her desk and pushed him into a chair.

"Freddy's in the psychiatric ward. He's strapped to his

bed and under heavy sedation. He went berserk yesterday afternoon after the bunyips attacked those two professors on the fifth floor. It might have been a psychotic reaction to all the pain killers he's taken over the past several weeks. Or maybe he got ahold of some grog and it interacted with the drugs. In any case, he's very dangerous right now."

Paul fought to control his anxiety. "Sheila, if anyone attacked those bastards, I promise you they had it coming."

She leaned against her desk and sighed. "All I know is that the man I saw was a bloody, raving lunatic. It took three orderlies and two guards to hold him down while I sedated him. He kept screaming about no one having the right to put the bunyips in cages."

The blood drained from Paul's face. "*Cages?* They put them in *cages?*"

"I was upset too, Paul. I realize how intelligent they are. But this is a hospital after all and, from what I understand, the bunyips started it by attacking—"

"Of all the cruel, stupid . . . " Paul spoke under his breath as he rose to his feet. "Those bastards!"

Sheila tried to calm him, but Paul's shock rapidly evolved into fury. He ran back to the fifth floor landing and pounded on the door.

"Let me in, you fucking idiots! You can change the goddamn locks, but you can't keep me out!"

Getting no response, Paul ran back down the stairs. The fire equipment lay stored behind locked glass doors by the first floor landing. He kicked in the glass to the fire ax and headed back up the stairs with the ax in hand. All the while Sheila tried to talk to him, but he didn't hear the words.

Panting and sweating from running the stairs, Paul still managed to throw all his strength behind the ax. The blade bit into the door. Solid wood, judging from the dull resonance. Paul hacked into it even harder, this time unleashing a spray of chips. Working with feverish intensity, he chopped into the door over and over until it finally shattered.

He kicked it open and lunged defiantly into the lobby. Pike and Andrews weren't in sight.

He ran to the old polio ward.

"Oh, God damn!" he screamed, tears of anguish mixing with the sweat pouring down his face.

In front of him were rows of stainless steel dog cages, so small and restrictive that their tiny inhabitants couldn't even stand up. He ran to Maude's cage first.

"Get back from the door, Maude. I'm gonna break the hasp with this ax."

Paul raised the ax overhead and took careful aim. Just as he was about to let fly, someone grabbed his arms from behind. Instinctively, Paul released the ax and dropped to his knees, flipping the assailant over his shoulder. In his frenzy, Paul didn't even notice that the man he'd sent sprawling in front of him wore a police uniform.

He stood up to retrieve the ax, but was jumped by two men in white. He decked one with a right cross, then kicked the other in the balls, grabbed him by the neck and rammed him headfirst into the opposite wall. With single-minded determination he went back for the ax. A hand from behind caught him around the ankle, tripping him. He hit the floor with a thud and was immediately jumped by at least four men.

Unable to breathe from the crushing weight on his chest, Paul nearly blacked out. Someone handcuffed his wrists behind him. A searing pain stabbed through his shoulders as he was jerked upward by the elbows onto his feet. Andrews stormed into the room after Paul had been subdued. He'd obviously been in an altercation himself. His purpled left eye was swollen shut, bite marks covered his left cheek, and a gauze bandage obscured most of his right cheek.

Paul tried to lunge at Andrews, but the two officers pulled him back.

"Andrews, you stupid, immoral son of a bitch!"

"We had to cage them!" Andrews sputtered. "They tried to kill us! Besides, you can't just let a bunch of wild animals go running around a hospital. The medical staff director himself insisted that we confine them."

The handcuffs dug so tightly into his wrists that Paul could already feel his fingers going numb. He realized his present helplessness. "How could anybody be so fucking stupid?"

"I don't have time for this nonsense. And in thirty-five years of university life, I've never seen a graduate student conduct himself in a more disgraceful manner! You're sacked. You can go back to Kansas to write your dissertation, because I'm canceling your grant and ordering your visa revoked. I suggest you start packing the minute you get out of jail."

Andrews spun around and stormed out of the room.

"Awright, Yank, let's go. Yer in enough trouble already." The officers led Paul past a tearful Sheila and into the waiting police car.

As he lay on the bunk in jail that night, Paul had more than enough problems of his own to worry about. But his thoughts kept drifting back to Maude. He wanted to comfort her, to apologize to her, anything. But they were beyond the range of each other's thoughts.

* * *

Maude held her pouch open and admired little Alexis. She thought about Nate Townsend's group and what they'd done to Alex. Would Andrews and Pike do the same thing to Alexis? She'd learned a new emotion from her contact with humans: hatred. Boiling, bitter hatred. She reached in her pouch below the feet of little Alexis and pulled out her homemade lock picks. She rolled them between her palms as she thought. And planned. Finally a wicked little smile tugged at the corners of her mouth.

12

"Y'got a visitor, Yank, an' a damn pretty one at that. Best of all, yer can go home with 'er."

The jailer, bent-nosed, acne-scarred and with little wrinkled slits for eyes, had earlier bragged of being a former middleweight boxing champ. He certainly looked the part.

Paul sprang from his bunk.

"Sheila?" She was here already? He'd only been brought in a few hours before.

"What am I going to do with you, Paul?"

Bent-Nose laughed suggestively. "I'm sure yer'll think of somethin', ma'am. Meanwhile, Yank, yer free to leave—on one condition."

Paul looked warily through the bars. "What's that?"

From her purse, Sheila pulled an alcohol swab and a syringe filled with a yellow fluid. She beckoned Paul with an index finger.

"On condition that I get a shot? What kind of law says I have to get a shot?"

"The authorities want some reassurance that you're not going back to the hospital to start more trouble. Besides that, Paul, I'm not taking a lunatic home with me, especially not with P.J. there. Now the sooner you step over here, the sooner I'll get you out."

If anyone but her had made the offer, he'd have made

an anatomically specific suggestion of what to do with that syringe.

"No, Sheila, I'm not letting—"

"*Please*, Paul! I want you home with me," she pleaded, eyes rimming with tears. "But I'm scared of you right now, and we have our son to think of."

Sheila rarely showed vulnerability. But when she did, the effect was more powerful on Paul than any sedative.

"Darling, I promise you I'm under control," he said softly as he reached through the bars and touched her cheek. "I swear I won't cause any more problems tonight. So instead of the needle, let's go to your house and you can fix me a scotch."

"A double?" She smiled a little.

"Maybe even a triple."

She kissed his hand lightly. "All right, then. Officer, you can let him out now."

The hinges squealed as Bent-Nose pulled the cell door open. "Th' injection prob'ly wouldn't have made much difference anyway, ma'am, quiet as he's been since he got 'ere. Y'know, I'd hate this job if I had to put up with his kind ever' day. Most gawdawful borin' prisoner on earth. All 'e did was sit around feelin' sorry fer himself. Good riddance t' his kind. Gimme a drunk, screamin' larrikin any day."

Insulted by such condescension, Paul felt obliged to defend his capacity for masculine misconduct. "What is this? I'm being *thrown* out of jail? You don't think I have the balls to be a *real* criminal? Well, lemme tell ya, pal, just a few hours ago I took on—mmmmpphhh."

Sheila clasped a hand firmly over his mouth. "One more word out of you, and it's the needle."

Paul awoke the next morning on the couch, his head pounding. P.J. had obviously gotten up sometime during the night and squeezed in next to his dad. Paul found one of his son's arms draped over his chest. He carefully extricated himself and dressed, then headed for the kitchen with a desperate craving for coffee.

"Good morning, Paul. How do you feel?"

He answered with a groan.

"I guess I did go a little heavy on the grog last night." She led him by the arm to a chair and put a mug of coffee on the table in front of him. "At least a hangover should keep you out of mischief while we scheme our way out of this mess."

She stood behind him, rubbing his neck and shoulders.

"Sounds reasonable. Aren't you gonna have to head to work soon?"

"Another doctor is covering for me. You've got a lot of legal problems right now, and you'll need help sorting things out. We'll start by making some telephone calls as soon as I get P.J. off to school."

An entire day of phone calls produced nothing but frustration. Clarence had just left on a three-week sailing holiday, and no one at his office knew how to reach him.

Officials at the University of Sydney confirmed that the situation was, indeed, grim. Andrews had sent orders terminating Paul's grant and student visa that very morning. He obviously wanted Paul out of Australia as soon as possible.

"With me gone, that bastard can do whatever he wants to the bunyips," Paul fumed.

He called Jim Knox, his advisor back at the University of Kansas. Yes, Knox could get him a graduate assistantship—but certainly not to stay in Australia. He'd have to come back to Kansas.

Paul phoned a solicitor friend of Sheila's, who made some calls of his own.

Paul faced charges, from malicious vandalism to assaulting a police officer. The best the solicitor could do was a pledge from the magistrate to drop all charges if Paul left the country by the end of the week.

"Here's a capsule summary," Paul sighed as he collapsed onto the couch. "I'm unemployed and under indictment. If I don't leave the country immediately, I'll be deported—*after* serving time in prison. The only place I can resume a normal life right now is Kansas."

"What if you hold out until Clarence gets back? He seems to have quite a bit of influence. Maybe he can help."

"It's too late for that. Besides, the only arm Clarence can twist is Andrews'. How could he help me with the criminal charges? Can you imagine my getting an academic job after serving time in prison? Right now, I can't even afford a solicitor to defend me."

"Paul, I don't have much money, but I could at least help out."

"No. In the first place, I couldn't take it from you. Besides, even your solicitor friend is advising me to accept the magistrate's offer and leave. Let's remember that every one of the charges pending against me is true. Unfair, but true."

"What about the bunyips?"

"There's nothing I can do for them. I've got no jurisdiction whatever. I'm sure Clarence will order them freed once it's safe. As far as the archives go, I can't transfer them back until Aristotle has completely recovered. I can always fly in for a few days when that time comes."

"So now what?"

"I'll have to go back to Kansas, for a little while, anyway. I'll finish my degree in May, then I can come back as *Doctor* Paul McDaniel. The criminal charges will have been dismissed and probably forgotten, so I'll be eligible for an immigrant visa."

"I'd like to believe in your dreams as much as you do," she replied. "But what in hell is *Doctor* Paul McDaniel, aspiring young biologist, going to do in Silver Hill?"

"Clarence will probably create a job for me so I can

look after the bunyips." Paul hoped that his voice wasn't betraying his own uncertainty. "If not, I'm sure I can get a position somewhere. Besides, we don't have to stay in Silver Hill. You can practice medicine anywhere. I'm sure we'll find a place where we can both get the jobs we want."

They talked into the night. Despite many reservations, Sheila finally agreed to Paul's plan. After all, what choice did he have? Still, Paul detected a distinct chilling of her attitude toward him. He knew without her having to say it that he'd be sleeping on the couch until he left.

Five days later, Paul stood on the station platform waiting for the train that would begin the first leg of the long journey from Oz back to Kansas.

He'd wanted a few minutes alone with P.J. to say good-bye, so Sheila had taken the money and was in the station house buying his ticket. He'd put off getting it until the very last minute, as if the mere act of buying a ticket would bond him to using it. Now, the time had come to face reality. It was time to part.

Paul was no stranger to grief and heartache. But few things could hurt as deeply as the tearful hug of a six-year-old boy.

"Please don't leave us, Daddy! We love you! Don't go away. *Please*?"

Paul tried to find the words to comfort him but nothing worked. No sooner had P.J. found a father than he'd lost him again. Paul would be back in six months, but to a child it might as well be eternity.

The train had already pulled up as Sheila returned and handed Paul a white envelope.

"Here's your ticket. Reckon it's good-bye, then." Her voice carried an almost clinical detachment.

Paul fought back the tears as he embraced her. How could he leave her again? How could he leave his son, who now stood sobbing quietly at his side, holding on to both parents as if his tiny arms were the only thing left that could bond the three of them together?

None of them wanted to break the embrace. To let go now might be saying good-bye forever.

A loud blast from the train's air horn intruded.

"All aboard, please!"

The tears would hold back no longer. "God, I love you, Sheila. I can't wait to come back to you."

She didn't answer. He knew that, regardless of what he said or promised, she didn't really believe him. Why should she? What had he ever given her to hold on to? Yet here he was, leaving her behind again.

The train whistle blasted again to signal departure. But something within Paul refused to let go.

A conductor rushed over and tapped him on the shoulder. "C'mon, mate. Train's pullin' out."

Sheila squeezed him tighter. How many times had he longed to hold her like this?

"C'mon, sport. Train's movin'!"

Paul could barely breathe, Sheila held him so tightly. He wasn't about to be the first to let go.

"Awright, then, have it yer way." The conductor ran back to the train. As he grabbed the rail to the passenger car, he turned and shouted, "Good on yer, mate! I wouldn't leave 'er behind, neither!" He shut the door behind him as the train rolled off.

"I love you, Paul," Sheila whispered. This time, the voice came from the present.

Only when the train had rolled safely out of view did the McDaniel family finally relax its embrace.

"Y'know, it scares me that I could be so goddamn stupid that I'd even *consider* getting on that train."

"You do have a remarkable capacity for idiocy, love. At least you're learning to overcome it. So what's your scheme?"

"I'm gonna stand up to them—Andrews, Pike, Coburn, the magistrate—all of them. I did the right thing, damn it! I've got nothing to hide or be ashamed of, and I'll take my case in front of every television camera in Australia. I'll tell the whole world how I tried to defend the bunyips against those bastards' mindless cruelty. Let them be the ones to explain why I should go to prison for that!"

"Good on yer, love! I've been waiting all week to hear you say that."

"In the meantime, the money from my tickets will keep me going for a little while."

Paul tore open the envelope. But instead of the ticket, he found the money he'd given Sheila to buy it. He looked at her in confusion.

A sly smile curved her lips. "You didn't really think I was just going to stand here and let you ride away, did you? If you hadn't come to your senses at the last minute, I'd have stalled you a little longer."

P.J., who was beginning to understand that he'd still have a daddy in the morning, now hugged Paul's waist tightly.

For once in his life of endless caution, doubt and circumspection, Paul had no question but that he'd made the right decision. A decision that had been risky, illogical—and straight from the heart.

The family hugged again, this time out of pure joy. Through closed eyelids, Paul saw Plato embracing Minerva. A sudden realization dawned. *This is our Rosetta stone, isn't it, Plato? Our love for them is the common link of understanding. That's what allows me to decipher the archives.*

Plato looked at Paul and smiled, then turned back to Minerva.

* * *

Back on the fifth floor of the hospital, Andrews was

leaving for dinner. Pike never really cared much for him as a person, and knew the feeling was mutual. Still, Andrews always carried out his polite little charades.

"Would you care to join me for dinner, Larry?"

"No thanks, Charles. Too much work, too little time."

"Yes, I suppose so. Well, good night then."

From a window Pike secretly watched Andrews get in his car and drive off. Moments later, he was on the phone.

"He's gone now. I don't expect him back for at least an hour."

"Thank you, Professor Pike," said the voice from the receiver. "I shan't be but a few minutes getting there."

* * *

P.J. had just gone to bed. Although it was still early, Paul decided to turn in too. He hadn't slept well in several days. Now, having made the commitment to stay—come whatever—he could at last rest easy. Tomorrow, he'd start working on a plan to free the bunyips and Freddy.

After a long shower, he wrapped a towel around his waist and prepared for bed. He still slept on the couch alone, but had been instructed to make himself comfortable around the house. From the certain way Sheila's eyes followed him, Paul concluded that she rather enjoyed watching him walk around bare-chested. Back in Kansas, she'd often told him how appealing she found his broad shoulders.

The linens he slept on were stored in the hall closet by day. He'd just opened the door to get them when a husky purr rose from behind.

"I don't think you'll be needing those any more."

Paul closed his eyes in quick prayer. *Please, Lord, let this be what I hope it is.* He turned around to a sight that stopped his breathing. Sheila leaned against the doorway to her bedroom, wearing only a black lace peignoir, blonde hair streaming down her shoulders.

She walked slowly toward him, removing her robe to reveal the merest shadow of a bra underneath. She draped the robe temptingly over his shoulder, then pressed herself against him as she drew his lips to hers. Paul closed his eyes and savored the seductive scent of her body.

But the heat, the simple body heat, was what captured him. The firm shoulders, the strong hips pushing against him, those incredible breasts, and the tongue that seemed to probe all the way into his soul—all these had haunted his dreams for seven years. Now the body heat connected those dreams with the woman he finally held in his arms once again.

She broke off the kiss and pushed him back. Those intense blue eyes of hers, always charged with energy, locked in to his as she pulled the towel from his waist. Slowly she unfastened her bra, looped it around his neck, then led him by the straps to her bed, never once breaking that electrifying eye contact.

As they reached the bed, Sheila lowered her hands to the tiny black bows at her hips. With a slight pull on the ties, her panties floated to the floor. Then she pushed Paul backwards onto her bed and crawled on top of him.

* * *

Pike opened the stairwell door in response to a light rapping.

"Good day, Professor Pike. Well, I can finally recognize your face again now that they've removed all the stitches. Although I imagine you'll still need a little plastic surgery after the swelling has gone down."

"Yeah, and thanks to you I'll be able to afford it. I have 500 cc's of bunyip blood this time."

Dr. Lee patted the briefcase he carried. "And I have $50,000 for you."

"I don't know how much longer we can do business.

Eventually, we'll be ordered to release the bunyips back to the wild."

"Yes, and we need to begin preparations for that. My clients won't appreciate having their supplies interrupted, even for a little while. Perhaps you could gather a reserve of blood while I try to come up with a long-term plan for guaranteeing the supply after they're released. Our job would be much easier if you could, perhaps, entice Professor Andrews into joining forces with us."

"Forget it. That egotistical little bastard is motivated by a lot of things, but money isn't one of them. He'd have us all thrown in jail if he knew about this. Maybe we could substitute the blood of some other marsupial. I mean, who'd ever know the difference?"

"Tut-tut, Professor Pike. I may be many things, but I'm first and foremost a reputable business man. If I sell someone bunyip blood, I guarantee that it is, in fact, the blood of a bunyip. Before you feel tempted to try something on your own, let me inform you that I personally cross-match the blood to make sure it's authentic. Reputation is everything in my business."

"All right, then. Have it your way. I'll try to suck some extra blood whenever I can. I should have two liters by next week."

"Excellent. And I will bring $200,000—in cash, of course."

* * *

"Wake up, darling. I brought you some coffee."

Paul opened his eyes. Sheila, wearing a bathrobe, sat on the bed beside him with a mug in each hand.

"You mean they serve coffee in heaven?"

She giggled as he took one of the mugs. Then she straddled his legs with hers. "You certainly seemed to enjoy yourself last night."

"Any more and I'd be in a wheelchair. In fact, I haven't tried my legs yet to make sure they still work." He maneuvered his right foot, still under the covers, between her thighs and rubbed it against her.

"They work just fine, as far as I'm concerned." She held the foot close as she pushed up against it.

"Last night was incredible. I mean, we've had great sex in the past, but . . . "

She beamed back at him. "I'll have to admit, I did plan it that way. I didn't know whether you'd be dumb enough to try and board that train or not. I figured I'd have to provide you with either a damn good reason for not hopping on the next one or a reward for coming to your senses in time."

She pulled off her bathrobe and stuck out her chest as those bright blue eyes of hers locked back into his.

"P.J.'s already at school, and I have two more hours before I have to leave for work. Any ideas how we can pass the time?"

Two memorable hours later, they were just leaving the house when the phone rang.

"Paul, it's Clarence! I just called my office for messages and learned what happened to you. Now don't worry. I'll make sure you don't get punished any further! I already have a solicitor friend lined up to take your case."

Clarence tended to excite easily, Paul had observed. Thanks to Sheila's attentions, Paul himself had lapsed into a serenity worthy of Buddha. "That's nice, Clarence, but I've already decided to—"

"I know you've had a rough time. I'll put this story on every telly in the world if I have to. Imagine how it would look—a graduate student going to prison for defending the bunyips! I'll see to it that Pike and Andrews are ruined and the magistrate crucified if they even dare *discuss* putting you on trial."

"Well good, and I—"

"Just calm down—*calm down!*—and let me put a stop to this nonsense. I'll have those charges dropped within a week."

"Fine. Y'know I've already decided—"

"Listen to me, Paul. You do not, I repeat, *you do not* have to leave Australia."

"Whatever you say, Clarence."

"So what else did Clarence tell you?" Sheila asked during the drive back to the hospital.

"That he can't get the bunyips out of their cages immediately. Coburn still has final say around the hospital, and that goes for getting Freddy out of the psychiatric ward too. Besides, Clarence feels that the genetic and immunological studies being done by Andrews and Pike are essential for guaranteeing the bunyips' long-term survival. In any case, their home range isn't safe yet. Clarence did promise that the bunyips will be released to the wild within two months. He'll also make sure that I'm allowed back on the fifth floor until then. He wants me to wait a few days, though, for the emotions to cool off a bit."

"What about your employment?"

"My grant was canceled. It's already too late to save it. He offered to create some kind of make-work job for me. It wouldn't pay very much, but enough to keep me going while I finish my dissertation."

"Y'know, darling, a job like that would only slow the progress on your doctorate. Why don't you just live with me? You can help with the cooking and housework and spend the rest of your time writing."

"Be a house husband? Jeez. I'm not sure I'm . . . "

Her hand slipped between his legs and began stroking his inner thigh.

"Come on, now. None of that macho bullshit. You know how rotten I am at domestic stuff, and you're already doing most of it, anyway. Just like you did back in Kansas. You'll finish your dissertation a lot quicker if you're not distracted with another job. Especially since I intend to provide you with all the distractions you can possibly handle."

Paul mumbled something about taking her offer into consideration. At the moment, it was all he could do to concentrate on driving.

Once inside the hospital, Sheila sat at her desk reviewing patient charts. Paul sat in one of the chairs across from her, eyes closed.

"What are thinking about, Paul?"

"I'm making contact with Maude."

Sheila turned to her charts with a sigh. "I still don't understand what all this 'psychic communication' stuff is about. I just hope it doesn't land you in the booby hatch with Freddy."

So do I, he worried to himself.

P.J. joined them at the end of the day. Then they all headed out to eat.

"So, Paul, what did you learn from Maude today?" Sheila teased.

"He learned that Maude wants him to come back tonight, after those stupid professors are in bed." P.J.'s own voice reflected irritation with his mother's lack of understanding. "Right now, Dad's trying to figure out how to tell you so you won't think we're all mad."

Sheila looked at Paul, who turned away with an embarrassed smile. Then to P.J., "How did you know that, son? Did Daddy tell you that?"

"No, but that's what he's thinking. Isn't it, Dad?"

"Uh . . . yeah. Uh-huh."

"Look, Paul, I realize that there's a lot going on here, even if I'm not tuning in on the mental telepathy. I also know that it's very important. But P.J. and I are important too. I want you to promise me that you won't do anything that might even possibly get you into more trouble."

"I swear. Maude just wants some information from me. I have no idea what kind."

"Okay, but I'm going with you. We'll get a baby-sitter for P.J."

They returned to Sheila's office at around eleven and waited. Paul worked on the outline of his dissertation while Sheila used the time to catch up on her paperwork.

Maude contacted him around midnight. Paul covered his face with his hands. He saw a blue flash, then found himself viewing the world through Maude's eyes. She'd evidently picked the lock to her cage and was now in the fifth-floor laboratory, standing on a chair in front of a shelf filled with jars and bottles.

She picked up a large brown bottle filled with a clear liquid and held it close to her face so that Paul could read the label. Formaldehyde.

You want to know what it's for? Is that it?

She didn't respond. Although Maude could understand words spoken aloud, she still wasn't fluent in following them from the visions. Paul pictured a hand pouring the formaldehyde into a jar. Then he pictured a pair of hands cutting the heart out of a dead rabbit and dropping it into the jar. Then the hands put the jar on a shelf filled with similarly preserved specimens.

Hopefully, Maude would be able to abstract enough from that scene to understand him. Then, as a warning, Paul pictured a man picking up one of those jars and drinking from it. The man immediately clutched his stomach and vomited, then collapsed to the floor. Paul could only wonder what Maude was getting from all this.

The next item was a bottle of nitric acid. Paul pictured the acid dropping on bare skin and dissolving it away.

Jesus, Maude, I hope I'm not giving you any wrong ideas here. Nobody's gonna pour that stuff on you.

The next item was a jar of potassium cyanide. Paul wondered if he might be giving the bunyips the impression that Pike and Andrews were setting up some kind of extermination camp. He focused on the skull and crossbones on the label.

That means you can't eat it. But nobody's gonna feed it to you.

He pictured a small boy picking up a jar with a skull and crossbones on it. Then the boy's mother jerking the jar out of his hands in horror and pointing to the label while shouting "No! No! No!"

It's a warning sign. That's all, just a warning.

Maude slowly circled the emblem with her index finger.

Yes—that sign is a warning.

Maude tapped the label, and Paul found himself standing next to Plato in a room filled with shelves of books. Paul looked around and realized that the archives had taken him into his memories of the library at the University of Kansas. The shelf in front of him contained books on poisons and toxicology. Plato pulled a thick volume from the shelf and handed it to Paul. Then Plato tapped him on the forehead, and everything went blank.

A while later, Plato came back. This time, Paul dreamed that they were at the airport. Sheila and P.J. were there, too, climbing aboard an RFDS plane with their suitcases. Then Plato boarded the plane, and Paul followed. From the window, he saw a smiling Maude standing on the runway, waving good-bye.

* * *

"Paul! Paul!"

He snapped back to consciousness as Sheila shook him by the arm. "Sorry. I guess I . . . "

"It's five in the morning, Paul. I fell asleep at my desk. When I woke up, you were just sitting there, not moving a muscle. I wondered if you were still breathing."

Still disoriented from his session, Paul tried to allay her concern. "I'm fine. We're done now. At least, I think so."

They headed back to the car, arm in arm. Sheila took the keys from him and pushed him into the passenger seat.

"So what was on Maude's mind?" she asked once they were on the road.

"She wanted to learn about the chemicals in the lab, especially anything poisonous. At first, I thought she just wanted to know what Andrews and Pike would be doing with them. But she's after a lot more than that. My mind sort of went blank after a while. She's up to something, but she won't let me know what. In fact, I even got the impression that she wants . . . no, never mind. You already think I'm crazy."

"You got the impression that she wants the three of us to leave town, to go off somewhere with the RFDS."

Paul gave her a puzzled glance.

"She sent me the same message. It was the first one I've gotten. I imagine it has something to do with a phone call I received last week. Andrea Forster, one of my chums from medical school, works out of the Flying Doctor base in Cairns. She's about to have a baby and is taking a six-month maternity leave. The doctor who's scheduled to cover for her has been delayed for a month. Andrea called and asked if I'd like to fill in for December."

"What did you tell her?"

"That I'd love to, but that my personal life was rather complicated at the moment. Besides, we'd have to leave next week, and that would mean P.J. would miss his last week of school before summer holiday as well as—"

A sense of urgency overrode caution. Without understanding why, Paul cut her off. "Let's go to Cairns—as soon as possible."

They pulled into the driveway. As Sheila turned off the engine, he put his hands on her shoulders and kissed her.

"Are you serious?"

"Very. Something important is about to happen. I dunno what it is, but the bunyips have some pretty heavy scores to settle. And I sure as hell don't want any of us in the line of fire. If they want us out of Silver Hill, there's a reason. And if there's one thing I've learned about bunyips, it's to follow your instincts around them."

"Today's Thursday. I suppose we could leave as early as next Friday."

"I'll make our reservations as soon as the travel offices open."

"Well, all right . . . I reckon . . . "

"What? I know that tone. What's bothering you?"

"Maude showed me a few other things too. Things about you. Right now, I'm not sure . . . "

"*What* things? Tell me." Paul felt his heart sink once again.

"No . . . not yet. I need some time to sort them out myself first. We'll discuss them later."

"Jeez! You're gonna torture me by making me guess?"

"No, at least I'll try not to. Let's go to Cairns. I think we both need the change of scenery."

Paul started back to the hospital that afternoon, but Maude warned him away as soon as he came in range. He was not to return there until after the trip to Cairns. He acquiesced, although he still didn't understand why.

A week later, the McDaniels departed for the Coral Seaside town of Cairns in far north Queensland.

* * *

Maude smiled to herself as she rolled a lock pick between her thumb and fingertips. With Freddy still locked up and sedated and Paul half a continent away, neither man could be held responsible for what was about to happen. The reckoning would now begin.

13

The McDaniels arrived in the holiday town of Cairns with plenty to celebrate. Not only had all the charges against Paul been dropped the day before they arrived, but the police records of his arrest had mysteriously disappeared.

"Once they realized how bad they'd look to the public, I reckon everyone involved decided to pretend the incident never happened," Clarence surmised.

The family rented a fourth-floor holiday flat facing the Esplanade, the main thoroughfare along the Cairns waterfront. Although the rainy season normally started in December, the weather remained sunny. Every morning they had breakfast on the patio and watched as the marlin boat crews busily prepared to haul in their daily catch of wealthy sport fishermen.

After breakfast, Sheila headed for the RFDS base while Paul worked on his dissertation. P.J., like many children raised by single professional women, was used to entertaining himself quietly and posed no major distraction during the long hours that his father stared into his computer screen. Except for a half-hour lunch break, Paul worked until Sheila returned, usually around five. They'd have a quick dinner, then go out for a movie or maybe just a long stroll along the Esplanade. Weekends were spent snorkeling or sailing or anything else the normally landlocked McDaniels could find to do on the water.

At nights, Paul would wonder what Maude was up to, but only until Sheila came to bed. It had taken everything he had to rekindle the spark between them. Now it took at least that much to control the flames.

Still, nothing matched the simple joy of waking up with her cuddled next to him.

* * *

Back at Silver Hill, Maude had work to do. Dr. Lee would be coming the following night. Around midnight, she picked open the lock to her cage and slipped quietly into the lab. There she grabbed the bottle marked "mercury bichloride" and headed for the refrigerator where Pike stored his blood supply in an inconspicuous plastic jar. She salted the blood repeatedly with the white crystals as she stirred with a spoon. She washed the spoon, put everything back in place and returned to her cage.

Within days, pills made from the contaminated blood would reach consumers. From Paul's memory Maude had learned of the pernicious nature of mercury. A slow poison when given in small doses, its effects wouldn't begin showing themselves for weeks or months. By then, most of the damage would be irreversible.

A fast-acting poison wouldn't work for Maude's purpose. The contaminated batch would be identified and isolated as soon as someone dropped dead with a bottle of pills in hand. And the incident would soon be forgotten. With a slow-acting poison, however, the damage would be widespread long before it was even noticed. Some victims would go insane, mad as the hatters of centuries past whose bodies had slowly absorbed the mercury bichloride used in making felt hats.

As victims sought medical help for their numbness and

tremors and other symptoms of nerve damage, the source of their misery would gradually be identified. By then, almost everyone who used bunyip blood products would be afflicted to some degree, and the scandal would attract worldwide headlines. The market for bunyip blood would be destroyed forever.

The next day, after Lee had picked up the contaminated blood, the bunyips began preparations for Step Two.

* * *

"I'm surprised you weren't scared when that shark swam by, P.J.," Sheila said as she pulled off her flippers and followed her son up the steps to the boat's main deck.

"Nah. It wasn't that big. Besides, I always feel safe when we're with Dad."

Paul, bringing up the rear, had already advised that they were likely to encounter a reef shark or two. But the expression of trust still warmed him.

They deposited their snorkeling gear in a large plywood bin, then found a seat among the twenty-odd passengers crowding the boat's stern.

"Enjoying yourself, son?" Paul asked as he toweled P.J. off.

"Dad, this is the best time I've ever had in my whole life." Then in a voice much louder than it needed to be, "Mum, are you and Dad *ever* going to get married?"

Sheila immediately reddened. Paul felt a little embarrassed himself at having this discussion in public but . . . well . . . it would be nice to hear the answer.

"Dad has a few things in his own life he needs to work out first," she replied in a low but even tone. Then she looked straight at Paul. "The matter will not be discussed further until then."

Paul nodded his acknowledgment, but wondered what

he was supposed to work out. Ever since she'd gotten that message from Maude, Sheila seemed to talk in riddles.

"By the way, I hope you're ready for a trip," she announced, apparently eager to change the subject. "Next Thursday I'm doing an overnight clinic at the Timburru Aboriginal Mission up north of here, near Cape York. Since that's only a week before Christmas, and since any number of things might strand us there for several days, I've arranged for the two of you to ride along. That way, we'll all be together for Christmas, no matter what."

"Yay! We're going flying, Dad."

"Is that all right with you, Paul?"

"It wouldn't matter to me if we spent Christmas slopping hogs back in Kansas. As long as we're together, I'll be happy."

Sheila smiled, then leaned over and kissed his cheek. "You're learning," she whispered.

* * *

Travis took being caged the hardest, tortured by the separation from his juvenile charges. Unlike Crockett, who'd occasionally tire of the little ones' frolicking and turn stern and aloof, Travis invariably delighted in their antics.

When they were free, Travis could usually be found carrying a child in each arm while two or three clung to his legs, forcing him to shuffle along like some animated carnival ride. Whereas Crockett would push away fidgeting little hands that tugged his hair, Travis patiently endured. As a result, his thighs and upper chest had been plucked nearly bald.

Pike entered the ward with a tray of needles and blood collection tubes. With slow deliberation he pulled on the heavy leather gloves that protected him against little teeth and unlocked the cage of one of the juveniles. He grasped a tiny arm with one hand and shoved a needle in it with another.

Across the room, Travis pounded the steel bars of his cage in helpless fury. Bitter tears streamed down his face as Pike went from cage to cage.

Once the gentlest of all the bunyips, even Travis had been rendered vicious by anger and frustration. With each passing day, his lust for vengeance grew ever more dangerous.

Still trembling with rage, Travis looked across the room into Maude's eyes. A blue flash passed between them. Then he sat down in the corner of his cage and smiled.

* * *

The Timburru Aboriginal Mission was a pleasant seaside village of about twenty simple white-washed cinder block houses with corrugated tin roofs, all built around an Anglican church of the same architecture but on a larger scale.

A small guest house next to the parsonage doubled as the clinic. Paul helped Sheila and the field sister set up the medical equipment as patients gathered on the small verandah that served as a waiting room. P.J. immediately made friends with a group of aboriginal children about his age, and went off to play.

Paul had nothing to do once the clinic started, so he went for a walk on the beach. It was a warm, sleepy afternoon, and after a while he sat down and rested against a palm tree. He closed his eyes, and Plato was back with him. Plato walked to the water's edge and showed happy surprise as a wave crashed into him. He was reliving Paul's first memory of the sea.

You like it here, don't you, Plato?

Plato smiled back at him.

The McDaniels returned from Timburru on schedule the

next day. Plato remained oddly enchanted with the beach, and tried repeatedly to probe for knowledge on the subject. But as a native Kansan, Paul didn't have much to offer.

* * *

Pike stuck his pistol and a handful of darts into his lab coat and carried his blood-drawing tray back to the polio ward. After his altercation with the adults, Pike didn't dare so much as touch one of them without first sedating it.

He put his tray on top of Crockett's cage and pulled out the pistol. He prepared to load it, but noticed Crockett's outstretched arm protruding between the bars.

"Finally decided to make it easy on yourself, eh?"

Still wary, Pike gingerly applied a tourniquet just above the elbow. The bunyip didn't flinch as the needle slid through his skin and into a vein.

As the blood streamed into the vacuum tube attached to the needle, Pike glanced into Crockett's face. The bunyip's eyes were already fixed on his.

Pike shuddered. "What are you grinning about? You can't be enjoying this. What's going on here?"

He didn't expect an answer and didn't get one. He finished with Crockett, then moved on to the next cage. Again, a small, hairy arm extended itself for his needle. Again, a pair of eyes bored into his, the mouth set in a malevolent little grin. So it went at the next cage.

The experience unnerved Pike. By the time he'd finished the fifth bunyip, his hands shook. He stared into the leering face of the sixth for a moment, then wordlessly picked up his tray and headed back to the lab.

Pike couldn't have known it, but the bunyips really did want him to take their blood. The quicker he built up his supply, the sooner Dr. Lee would return.

* * *

"Paul, are you sure we're on the right road?"

"Yeah, we're just in the wrong vehicle. These mountain roads weren't meant for two-wheel drive, especially in this rain. What time are the Forsters expecting us, anyway?"

"Noonish. We Aussies are rather informal hosts, you know, especially on Christmas. Besides, I'm sure the new baby will keep them occupied until we get there."

Paul used his bandana to wipe the steam fogging the inside of his windshield as he strained to follow the twisting mud path through the jungle in a tropical downpour. "Why would a doctor live all the way up here, anyway?"

"Andrea was always the outdoors type, even in medical school. I remember how she and Dave used to keep their rucksacks packed and ready to head for the bush any chance they could."

The rain intensified, and even the frantic slapping of the wiper blades failed to clear the windshield. Paul stuck his head out the window. Sheila did likewise, although Paul suspected she did it more to share his misery than actually help him navigate.

Suddenly, he felt his rear wheels slip. "Brace yourself. We're sliding."

Paul let off the gas pedal, then floored the clutch and allowed the car to coast backward a little as he maneuvered it closer to the ascending slope of the mountain. The opposite slope was an almost sheer drop-off, and he wanted to get as far away from it as possible. The car suddenly lurched sideways and down with a thud.

"Shit!"

"What happened, Paul?"

"Must have dropped one of the rear wheels into a pothole. I couldn't see it for all the water pouring down the mountain. Let me see if I can drive us out."

The wheels spun uselessly.

"So now what?"

"You take the wheel. I'll get out and try to push us free."

It was not to be. After half an hour of standing in the rain and pushing against the rear bumper while being sprayed with mud from spinning tires, Paul conceded defeat. Sheila, too, had been thoroughly drenched.

He climbed back in the car, and Sheila kissed him. "Don't worry, darling. It's already after two, and Dave said he'd come looking for us if we weren't there by three."

Paul wiped his hair back from his forehead and sighed. "Oh, I know. I'm really not worried. It's just a hell of a way to spend Christmas."

From the back seat P.J. leaned forward, wrapped his arms around Paul's neck and hugged. "That's okay, Dad. It's still my favorite Christmas ever."

"Mine too," Sheila added with a determined smile.

As for Paul, that went without saying. But he said it anyway, out of pure joy of rolling the words off his tongue.

A few hours later, the McDaniels were showered, changed, and gathered around their friends' dinner table. They ate and talked until well after midnight before their hosts showed them to their room. No sooner had Paul's head hit the pillow than Plato returned.

Can I ask the questions this time?

Plato gave him a bemused smile and nodded.

How far back in time do the archives go?

Plato stretched his hands as far apart as he could.

Can you take me there?

The bunyip gave him a quizzical look.

Yes! I want you to take me as far back in time as possible.

Plato replied with a demure smile.

Yes, I'm sure! I want to go there.

Plato took Paul's hand, and they again walked the Outback by starlight.

Instead of prickly spinifcx and scrub, a lush plain of waist-high grass spread out before them. A troop of about a dozen bunyips approached. The leader, a graying male with wide-set eyes and a slow, arthritic gait, stepped up to Plato. They rubbed their knuckles against each other's cheeks in greeting.

Plato pointed to Paul, and the leader stepped over to greet him too. Paul reciprocated, not at all surprised that his own outstretched arm was covered with reddish-brown hair.

Are you the first, the original keeper of the archives?

Paul himself didn't know whether he'd spoken the words or thought them. In any case, the old one smiled and nodded. Paul dubbed him Methuselah.

Methuselah's troop resumed its walk, with Paul and Plato joining them. The warm, damp air smelled of earth and wildflowers, resounding with the merry chirp of crickets. Under the full moon, the landscape appeared as bright as daylight to the bunyips' nocturnal eyes.

In the distance, Paul noticed a low sandstone mountain spread out like a sleeping camel. He stepped over to Methuselah.

I know this place, I think. Except the mountain I remember is in the desert now. It hasn't been surrounded by grasslands since the Pleistocene. How far back in time are we?

Methuselah pointed to a large animal grazing in the distance. Paul didn't recognize it, so he walked in closer. It seemed to notice him, yet showed no sign of concern at his approach. Bigger than a cow, it vaguely resembled a hornless rhinoceros.

What kind of animal is this?

He stepped up to the beast and stroked its neck with one hand. Its sandy yellow hair, about three inches long, reminded him of pig bristles. The animal snorted and walked away. Paul glimpsed a small head protruding from a bulge in its abdomen.

It's a marsupial? Who ever heard of a—? Something clicked in Paul's head. *My God! Of course. It's got to be a diprotodon!*

Paul rejoined the others on their walk. A flat-faced kangaroo reared itself to its full ten-foot height, then bounded away in leaps of thirty feet or more as they approached. An emu-like bird, as tall as a house, wandered by.

Paul smelled smoke, then heard the gentle murmur of human voices being carried on the wind. Methuselah turned to him and pointed toward a large sandstone outcrop about two hundred yards upwind.

Paul silently made his way to the outcrop. Twenty or so dark-skinned humans sat naked in a ring around a large wood fire. A shriveled man with white hair and beard, his back to Paul, raised his hands heavenward and spoke as the others listened in silence.

Paul watched in rapt attention. Suddenly, the old man turned around and looked straight at Paul, motioning for him to join them. Paul fought the urge to run. The old man clearly intended no harm. Paul took his place in the circle, and the old man continued his story, speaking in a language Paul had never heard before but somehow vaguely understood. The old one spoke of the great Rainbow Serpent, who would protect them from the time of darkness about to come as one of the giant Kadimakara moved so close to the earth that its very shadow would soon hide the moon.

A woman gasped and jumped to her feet, pointing to the sky. The moon was beginning to darken. Instantly, the others were also on their feet, yelling. The men waved their spears threateningly at the sky. Paul watched as the moon slowly disappeared altogether.

Paul stared at the sky. *The planets! I must remember the location of the planets. That's Jupiter, there's Venus, there's Mars and—*

"Paul! Wake up."

"Huh? What? Where are we?"

Sheila switched on the bedlamp. "We're in Andrea and Dave's guest bedroom, remember? You started hyperventilating. I didn't know if you were having a bad dream or some kind of seizure."

He sat upright. "I was in the archives again, *way* into them. God, it was wonderful! They seem to get more realistic all the time. I mean, I actually saw a diprotodon, a living, breathing diprotodon."

"A what?"

"A kind of hornless marsupial rhinoceros. They've been extinct for over fifteen thousand years. Yet, I actually reached out and touched one. And I saw a giant kangaroo and, oh God, I can't begin to tell you everything. But I've got to copy something down first."

"You've got to *what?*"

He jumped out of bed and rummaged through his day pack, producing a marking pen. "Copy something down. A sky map. I made a mental image of one just as you woke me up. But I don't have a piece of paper big enough to do the job."

He scanned the room as Sheila stared at him in obvious bewilderment.

"The sheets! Of course. A white sheet will be perfect."

He pulled the top sheet from the bed and spread it on the floor as Sheila shook her head and muttered something that he probably didn't want to hear anyway.

"Turn off the light, Sheila. I can project my mental picture right onto the sheet."

She reluctantly complied.

From the darkness, Paul continued, "Okay, Mars is right here. Venus here, the Southern Cross right here, Mercury here . . . "

14

Sheila had fallen back asleep by the time Paul finished plotting the night sky of his dream. He folded the sheet and put it in his day pack, then crawled back into bed. Eventually, the information on that sheet would help him discover just how real the events he'd witnessed had been. But that would come later, after the bunyips were safely released to the wild. For the present, his mind already crawled with more strange visions and thoughts than any human brain was designed to handle.

He tried to sleep but couldn't. He didn't believe for one moment that it had only been a dream. He could only hold Sheila in the darkness and wonder where all these events were headed.

* * *

Maude was getting anxious. She didn't like the images racing through Pike's brain as he sat alone in his lab, two days after Christmas. She still couldn't interpret his thoughts clearly, but enough to know that Dr. Lee would be coming by that night for another pickup, and Pike was still almost a liter—$100,000 worth—short of what he'd promised. Andrews had grown testy about the amount of excess blood being drawn and insisted that collections be cut back.

On top of that, the bunyips were scheduled to be set free in only a month. Maude realized that Pike despaired of not having dissected one. Since Aristotle and the burned ones had almost fully recovered, it didn't look as though the professor had a candidate, either. The two men had already accepted a sizable advance for a textbook on bunyip anatomy. Without a dissection, there wouldn't be enough data to write it.

Pike loaded a dart with enough anesthetic to put down an elephant. Every bunyip was on to his plan as he entered the polio ward.

Desperately, Maude tried to think of a way to stop him without using her lock picks. All would be lost if they were seen and confiscated.

Pike paused in front of Crockett's cage. "If you weren't in your prime breeding years, I'd be only too happy to carve on you, you little bastard," Pike mused, pointing the gun at him and pretending to pull the trigger. "But no, I'll have to settle for one of the old, decrepit ones. I reckon the one they call 'Moses' is most expendable."

Instantly, Crockett lunged forward. With one hand he caught Pike's pant leg and pulled the man close enough to seize his thigh with both hands. The bunyip jerked hard, lifting Pike off his feet as he yanked the man crashing into the cage door. The bars dug into Crockett's cheekbones as he attempted to sink his teeth wherever he could find purchase.

Pike's face froze in alarm. Either by accident or intention, the pistol discharged its lethal dart into Crockett's neck.

Seconds later, Pike wrenched free of the bunyip's grasp. He stared breathless and shaking as Crockett convulsed, then finally collapsed. The man seemed oblivious of the others, who clutched the bars of their cages in silent shock.

Pike carried Crockett to the lab and spread him out on the dissecting table.

Maude switched into Andrews' mind. She could follow

his thoughts easier than Pike's, even if neither professor seemed attuned to hers.

Andrews opened the door to his room in response to Pike's knock. Pike had regained his composure and now stood at the doorway looking almost remorseful.

"One of the bunyips died, Charles. He must have been hypersensitive to the anesthetic."

"Damn you! I told you that dart gun was overdoing things. Why do you have to be so rough?"

"Look, if we didn't use darts, we'd probably have killed one anyway whilst wrestling with it. It's a calculated risk either way. The point is, we now have a body to dissect, and a warm one at that. So let's get at it. This will probably be the only chance we'll ever have."

"All right, Larry, but I don't like this," Andrews said as he followed Pike to the lab. "Something's going on around here that just isn't right. The longer I stay on this floor, the more I'm convinced of that. And I'm beginning to wonder if you're not a part of it."

Pike shot back a hostile glance but didn't speak.

Maude decided to take some kind of action, no matter what the risk. She pulled out her picks and set to work. Her fingers trembled with panic, jerking the picks uselessly across the tumblers.

She closed her eyes and focused into Andrews' mind.

In the lab, Andrews paused and rubbed his hand against his forehead. "Larry, something's wrong here. Don't do any cutting just yet."

Pike paid no heed, and sliced into Crockett's abdomen with a scalpel.

"Stop, Larry! I just remembered something from back at the field station. The bunyips have a fainting response that mimics death—no pulse, no respiration. Let's make sure he's really dead before we cut anymore."

"Oh, for Christ's sake. You're getting as silly as that damned McDaniel. Now stop talking nonsense and—"

A spurt of blood from a severed artery filled Pike's mouth.

"God damn it!" Andrews yelled. "Now I suppose you are going to tell me that a corpse is producing blood pressure?"

"Oh, belt up! It's just some kind of post-mortem muscle contraction. See? It's stopped."

"Maybe the heart's only beating once every minute or so. Now I'm telling you to wait until—"

"And I'm telling you to belt up and let me work."

The time they spent bickering gave Maude one final chance. She forced her mind clear of emotion and turned back to the lock. Seconds later, she swung her cage door open and ran for the lab.

"I'm going to call a surgeon up here," Andrews was insisting as Maude entered the room. "Until then, let's stop and—Hey, what's this?"

Maude jumped onto the dissecting table and shielded Crockett's body with her own. Desperately, she looked up into Andrews' face.

The man froze, then shuddered as his eyes locked into hers. "What are you telling me?"

He leaned forward intently. Pike shouted something, but Andrews ignored him. "You're trying to tell me something . . . what?"

He shuddered again. "What are you telling me? I want to know."

A flash of blue light.

"Oh . . . my . . . God. Oh my God, no! What have we done?"

"Get her out of here!" Pike screamed.

Andrews grabbed Maude by the arms and lifted her off the table. Crockett sat up, his eyes filling with shock and terror as his intestines spilled out onto the table. Andrews carried Maude out the door.

"There's nothing you can do," he said. "Back to your cage whilst I see about saving your friend."

Maude flailed her arms and legs, struggling to break free. But Andrews held firm as he pushed her back into her cage and relocked it.

"Stay here. You'll only get in the way," he commanded. Desperately, Maude linked his mind into Pike's.

"Shit!" Andrews yelled.

He scrambled back to the lab, leather soles slipping on the vinyl tile.

The scene that awaited him was something out of a slasher movie.

"God damn you, Larry, stop it!"

Andrews lunged forward and grabbed Pike's arm before it could plunge the scalpel into the bunyip's heart again. With his other hand, Pike held Crockett pinned by the throat to the dissecting table.

Andrews smacked his palm into the larger man's face with enough force to send him reeling across the room. Pike hit a table and knocked it over with a crash, shattering beakers and specimen jars in every direction.

Andrews turned back to Crockett, who lay quivering on the table. His heart still twitched erratically in the pool of blood overflowing his chest.

"Mother of God! What have we done?"

Crockett's eyes rested on Andrews', and the two regarded each other in silent mutual horror. A moment later, the bunyip's eyes glazed and the heart stopped.

Andrews turned to his colleague and spoke in a voice of barely restrained outrage. "You immoral, lying son of a bitch."

"Have you gone mad? What the hell did you expect me to do? How was I to know it was still alive?"

"You killed him deliberately. The anesthetic overdose was no accident."

"It *was* an accident, I tell you. And once we'd gutted it,

it would have died anyway. I was just putting it out of its misery."

Andrews glared into his colleague's blood-spattered face without speaking. Finally, he headed out the door and down the stairs.

Pike calmly began scooping up the spilled blood and funneling it into his jar.

Maude pushed aside her grief and instead stoked the raging fires of hatred. In the cage across from her, Minerva reached into her pouch and retrieved the loaded syringe that Maude had given her to hide. Mother and daughter stared into each other's eyes, sharing strength and comfort. For now, they could only wait and hope.

* * *

Paul and Sheila returned to Cairns, leaving P.J. to spend a few days alone with Andrea and Dave, his frequent baby-sitters from back when Sheila was in medical school.

The next morning began with a pre-dawn phone call for Sheila. After a couple of minutes repeating, "Yeah, okay," she closed the conversation. "Tell him I'm on my way. I'll be at the airport in ten minutes."

"What's up? Another emergency run?"

"Afraid so. Some miner gashed his leg. Tried to bandage it himself, but now it's infected. I need to get to him before gangrene sets in."

"A long trip?"

"Yeah. He lives on some island up in the Gulf of Carpenteria."

Paul felt an odd compulsion. "Can I ride along?"

"Sure. Always glad to have you around. Any particular reason?"

"No. Just another one of my—"

"—instinctive gut reactions? Good. I like those better than your usual, hyper-analyzed responses reasoned out to the two-hundredth iteration."

Minutes later, as a red sun seemed to bob out of the eastern sea, they were airborne. The field sister sat with the pilot in the cockpit of the twin-engine Beechcraft, and Paul and Sheila sat across from each other in passenger seats. After they'd been aloft for an hour or so, Sheila leaned across the narrow aisle and kissed him. "You're being awfully quiet, darling."

She'd brought him back from his own little world. "I know. Sorry."

"Worrying about the bunyips again?"

"Yeah. I dunno what to do now. They'll never be safe or happy around humans. The Outback was like the Garden of Eden to them. It was all they ever wanted."

"So take them back. I thought that was your scheme all along."

"It's not that simple. Now that they've been discovered, people will *never* leave them alone. There's always gonna be somebody trying to exploit them." His ears burned with shame. "Like I did."

"Where else can the bunyips go?"

"That's the problem. Where *can* they go? They don't know anything about the rest of the world. How can we protect them without making them virtual prisoners?"

"Let the archives guide them, Paul. That's why the information is kept in the first place, remember?"

"Yeah, you're right." Paul's eyes narrowed. "Y'know, you seem to know an awful lot about—" He caught something out of the corner of one eye, then jerked about suddenly to stare wide-eyed and gape-mouthed at the seat behind Sheila. The blood drained from his face.

"Uh-oh," she said, handing him an airsickness bag.

"No, it's not that. It's Plato. He's sitting in the seat behind you!"

She turned about quickly, then sighed with relief. "Your imagination is getting away from you. There's nothing there, see?" She passed her hand right through Plato's smiling face.

Paul leaned over and passed his own hand through Plato's body.

"I still see him, though. I see Plato as clearly as I see you right now."

"Can't your little friend confine himself to your dreams? Next thing I know, you'll be insisting that he's real and *I'm* the figment of your imagination."

"No, it's okay. I think I understand. The archives have been teaching me how to use them. At the same time they're learning about the human brain. Apparently, they've figured out how visual perception works. So what I'm seeing is just a projection within my own mind. Right, Plato?"

The bunyip smiled.

Sheila nodded and spoke to herself. "Aha."

"What do you mean, 'Aha?' What do you know about this?"

"Nothing important. It's just that things are beginning to fall in place. I'll explain later. In the meantime, you go play with your little friend. I have reading to catch up on." She buried her nose in a medical journal, obviously suppressing a smirk.

It's a conspiracy, Paul thought. *They're all trying to drive me crazy!*

The plane banked as the pilot prepared for landing. From his window Paul saw an island consisting of two jungle-covered mountains connected by a stretch of flat forest and rimmed by a narrow ribbon of sand.

The plane landed on a strip of cleared land parallel to the beach. As they disembarked, the pilot explained that the island had been nicknamed 'Fourex' after all the cases of Castlemaine's XXXX Beer that the pilots from Cairns had flown there. The only inhabitant was Charlie Struthers, a retired opal miner who'd bought the island twenty-odd years earlier.

Charlie wasn't waiting for them at the airstrip.

"His cabin's up this way." The pilot pointed toward the base of the nearer mountain. "Reckon with a crook leg he's not gonna be walking down to us."

Everyone followed the pilot as he started up the narrow footpath leading into the jungle. Then Paul noticed Plato off to one side, beckoning him back toward the beach.

"Why don't the rest of you go ahead?" Paul said. "I'll stay back here and have a look around."

"Plato," he mouthed voicelessly in response to the quizzical look Sheila gave him.

She rolled her eyes in amusement. Paul desperately wished he could tap into her brain and find out what she knew. But the mind link only worked through a live bunyip intermediary.

Moments later Paul followed Plato up the beach. He took off his boots and walked barefoot, enjoying the crunch of warm sand under his feet.

"You like it here, don't you?" As real as the vision had become, Paul now spoke out loud to it instead of thinking his communications.

Plato smiled.

"Hey, yeah! Maybe we could find the bunyips an uninhabited island. That might work."

Plato nodded and smiled.

It was rather eerie when Paul thought about it. Plato, of course, was no more real than the images on a movie screen. The only perceptions the bunyip could experience were those already in the archives or those drawn from Paul's experiences. Everything Plato smelled, felt, touched or saw on this island was simply an extension of Paul's own senses.

Plato turned to him with an inquisitive look, rubbing his belly. Paul felt a hunger pang.

"You want to know what's edible here? Is that it?"

Plato smiled.

They were walking along the beach as the tide went out. A miniature spring poured from a pencil-sized hole in the sand.

"Clams!" He dropped to his knees and dug furiously with his hands as Plato crouched nearby. Presently, he produced a clam the size of his palm for the bunyip's inspection.

Plato looked it over and smiled, then gave Paul a series of gestures.

"Eat it? *Raw*?" He was aghast. He'd always adhered to Miss Piggy's advice on the consumption of raw shellfish; that eating something slimy out of an ashtray was simply beyond comprehension.

But bunyips, after all, did not cook their food. Simplicity was the essence of their lifestyle, and even fire presented an unwanted intrusion. Warmth came from huddling with loved ones. And rather than cook their food, they sought out whatever could be enjoyed the way Nature had created it.

Plato mustered his best "Give 'er a go, mate!" expression.

Paul groaned as he pulled out his pocket knife and forced the shell apart. He closed his eyes and swallowed the contents, then shuddered as the malodorous glop slimed its way down his esophagus.

His stomach heaved. But Plato, long accustomed to biting the head off his evening meal and eating while it still wriggled, found the vicarious experience delightful. The bunyips would definitely enjoy raw clams. What else was there to eat?

Something scampered across the beach, and the bunyip scrambled after it.

"Oh, no . . . not raw crabs!"

But Plato insisted. By the time the others returned, Paul had sampled the meat of a dozen life forms that he normally wouldn't have eaten cooked, let alone raw. He was only too glad to head back to Cairns.

* * *

With fiendish delight, Maude tuned in on the brain waves of Dr. Lee. He'd just arrived back on the floor that night with his customary smile, neatly-pressed silk suit, and briefcase loaded with cash. This time, instead of just picking up the blood, he felt an odd compulsion to drop by the polio ward. Maude was learning to do more than just eavesdrop on human thoughts. She was learning how to influence them.

"Would, uh, you excuse me a moment, Professor Pike? I'd like to see how our little golden geese are doing."

"Why?"

"No reason . . . really. Just a—"

"Take your time. I'll be here when you're done."

Lee strolled among the cages until he noticed Minerva beckoning him with one hand. He walked over, bent down and peered into the cage.

"And what is on your mind, little one?"

Minerva pulled the loaded syringe from behind her back and shot the contents into Lee's face.

He jerked back and reached for his handkerchief. Too late.

"Eeeaaaiiieee!"

Minerva clasped her palms over her ears against the piercing shriek.

"My eyes! My eyes!" He groped blindly toward the door with one hand, vainly scrubbing the handkerchief against his face with the other.

Pike burst through the double doors. "Christ! What happened?"

"My eyes! They squirted something in my eyes!"

The professor grabbed Lee by one arm, then half-led,

half-dragged the man to the lab and stood him under the jerry-rigged emergency shower.

"I don't know what you got into, but we're gonna have to wash it off."

With one hand he opened the valve while prying Lee's hands away from his face with the other.

"Open your eyes and look up! It's a shower. Let the water wash that crap out of your eyes."

Lee kept screaming as the other man wrenched his face upward into the spray.

"God, what's that smell?" Pike asked. "Ow! What the hell?" He jerked his hands back and looked at them. His skin smoked and bubbled, dissolving wherever the shower had touched it.

"Shit!" He turned his back on Lee and plunged his hands into a bucket of soapy water he'd used earlier to wash up the mess from Crockett.

Frozen in shock, Lee stood motionless as the full spray of the shower continued to rain down on him. His suit melted like plastic wrap draped over a hot stove, fusing into his blackening skin.

"Pike! Help me!"

The professor rushed to the chemistry shelves. "That stuff's gotta be some kind of acid," he said to himself in a voice of barely-controlled panic.

He grabbed the jar of bicarbonate of soda. "This'll stop it." He dumped the contents into his bucket and resumed scrubbing himself.

"Pike! Where are you? Eeeaaauuuggghhh!" Lee collapsed to the floor where the deadly rain continued to pour over him until spent.

Sitting at her third-floor station, nursing supervisor Sandy Harris sighed with annoyance and cradled her forehead in her hand as she dealt with the twelfth phone call in twenty minutes. "I'm sorry the lines were busy, Mrs. Gordon, but several others have called about the noise, too . . . No, we don't know where it came from yet. Our staff are tracing the source now . . . Absolutely not! I *promise* you, Mrs. Gordon, our anesthesiologists are not on strike!"

Even as she spoke, a security officer and three orderlies entered the lab. The stinging, suffocating vapors drove them back at first. Finally, two of the orderlies held their breath while they rushed in and pulled Pike, who'd been overcome by the fumes, to safety. Except for his grotesquely burned hands and arms, Pike was in pretty good condition. The orderlies hauled him down to the emergency room.

Back on the fifth floor, the officer poked a peculiar, corroded object with his pen. He peed his pants when the blackened crust broke away to reveal a human eye socket.

Maude and Travis smiled at each other from their cages. One down, two to go.

* * *

Late that afternoon the RFDS plane took off for the return flight to Cairns. Charlie, the owner of Fourex Island, had joined the flight. The infection in his cut was already dangerous and, after much pleading and cajoling from Sheila, he'd consented to being treated in the Cairns hospital.

Charlie lay on the gurney and Paul sat beside him, talking. The miner was a skinny little man with white hair, a scraggly beard and pale blue eyes that seemed to glow in the dim light inside the plane. Paul found him surprisingly outgoing for a hermit.

"Say, Charlie, I have some, uh, friends who are looking for their own island around here. One about the same size as yours, but with no people on it. They like a lot of privacy. Any ideas?"

Charlie's eyes narrowed. "How much d'yer reckon they's willin' to pay, mate?"

"I dunno. How much would it take?"

"Well, if they's got a quarter of a million dollars—I'm talkin' cash foldin' money, now—I'll sell 'em me own island."

At that price, Paul realized, the bunyip habitat would be the bargain of the century. "You sure?"

"Yeah, I'm sure. I reckon it's about time I got back to civilization. Y'know, I'm 58 years old. It's time to get meself a wife an' settle down. A bloke can't just spend his entire life enjoyin' hisself."

Paul was hard pressed to follow up on that last comment, but he soon regained his stride. "Y'know, Charlie, I think we just might be able to work something out . . . "

* * *

Two nights after Lee and Pike's "accident" Maude again picked the lock to her cage. She'd have to work fast. Pike had a private patient room on the hospital's second floor, but would be transferred to Sydney in the morning. It was now ten p.m., and Andrews had just gone out for dinner. He invariably returned to his room by midnight, and Maude needed everything in place by then.

She headed straight for the storeroom and retrieved the cardboard box she'd stashed there the previous night. That had been a busy time for Maude. She'd sneaked into the hospital pharmacy and helped herself to a number of supplies. She'd also swiped Pike's dart pistol.

Next, she freed Minerva, Aristotle, Travis and Moses. They all headed down the back stairwell. Pike was asleep, and the bunyips slipped into his room undetected.

Already on painkillers, the man didn't stir at the prick of Maude's needle as she pumped in enough morphine to fully anesthetize him. The bunyips then spread-eagled him on his bed and used surgical tape to bind him very tightly in place to the bed rails.

After his mouth had been taped shut, Pike was brought back to full alertness—and pain—with a syringe load of naloxone followed by a pitcher of ice water in his face.

Perhaps he thought he was just having a bizarre nightmare when he came to. The lights had been turned on, and Minerva sat at the foot of his bed grinning at him. Revenge was only fun when the target knew who was behind it and why.

He tried to pull free. His arms, already stripped of skin, could bring nothing but searing pain as he jerked and strained against his bonds. He tried to scream, but could only manage a muffled squeaking through his nose. After several minutes of fruitless struggle, he finally settled back down, his only option to stare at Minerva in bug-eyed terror and wait.

Maude boxed her remaining supplies and headed back upstairs alone to carry out the next step.

Andrews returned to find his bed littered with IV equipment, medicine bottles, and spent rolls of surgical tape. He dumped these into the cardboard box left beside the bed. The last item he discovered proved the most curious of all, Pike's medical chart. Andrews stuck the chart in the box and headed down to Pike's room.

A light shone from under the closed door, so Andrews walked right in.

"My God! What is this?"

Pike lay on the bed, wild-eyed, struggling to communicate. Andrews dropped the box and ran to free him. Just as he started to pull the tape from his colleague's mouth, he heard the discharge of a dart pistol and felt a stabbing pain in his left buttock. He reached behind, and his hand came back with a spent dart in it. Andrews turned around to observe the closet door being pulled shut from the inside.

"Who the bloody hell is in there?" he demanded, marching to the closet. He jerked the door open, then stared in astonishment at the five little figures who stood smiling ever-so-sweetly at him.

His reaction proved short-lived. His knees buckled as the dart's anesthetic took effect.

With rubber gloves on their hands, the bunyips removed the IV bottle, now covered with Andrews' fingerprints, from the box and mounted it on the IV stand by the bed. Using more tape, they arranged the connective tubing so that one end dangled about a foot above Pike's forehead.

Everything now in place, Minerva opened the valve on the tubing very slightly. Pike watched in frozen silence as the fluid slowly wound its way through the transparent tubing. Finally, a droplet dangled at the very end.

Drip.

If Pike had any lingering doubts about his fate, they were resolved by the acid searing into his forehead. Once more, he tried to scream. His cheeks ballooned outward as his face darkened to red, then purple. The tape held firm.

Drip.

The acid hit his forehead again, then traced a blistering path across his balding pate. Bedpans wedged between his head and the bed rails blocked him from moving out of harm's way. He slammed his head against one of the bedpans, trying to dislodge it. No luck.

Drip.

This time, the caustic fluid struck just behind his left ear. He tried slamming his head against the opposite bedpan.

Drip.

This one caught him on the right temple.

Drip.

The left temple.
Drip.
Drip.
Drip . . .

The hysterical screaming of a nurse awakened Andrews around five a.m. Pulling himself to his feet, he saw what had upset her. The top of Pike's head had been dissolved to a smoking, bubbling goo that had eaten all the way through the bed and now spread across the floor.

The police arrived within minutes. Andrews, still groggy, couldn't have offered a believable explanation even if he had one.

* * *

Mid-afternoon that same day found Paul and family enjoying their last weekend in Cairns when the phone rang.

"Paul!" Clarence Richmond yelled excitedly, "I'm in Canberra, getting ready to fly back to Silver Hill. I need you here with me immediately."

"Well, Sheila's replacement should arrive in a few days—"

"Won't work. I need you on the next flight to Sydney. I'll meet you at the airport there and have a charter waiting to take us to Silver Hill."

"What's going on?"

"I don't know myself. All I do know is that Pike is dead and Andrews is in jail for murder. So now I'm doing what I should have done in the first place. I'm putting you in charge of the bunyips."

A long pause followed while Paul absorbed the new developments.

"Paul, my secretary just handed me a note. There's an

Australian Airlines flight leaving Cairns for Sydney in three hours. I'll have a ticket waiting for you at the gate."

Three hours later, Paul settled back into the narrow confines of a 727's center seat. He still had no idea what had happened. On the other hand, he could hardly regret being out of town when it did.

Paul and Clarence made it to the hospital by late evening. Each carried a large box, generously provided by the Taronga Zoo, of raw emu eggs, live lizards and other bunyip delicacies that Paul would rather not watch being consumed, thank you.

As the elevator approached the fifth floor, Paul felt increasingly light-headed. So did Clarence, judging from the way his eyes widened.

"Brace yourself, Clarence. This is gonna be wild."

The door opened to a scene of Maude chasing Aristotle across the lobby while spraying him with a can of Foster's. Aristotle's foot hit a large patch of liquid and slipped out from under him. Maude crashed into him, and the two of them tumbled together in a heap, laughing hysterically.

"This should be quite an experience, Clarence. I don't think I've ever been vicariously drunk before."

The two men carefully stepped off the elevator. Not only were they unsteady from the bunyips' transmitted inebriation, but intermittent beer puddles made the floor treacherous.

No sooner had Paul set his box down than a dozen eager hands tore it open. A ten-inch lizard scampered out and headed down the hall, immediately pursued by a cluster of jubilant partiers.

Paul felt a spray of cold liquid up his back and turned around to see Moses grinning sheepishly as the beer he'd just opened gurgled out in a fountain of foam.

Freddy entered the lobby from the polio ward. " 'Fore

yer starts in on me, mates, I ain't the one responsible fer the beer. It's me birthday, an' George an' Wendy had three cases sent up here whilst I was gettin' checked outta the booby hatch. The bunyips was already into 'em by the time I got here."

"Oh hell, I guess we could all use a break. Right, Clarence?"

"Right-o. By the way, Freddy, any idea what happened between Andrews and Pike?"

"Sorry, mate. Wish I knew, but them tranquilizers they's had me on sorta messed up me communications with the fifth floor. Even tried askin' Maude if she knows. If she does, she ain't tellin'."

"Yeah, well I have no doubt but that she knows every tiny detail," Paul replied. "Something tells me that we're not gonna get any rest until we sort this out. In fact, I'll bet that . . . screw it. Let's just have a beer and worry about this shit tomorrow."

"Sounds right by me, mate."

"Same here. If you'll excuse me for a few moments, gentlemen, I'll go phone my office first. See you in a few minutes."

The party gained momentum as Aristotle demonstrated how a huge beer puddle made a wonderful slippery slide when hit at a full run.

Paul noticed that none of the juveniles took part in the festivities. He wandered into the polio ward to see what had become of them. Travis, who'd apparently herded his charges into one of the iron lungs, now sat sulking with his backside barricading them inside. Paul had observed that Travis had little tolerance for irresponsible behavior. Now, with Crockett dead, his guardianship of the little ones had probably become an obsession.

A young adult female, only slightly intoxicated, walked in, pulled up a chair, and sat directly in front of Travis. Freddy had named this one Melissa, after his long-lost daughter, because both shared a penchant for bringing attention to themselves. Melissa smiled quietly at Travis, who responded with a frown, crossing his arms and looking away while almost certainly blocking out any mental communications.

Yet Paul noticed that Travis stole a furtive glance in her direction, and he didn't pull away when Melissa stretched out her legs and clasped his feet between hers.

Paul caught Travis' eye and gave him a wink. Travis turned away and actually blushed.

Paul returned to the lobby for another beer. A few minutes later, Clarence rejoined them. "Well, everyone, I have some news you'll find interesting. Nate Townsend's gang was cornered in southwest Queensland earlier today whilst trying to sell a load of kangaroo meat. There was a shoot-out and the police killed two men and took two others prisoner. The one they call Big Al, the one who helped stomp your friend, Wendy, was captured."

"If the coppers is lookin' fer approval, they's got mine."

"Yeah, but what about Nate?" Paul asked.

"No word on him as yet. Apparently, he's still on the loose."

"Shit!"

"Don't worry, Perfesser." Freddy clasped a hand on Paul's shoulder. " 'Sides the police, ol' Nate has you, me, Wild Wendy, an' four dozen bunyips on his arse. It may take a while, but one of us is gonna git him."

Paul raised his beer. "A toast to the quick demise of Nate Townsend."

Freddy smacked his beer against Paul's with a hearty "thonk."

"An' the bludger better hope the coppers gits him first."

15

Paul awoke in his old fifth floor bed just before dawn the next morning. The bunyips were eager to learn the state of the archives, and the early morning quiet offered the best time for undistracted communication.

Maude and Aristotle, already waiting outside his door, entered in response to his unspoken invitation. They seemed a little shaky, but not quite as hungover as he'd expected.

"I have a surprise for you." There was a blue flash as Paul conjured up a vision of Plato, which he could now do at will.

Maude and Aristotle exchanged glances of wide-eyed wonder. Before this, the archives had only produced comparatively faint, dream-like images best seen through closed eyes in a mind relaxed almost to sleep. The Plato being generated in Paul's brain rivaled reality itself in clarity.

The archives had grown enormously in size and complexity during the weeks of wandering through Paul's mind. They'd copied almost all of his memory, most everything he'd read, seen, heard, felt, and even thought over the course of three decades. Combined with what the living bunyips had learned on their own from humans, the archives could become a force of unbelievable potency.

But not yet.

Aristotle entered the archives by calling up the index

sign of a full moon, then watched in bewilderment as Neil Armstrong strolled across the lunar surface. Fascinating stuff, no doubt, but hardly the stellar navigational plots he'd been attempting to call up.

Apparently, the archives had reorganized themselves.

Aristotle called up the image of an emu egg, one of the many index signs for food, only to gaze in consternation at a museum exhibit of fossilized dinosaur eggs.

It quickly became apparent that he couldn't retrieve the archives until he'd learned about their recent structural changes.

To increase concentration, Paul laid back down and closed his eyes. The bunyip stretched out next to him. Plato appeared again, obviously amused at Aristotle's confusion, and the lessons began.

After a couple of hours, Paul interrupted. "Enough for now." Plato disappeared as Paul sat up and opened his eyes.

He turned to Aristotle. "I need breakfast, and I also need explanations from you. Suppose we start with how Andrews wound up in jail?"

The bunyip slipped to the floor, shrugged, and walked out the door.

After shoveling down a quick meal of the pale green clots that hospital cafeterias serve in the guise of "scrambled eggs," Paul headed for the jail.

"Paul! Thank God you're here. You can't imagine what's been going on since you left." An ashen-faced Andrews peered from behind the bars of his cell. Paul found it hard to believe that his entire career had once lain at the mercy of this frightened little man.

"Right now, Charles, I'm prepared to believe anything."

Bent-Nose, the jailer, sneered as he let Paul into the cell. "Bloody poofter intellectuals," he muttered as he walked away, contemptuously neglecting to relock the door.

"Paul, the bunyips did it. I know it sounds completely mad. But it's the truth, I swear it. You have no idea how intelligent they really are."

"Maybe I do. Why don't you just tell me what happened?" Paul settled himself on the bunk beside Andrews. The hot, cramped cell smelled of sweat and urine.

Andrews sighed, apparently relieved that someone would finally hear him out. With one hand he pushed back the sweat-soaked strands of gray hair from his forehead. "It all started when Pike told me that he'd accidentally killed one of the bunyips . . . "

It didn't take Andrews long to tell his end of the story. " . . . and the next thing I knew, I was pulling a dart out of my buttock. I found the bunyips who'd done it in Pike's closet, but I don't remember anything after that."

"I have no idea how," Paul promised as he left, "but I will get you out of this."

Paul returned to the fifth floor and dragged Maude by the arm to one of the private rooms.

"Okay, this time I'm not letting you off. Tell me about the killings."

She mustered her most convincing look of Bambi-eyed innocence.

"No dice, lady. Now cut the crap and tell me."

She smiled demurely, trying one last time to put him off.

"Yes, I'm sure I really wanna know!"

A blue flash. Minutes later, Paul had more knowledge of Pike's fate than he ever wanted. To avoid repeating her story, Maude sent it simultaneously to Freddy and Clarence, who were elsewhere on the floor.

"Jesus," Paul sighed. "Now what am I gonna do?"

But Maude provided no answers. Just a smug little grin.

Freddy and Clarence came to Paul to confer. Although

the bunyips were physically excluded from the room, all three men knew that every word and thought were being followed. Even if the conference was moved out of the range of telepathy, the bunyips would simply tap into the men's thoughts the moment they returned.

"Undoing this mess will be trickier than hell." Paul popped the top of the beer Freddy had pulled from his ice chest. Since the "celebration," Freddy kept the beer supply confined to an ice chest that never left his side. "We know all about the killings, but can't explain how we got the information without getting committed to a lunatic asylum or further endangering the bunyips. Imagine what the military alone might pull if they learned about the bunyips' psychic abilities."

"That's right, mates," Freddy continued. "We can't even tell the authorities that the unidentified human mullock heap from the lab is what remains of Dr. Lee. They'd insist on us tellin' 'em how we knows."

"Okay, let's start with something simple," Paul said. "I'd like to show the two of you, as well as the bunyips, the new home Plato helped me find for them. Maude, if you're still tuning in—and I know you are—please link everyone's mind together for this."

Freddy closed his eyes and leaned back.

"No need for that anymore," Paul said as he unlocked the memory by calling up its index sign, a raw, slimy clam. "Leave your eyes wide open. It'll be just like watching a movie."

It proved far more realistic than that. Freddy and Clarence gasped in awe as they found themselves mentally transported to Fourex Island.

Freddy reached out to touch a coconut tree that seemed to be standing directly in front of him. "I'll be buggered!" he exclaimed as his hand passed through the three-dimensional image.

At the end of the tour, Plato, Methuselah and about

twenty other graying elders appeared. Moses walked over to them, and they exchanged greetings. Then Plato tapped Moses' forehead, and everything went black.

The sun had already set when everyone finally awakened. Paul's watch indicated that about four hours had elapsed. Moses now stood in front of them with a taut little smile, nodding his head.

"D'yer know what that last part was all about, Perfesser?"

"Yeah. Kind of a council of elders. Except this one includes leaders from *way* back. They don't seem too happy about it, but I guess they've voted to at least give Fourex a try."

"I don't know if I can allow this," Clarence interjected. "After all, I'm the one answering to Canberra. I'm not convinced we could take animals adapted to the open desert and put them in a restricted tropical environment when we haven't even studied—"

"Listen to yourself, Clarence! You're going to decide their fate for them? Don't you think they're smart enough to figure out where they want to live?"

"Shouldn't we at least split them into two or three groups? The way it is now, they could be wiped out by a single bout of some plague or—"

"No. They're a single population, and they couldn't exist any other way. I'm not letting you or anyone else interfere with them anymore. We take them wherever they want to go and release them. From that point on, they make their own decisions."

Clarence pulled off his glasses and leaned back in his chair. "I see our graduate student is rapidly coming into his own. Very well, soon-to-be-Doctor McDaniel. Carry on."

"Even if they change their minds about the island, we can always retrieve them and drop them off somewhere else. Of course, we'll still have to come up with $250,000 to buy Fourex from Charlie," he continued. "It would be best if we could fund it through private donors. If we get the money from the government, it'll be harder to keep our actions secret. Any ideas, Clarence?"

"Well, I do have some wealthy friends I could approach—"

A knock on the door interrupted him. Maude entered the room carrying a briefcase, as did the four bunyips behind her. The briefcases were lined up on the floor in front of the men and opened.

"Gawd!" Freddy exclaimed. "So that's what happened to the loot Lee gave Pike! Wonder how much is there?"

Clarence lifted a briefcase to the bed and began pulling out stacks of currency. "Well, gentlemen, I'd suggest we start counting and find out."

The total came to exactly $350,000.

"That's enough to buy Fourex, transport the bunyips there and still leave a healthy sum in the bank to cover future emergencies," Clarence concluded. "And we owe it all to Lee and Pike. What say we drink a beer in their honor?"

Freddy pulled open his ice chest. "Thought yer'd never ask. I'm dry as a kookaburra's khyber in Quilpie."

* * *

Paul, lying in bed next to Sheila, fixed his eyes on the ceiling as he pulled the sheet up to her chin before turning toward her.

"Why did you do that, Paul? You never look at me any more unless I'm covered up. What's wrong? Don't you like my body any more?"

The hurt in her voice tore into him.

"Oh, Jesus. I love everything about your body. It's just that the archives have extended the bunyips' communication range recently and . . . damn! . . . how do I say this without upsetting you even more?"

He looked into her eyes, searching for the words.

A blue flash.

"Shit, Paul! That's right. I forgot that they can see through our eyes."

He jerked back in astonishment. "My God! You—?"

"Yeah, me too. I reckon it's time you knew. Maude's been communicating with me and also linking me into the archives—the way she linked the two of us just then. The first time was in the hospital right before we left for Cairns. She's been doing it quite regularly since I got back last week."

"What? You mean . . . ?"

"The first time the archives were just trying to learn some basic human neuroanatomy. After all, love, a doctor does know more about the brain than a biologist. So, with Plato's help, I drew up a kind of road map for them. It was either that or they'd have to wander around your cerebral cortex blindly triggering synapses to see what happened. Then you *would* think you were going crazy."

Paul nodded in stunned silence.

"After that, Plato started questioning me about some of your memories that didn't seem to make sense. He needed an outside interpreter. I'm not sure I understood what he showed me, either, but I made some educated guesses."

"But why wasn't I—?"

"You weren't consulted, darling, because you had too many things going on in your brain already. The archives were beginning to wonder if all their activities weren't short-circuiting a few neurons. After some of the stuff Plato showed me, I have to wonder myself."

"What are you talking about? What kinds of—?"

"For one thing, they were a bit confused about the role of calculus in human sexual arousal."

"Huh?"

"Well, it seems they came across this memory of you churning out integrals whilst having a naughty with this screaming, tattooed Amazon named Wendy . . . "

"Oh, Jesus!" Paul felt a surge of panic that transcended mere embarrassment. "Now you've gotta understand—"

"—that it happened before I re-entered your life, and that you've been faithful to me ever since." Sheila's smile betrayed a sense of humor with sharply defined limits. "Otherwise, love, I'd have a little trophy jar of my own."

* * *

Aristotle had finally completed his preparations for retrieving the archives. Paul approached the moment with both relief and sadness. Carrying the archives proved a heavy responsibility fraught with constant annoyances, interruptions and bizarre dreams. But the archives brought with them a sense of community that Paul had never found among humans. The archives unified the generations of bunyips, past and present, into a cohesive whole that transcended life and death. Within them, any bunyip who ever lived could communicate with any other. And through them, Paul had explored a part of his own soul that he'd previously found inaccessible.

"Before you get the archives, I want your promise to help me free Andrews."

Aristotle rolled his eyes.

"I mean it. No promise, no archives."

The bunyip replied with a hard, steady gaze.

"Yes, I know he's an asshole. But he didn't intentionally hurt any of you."

The bunyip looked away, sighed, and nodded.

"Good. We'll do the transfer tomorrow night. That's a Friday, and usually the quietest time around here."

Paul arrived at the hospital at the appointed time. He stretched out on his old bed as Aristotle lay down beside him in the darkness. The other bunyips turned off their thoughts and voided their minds. The best way to assure that

Aristotle received the archives intact was to make certain there were no distractions.

It would also take time. Although Paul had received the archives in a matter of minutes, the result had been chaos. An orderly transfer would take several hours.

For a long while he lay still as Aristotle prepared his own mind. Then, just as Paul drifted toward sleep, came the blue flash, brighter than any he'd ever seen before. Slowly at first, like a sweater unraveling, the images began to pull away. The speed picked up. Lights and colors blurred into motion, then came in rapid, staccato bursts like dancers under a strobe light. Before his eyes a thousand generations unfolded one by one.

The final image was that of his friend and guide.

"I'm going to miss you, Plato."

Plato gave him a sad smile and rubbed Paul's cheek with his knuckles one last time. Then he was gone.

Aristotle had already left the room when Paul awakened with a hollow, aching sense of loss. He sent a mental message to Maude that he needed some company. But she didn't respond. For a long time, he sat alone on the bed and stared out the window. It was now Saturday, already approaching evening.

A light knock on the door, then Sheila entered. "I brought your shaving kit and a fresh shirt, love. Why don't you take a quick shower, then we can all go out for dinner. P.J., Freddy and Bronwyn are waiting downstairs for us."

He shrugged, pulling himself to his feet. "Yeah, why not?"

Sheila kissed him, then hugged him tightly. "Maude and the others haven't abandoned you, love."

"I know. It's just that for the first time I've learned what it's like to belong with others, to be a part of things, to have—"

"—a family. But *they're* not your family, *we* are. Now

that you've finally learnt what it's all about, the bunyips are stepping back to let us take over. They need to go their own way soon, and so do you."

For a long time, Paul embraced her without speaking.

"I know I promised not to rush you. But once I get the bunyips to safety, would you—?"

"Yes, darling, I'll marry you."

* * *

With the archives back where they belonged, the bunyips were ready for evacuation to Fourex. What to do about Andrews? Without the bunyips around to explain the truth, he'd almost certainly spend the rest of his life in prison.

Paul scheduled a meeting with Andrews' lawyer, Clayton Lomax. A stocky, middle-aged man with baggy eyes and a thick nose, Lomax was already familiar with Andrews' version of the killings. From the way he arched his brows during the discussion, it was clear that Lomax didn't believe a word he'd been told.

Paul had come to search for ideas, not argue. He sat in a worn leather chair across from Lomax's desk. A collapsed spring in the seat made comfort impossible, but the only other chair was piled high with books and papers. The air reeked of stale cigarette smoke.

"So what happens now?" Paul asked. "I have no idea how the Australian legal system works."

"It's about the same as your American system, actually. They're both based on English common law, with a few differences here and there. Instead of 'lawyers' we have solicitors and barristers. I'm a solicitor, and I'll prepare Andrews' case. The actual courtroom delivery will be handled by a barrister."

Lomax leaned back in his chair and lit a cigarette before continuing. "Next week, we'll take Professor Andrews in front of a lower-level judge called a magistrate. Assuming the magistrate finds sufficient grounds for trial, the case will be remanded to a supreme court in Sydney to be heard in front of a jury. Then we'll all go to Sydney and begin the process of jury selection—"

The glimmer of a plan sparked as Paul interrupted. "You mean that, if the magistrate rules that there's not enough evidence for trial, that Andrews would walk away, free and clear?"

"Yeah. But to be honest with you, mate, there's no bloody chance that—"

"And the magistrate hasn't yet made that decision?"

"No. The hearing's been put off until next Wednesday to give the forensic scientists from Sydney a chance to examine the evidence and—"

"That's where we've got to stop this, with the magistrate."

"That's bloody easy for you to say, Yank." Lomax had grown testy at the constant interruptions. "Frankly, I think an insanity defense is—"

Paul jumped to his feet, knocking his chair over backwards in the process. "Excuse me, Mr. Lomax, but I have to get back to the hospital."

Paul explained his idea to Aristotle, who agreed that it might work but would require some preparation. Before the hearing Aristotle would have to learn something about the way that particular magistrate's brain worked. Fortunately, the magistrate would be presiding over a series of unrelated cases the next day.

Paul waited in the visitor's gallery as the magistrate made his formal entry. Aristotle appeared to be a distressed child as he curled against Paul in his disguise.

A series of misdemeanor offenses were heard. Gradually, Paul noticed that the magistrate had begun showing signs of stress. A round-faced man with beady blue eyes, he'd displayed little more than boredom during the first two cases. Now his hands trembled as he used a handkerchief to mop the beads of sweat trickling across his bald head and down his reddened face.

Show me what he's seeing.

Aristotle complied, and Paul choked to restrain a laugh. The image was that of the gray-haired, wizened barrister pacing the floor as he quizzed someone sitting in the witness box. From the neck up everything was true and proper. From the barrister's neck down, the magistrate saw him as a voluptuous—and totally naked—olive-skinned woman.

Aristotle had already learned everything he needed to know about the magistrate's brain. This was just for fun.

Paul met again with Andrews in the small, stuffy room usually reserved for meetings between prisoners and their solicitors. The room had no windows and was almost devoid of features except for a scarred oak table and chairs.

It had taken Paul no small amount of arguing to convince Andrews to go along with the plan.

"Look, your own solicitor says it's a foregone conclusion that you'll go on trial. So what's to lose?"

Sweat beaded on Andrews' broad forehead. "Can't we at least explain to Lomax and the barrister what we're doing?"

"No, Charles. Sorry, but I'm not letting anyone else learn about the bunyips' abilities. I'd go to prison myself first." Paul folded his arms against his chest and leaned back. "Aristotle thinks we can pull this off. You'll just have to trust us and insist that Lomax and the barrister follow instructions."

By Wednesday morning it was clear that Andrews' case would be much more than a simple magistrate's hearing.

"Jesus, men, look at what's happening down there." Clarence didn't stop pacing as he pointed out the fifth-floor lobby window. "There are news crews from every corner of the globe down there. Murders are rare enough in Australia, let alone a double acid-bath killing. Add in Andrews' celebrity status, and we've got ourselves a bloody sideshow."

Paul was unworried. "Frankly, Clarence, I'm amazed you've been able to keep us out of the spotlight this long," he replied as he cuddled a bunyip toddler. Even without the archives, Paul remained so mentally attuned with the bunyips that they accepted him more or less as one of their own. Now that tensions on the fifth floor had eased, Travis no longer kept the little ones herded together but shared them around. The toddler, Laurie, had been assigned to Paul's care as a part of the bunyip equivalent of a daily duty roster. In response to Laurie's surprisingly clear request, Paul offered his little finger as a pacifier, then winced silently as tiny teeth dug in.

"Up until now, secrecy has been easy," Clarence replied. Politics came as easily to him as neurotic introspection to Paul. "The editor of the local paper is a friend of an old school chum. I just went over there, told him how important our privacy was, and promised him a worldwide exclusive interview the day after we got the bunyips to safety."

Clarence accepted the beer that Freddy held up in silent offering. "Even I can't control the publicity that a double murder attracts! By chatting up the populace, the reporters have found out about all the bunyips, too."

"Let's concentrate on getting Andrews off the hook." Paul best dealt with problems one at a time. "We'll figure the rest out later. The hearing is in four hours, and I'm sure the courtroom will be jammed. Our problem right now is getting Aristotle in unnoticed. I won't be able to sneak him in this time, since visitors will be searched."

Freddy's own wheels were turning. "How close does Aristotle have to get to the magistrate, Perfesser?"

"I honestly don't know. The closer the better. See, the messages—"

"—is bound to be energy-dependent an' subject to the physical laws that governs electromagnetic fields." Uncle Freddy was back. "Which means that if we's doublin' the distance to the receptor, we's gotta square the energy output o' the signal transmission or we ain't—"

Paul smacked Freddy's shoulder with the back of his hand. "I toldja to warn me before ya start that!"

The outburst startled Laurie, who protested by leaving a large wet spot on Paul's thigh.

In the end, getting Aristotle into the courtroom proved remarkably easy. Paul, wearing jeans and a blue worker's tank top, drove Freddy's truck to the rear service entrance of the courthouse. Then he carefully unloaded a large box that bore the markings of an industrial toilet paper manufacturer, placed it on a dolly, and pulled it inside.

He took the box up the freight elevator to the second-story courtroom and pulled it to the magistrate's private entrance. Aristotle, crouched inside the box, alerted Paul that no one was in the magistrate's chambers. The door was locked, as anticipated. But Aristotle could access Maude's knowledge of picking locks from the archives. He slipped out the escape hatch cut into one side of the box and quickly unlocked the door. From there, he slipped through the chambers, into the courtroom, and secreted himself in a compartment under the magistrate's bench.

Paul placed the dolly and now-empty box in the janitor's closet, then returned to the truck where he would wait until Aristotle was ready to be retrieved.

The hearing took place on time before a packed courtroom. Paul, Freddy and Clarence were relieved that they didn't have to be present. The less attention they attracted, the better.

The chief prosecutor called the nurse who discovered Pike's body as the first witness. Then he brought in the forensic experts, who testified that the only fingerprints on any of the evidence belonged to Andrews. Nurses, waitresses and bartenders alike recalled having heard Pike and Andrews exchange angry words on innumerable occasions. The obvious motive for Pike's murder was professional jealousy. The case against Andrews seemed unassailable.

Andrews was finally called to the stand as the only witness in his own defense. As instructed, the barrister remained behind the defense table during the questioning.

Andrews spoke in a slow, droning monotone as he explained that he had no earthly idea of how any of those horrible things happened. Meanwhile Aristotle unveiled the true events in a three-dimensional movie that played right there in front of the slack-jawed magistrate. For good measure, the chief prosecutor had also been linked into the magistrate's mind.

Both the prosecutor and the magistrate shivered as the acid shower dissolved Lee into a slush pile. Then they winced as the first drop of acid hit Pike's forehead while Minerva sat grinning at him from the foot of his bed.

From the visitors' gallery, press and spectators alike wondered what was behind the glassy-eyed stares of these two red-faced and perspiring men.

It took Andrews nearly two hours to complete his rambling and disjointed testimony. Spellbound, the prosecutor never once interrupted with an objection.

Finally, Andrews received a mental signal from Aristotle.

"That's all I have to say."

The vision evaporated, and neither magistrate nor prosecutor remembered anything Andrews had said.

"No further questions," Andrews' barrister said as he resumed his seat.

The prosecutor rose slowly to his feet. "I have no questions," he announced haltingly to the startled court.

The magistrate, citing the strain of public attention, recessed the proceedings until ten the next morning.

The magistrate took the rest of the afternoon off and went home seeking sanity. It was not to come.

As he sat alone in his study, the slayings replayed over and over in his mind like an endless-loop movie.

"I'm really not going mad," he said earnestly to his reflection in the mirror across from his desk. "I just need a vacation. Yeah, that's it, a vacation. A few days fishing, perhaps."

He leaned back in his chair and tried to focus on memories of sitting alone in his boat on the Murray River, fishing rod in one hand, beer in the other.

Suddenly, he saw himself back in court, ordering Andrews to stand trial for murder. An instant later, he was on his boat again, this time bound and gagged, rewatching the bunyips execute Lee and Pike.

After a brief pause, he saw himself in court once again. This time, he said the words, "Case dismissed." He was then treated to several minutes in his boat, unbound and unmolested, enjoying his tranquillity.

The same messages repeated themselves all night. Dawn found the magistrate still at his desk, feeling very much like a deranged Pavlovian dog.

The prosecutor, gaunt and bleary-eyed, stood before the bench as court convened the next morning. He exchanged pleading glances with the magistrate, then spoke in a quavering voice. "The state moves to dismiss the charges against Charles Wesley Andrews on the grounds of insufficient evidence."

"Granted. Case dismissed!" The magistrate hammered his gavel down with the exuberance of someone squashing a spider. "Adjourned."

The visitors and press didn't even have time to gasp in disbelief. Fifteen seconds after court convened, the magistrate and prosecutor headed for the exits. Caught totally off guard, Andrews' own barrister fought the urge to object to something—anything.

A public furor immediately went up, and both the magistrate and barrister very nearly lost their jobs. But they were restored to grace after Clarence released a statement praising the men's "invaluable contributions to wildlife preservation by not revealing certain irrefutable evidence proving Professor Andrew's innocence. Evidence that might, if made public, compromise Commonwealth efforts to protect the bunyips from human exploitation."

The Australian public would never know exactly what that statement meant. But if saving the bunyips required the occasional murder of a professor or two, then so be it.

"Paul!" Andrews chimed over the phone. "I'm down in the main hospital lobby. I want to thank you, and I know just how. I'm going to give proper credit for the discovery of the bunyips. I'm starting a press conference in five minutes. I want you and Freddy down here right now!"

"Charles, I'm glad you're off the hook. But as far as a press conference goes, there's no way that—"

"No false modesty, now. I want the two of you—"

"It's not false modesty! It's pure and simple—"

Andrews interrupted, oblivious of the desperation in Paul's voice. "Either you and Freddy come down here and accept the credit due you, or I'm bringing the press corps up to the fifth floor."

The phone clicked. Paul replaced the receiver, then pressed both hands to his face and slowly pulled downward. Clarence, the only person who could stop this, was out for dinner.

Freddy, sitting across from him, shrugged in resignation. "That's the way it goes, mate. Six months ago, we'd o' given everything we owns fer this. Now we'd strangle the bludger t' stop it."

Both men stood up and headed for the elevator.

"Will this shit ever end, Freddy?"

"Dunno, mate." Freddy wrapped an arm around his friend's sagging shoulders. "But if the bunyips starts lookin' around fer more acid, I'll help 'em find it."

16

It wasn't until the elevator door opened to camera lights and microphones that Paul and Freddy realized just how big a mistake they'd made.

"Now I'd like to introduce the real discoverers . . . " Andrews began.

Seconds later, the microphones turned to Paul. "Freddy and I would just like to thank Professor Andrews for having allowed us to continue our work in private by diverting public attention . . . "

"Freddy and I would just like to thank Professor Andrews . . . " Freddy mocked later that night, only half seriously.

"No act of kindness, no matter how small—"

"—is ever wasted. Yeah, I read fortune cookies too, Perfesser. Deep down, I agree with yer. But there's a lot to be said about—"

"—the sadistic joy of watching a cockroach squirm in the spider's web," Clarence joined in.

The mind link between the three men had grown so strong that it was only by force of habit that they even bothered to speak anymore.

"It's done, so let's forget about it," Clarence continued, staring once more at the crowded parking lot from the fifth-floor lobby. "Now we've gotta get the bunyips out of here.

Half the world knows by now where they are, and there are at least three television camera crews down there telling the other half. We're gonna have to figure some way to get our little friends to Fourex Island in secret."

"It shouldn't be that hard." Paul stepped across the room and peered out the window beside Clarence. "After all, nobody even knows about Fourex. They're expecting us to take them back to their old water holes. All we have to do is distract the press long enough to get the bunyips to the airport unnoticed."

"Any suggestions?" Clarence sat down, relieved to let Paul take the lead.

"Yeah. First thing we do is get a bus . . . "

After Paul had outlined his plan, Clarence wrinkled his brow as he cleaned his glasses with a tissue. "Yeah, y'know it just might work. After all, bunyips were rarely spotted in the wild before. Why would anyone expect the recent publicity to change that? I even have the perfect pilot, a friend of mine who's an amateur naturalist. If all goes well, you, Freddy, my pilot friend and I will be the only ones on earth who know where the bunyips are."

* * *

During the next two days, Paul gave the reporters plenty of hints that something was afoot. Signs were posted around the hospital that the north side stairwell was closed until further notice for "construction" and the area surrounding the north exit was closed off with a chain-link fence. Meanwhile Pete, the handyman, built an enclosed canopy of 2–by–4s and black plastic tarp leading the twenty-odd feet from the stairwell exit to the driveway.

On the third day, a bus with all its side windows papered over pulled up to the canopy at two in the morning. It was a small bus, the kind designed for off-road travel, bearing the logo of a popular Outback operator. More black plastic tarp was used to cover the distance from the canopy to the bus. From the street, all one could see was a blacked-out bus and a blaze of lights on the fifth floor. Two hours later the bus, with Freddy at the wheel and Clarence beside him, took off toward the bunyips' original home range. The press corps followed in hot pursuit.

At eight the same morning a road-weary two-axle truck rolled up to the hospital loading dock. The truck had obviously been bought second hand, since the words "Sutter's Meat Supply" were still visible under the weathered white paint that covered them. The present owner had settled for a crudely hand-lettered sign that said "RMS Hauliers" on the cab doors.

The driver, dressed in patched gray slacks and a denim shirt with the sleeves torn off, backed up to the dock and snapped the hatch open.

He strode over to Paul who stood alone on the dock.

"G'day, mate. I'm here to pick up a consignment."

Paul stared in horror at the thick, insulated walls and airtight hatch of the refrigerated freight compartment.

"I didn't order that truck! I ordered a—"

"Aw, give it a rest, sport. I asked yer if the cargo needed to be pertected from the heat. Yer said yeah. What the hell did yer expect, a bloody limousine?"

Paul spoke through clenched teeth. "No, but the cargo also has to be protected from freezing . . . "

"No worries, mate. It's only ten minutes to the airport, fifteen tops. We'll just turn off the freezer, an' yer packages won't even have time to get cold."

Paul didn't like this. For one thing the insulation would make it hard for the bunyips to communicate with him.

"Would it be all right if I rode in back with the cargo?"

"Fer all I cares, mate, yer can hang from the bloody rear axle."

Assisted by the driver, Paul reluctantly began loading

the truck with cardboard fruit crates that lay stacked just inside the hospital doors.

"Say, mate, what'cher got in all these boxes?"

Paul gave an answer intended to kill the trucker's curiosity. "Shit bags. There's an epidemic of diarrhea in the hospital. People crapping their brains out, and nobody knows why. We're sending specimens to a special lab to see if somebody can figure out what's causing it. Be careful with the stuff. It's extremely infectious."

"The bloody hell, y'say?" The driver stopped instantly and pulled on a pair of gloves.

Finally, all the boxes were loaded.

"I'm gonna get my pack. Be back in a second. You stay here and don't close the hatch until I return."

"No worries, mate. We're set to go soon's yer ready."

Paul ran upstairs, grabbed his pack and was giving the fifth floor a final once-over to make sure that nothing important would be left behind. Suddenly, he felt a stabbing anxiety.

Something was wrong!

But what? He shot down the stairs and exploded out the door to the loading dock.

The truck was gone. What did that stupid driver—?

"Where's me bloody truck?"

Paul spun around to see a very confused driver following him out the door.

"What the hell are you doing here? You were supposed to stay with the truck!"

"I was just gone a minute. Ran in to wash me hands. Now somebody's stole me bloody truck."

"Shit! Look, you go back inside and have someone radio the bus and tell them what's happened. I'll go hunt for your truck."

"Listen, mate, I'm goin' with you. After all, that truck—"

"I'll drive it up your ass! Now do what you're told!"

The fire in Paul's eyes warned that this was no idle threat.

"Aye, mate. On the double. An' good luck to yer!" The driver wheeled about and headed inside.

Paul ran for the parking lot. Thank God Freddy always left his keys in the pickup! He started the engine and squealed out of the parking lot. But a sudden realization hit home. He slammed on the brakes, ran around to the camper and pulled out Freddy's double-barreled shotgun. Back in the cab he loaded the gun and headed out. But which direction? Two major highways plus several unpaved trails led out of Silver Hill. Where was that damned truck anyway?

"Show me where you are!" he implored, hoping the bunyips were still within range.

Paul closed his eyes for a few seconds. He barely made out a driver's eye-view of the highway heading east from town.

Slamming down the accelerator, Paul took off in pursuit. He hoped he'd attract the attention of a cop or two along the way, but no such luck. He was still alone when the yellow Toyota pickup roared out of the city limits.

Surely he'd catch up with the truck eventually. All he needed was time and . . .

"God damn it!" The gas gauge hovered just above empty.

But slowing down to conserve fuel was no answer. He continued to pick up speed, passing traffic in his lane as if it were standing still. His heart pounded as he passed one car and narrowly missed side-swiping an oncoming truck.

"Where are you now?" At this speed he didn't dare close his eyes, even for a second. The flat ribbon of asphalt in front of him yielded no clues. Even with the accelerator jammed to the floor, the going seemed very, very slow.

"Where the fucking hell are you?" he screamed at the vacant road ahead.

He crested a low hill and caught sight of a truck on the

horizon. Was that the one with the bunyips? If not, they were in a lot of trouble. Paul was rapidly burning up his little remaining fuel.

"C'mon! Faster, damn it!" He pounded the Toyota's steering wheel with one fist. Slowly, he gained on the truck.

After what seemed an eternity he made out the faint letters on the back of the truck: Sutter's Meat Supply.

The hijacker didn't seem to be aware that he was being pursued and continued along at the fast but not breakneck clip of about 120 kilometers per hour. Paul pulled up behind.

What to do? He'd run out of gas soon. Yet, he still had a certain element of surprise, assuming the hijacker didn't know that Paul was trying to stop him.

That hope was shattered when he tried to pass the truck. He caught a brief glance of a pistol emerging from the driver's window before a hole exploded in his windshield. The bullet whizzed by, just inches from his head. Another near miss, and he felt the sting of glass fragments digging into his face.

Paul backed off and allowed the truck to outdistance him. Getting his head blown off would hardly solve anything.

He followed, groping for a strategy. The truck picked up speed, and he knew that the Toyota couldn't keep pace for long.

He stuck the shotgun out his window. For the first time ever, Paul—a right-handed shot—was glad that Australians drove on the wrong side of the road. He aimed at the truck's tandem right rear tires and squeezed both triggers at once.

The recoil bucked the gun out of his hand. Desperately, Paul grabbed for it and pinned it against the Toyota's door with his forearm while he fought to keep the pickup under control. The gun began to slip away. He braked hard as he concentrated on recovering the weapon. The truck sped on. Paul still didn't know the effect, if any, of his shot.

He stopped just long enough to pull two more shells from the glove box and reload. Heading back up the road, he prayed that he could still catch up.

He was relieved to find that the truck had not only slowed considerably but emitted a bluish smoke from the rear. Approaching closer, he saw that the right rear tires were now tattered shreds of rubber that flailed the road, deafening him with their steady, rhythmic slap.

Another truck, a huge "road train" diesel tractor pulling three trailers, barreled toward them from the opposite direction. Paul saw his opportunity and pulled over onto the right shoulder of the road while he hit the gas. If he could pull ahead of the truck while the road train passed between them, he'd be in a more commanding position.

Keeping control of the vehicle proved no easy task as it bumped and slid on the uneven sandy shoulder.

The road train plowed between them, air horns blasting in confused alarm. The second it passed, Paul steered left and braced himself as the pickup lurched like a runaway bronco back onto the blacktop.

"All right!" he yelled as soon as he'd steadied his wheels and saw the truck in his side mirror. Now what? A pickup could hardly run that truck off the road. Besides, the last thing he wanted was for it to crash with the bunyips still on board. Somehow he'd have to bring the truck to a safe stop.

He pointed the barrel of the shotgun backwards out his window, balancing it against his shoulder. He eased off the gas pedal and watched the mirror. The truck bore down rapidly. As expected, it came right for the Toyota.

The distance closed. Timing would be everything. He would only be able to get in one shot, so it would have to be good.

He held off until the truck's radiator filled his mirror. Steering with his left hand, he leaned out the window and leveled the gun, using gut instinct to direct his aim. He squeezed the trigger, and the shotgun kicked. He didn't even hear the blast over the roar of tires and engines.

He'd just pulled back into his seat when the bumpers hit. The pickup bounced forward, slamming his head against the rear window. Miraculously, he kept the wheels centered and quickly regained control. In the mirror, he saw the truck bearing down for another strike. He floored the accelerator.

The truck drew nearer, nearer. Then it began falling behind.

Paul saw what he'd been praying for. A thick plume of steam shot out the truck's radiator. Time was finally on his side.

The larger vehicle plowed on, and he kept pace ahead. Another mile or so passed. The truck's engine should seize up any minute now.

The Toyota gulped and sputtered. Grateful that it had brought him this far, Paul didn't even curse as it finally exhausted the last of its fuel. Instead, he pulled off the road and turned hard to the right. The truck's hijacker, probably unaware of Paul's vulnerability, kept going straight.

The pickup coasted to a halt. Paul reloaded his shotgun and started down the road on foot. Then a sudden realization hit home, and he slapped his forehead in disbelief of his own forgetfulness. "Freddy, I owe you one," he muttered as he went back to the camper, opened the hatch and pulled out the five-gallon can of petrol that his friend always kept there.

Minutes later, Paul sped down the highway again. About five miles further he spotted the truck, sitting motionless. He approached slowly, surveying the scene for any hint of motion. Nothing moved as he pulled up behind the truck.

The danger remained almost palpable.

"Tell me what's happening, Maude."

He didn't have to close his eyes to get the message.

"Shit!"

He pulled out of the pickup and walked warily toward the truck, gun at the ready.

"Okay, Nate Townsend. I know what you're up to. Let's talk!"

The passenger door opened, and Nate sat on the edge of the seat, grinning. On his lap, with a .45 pistol pointed at her temple, sat Maude.

"G'day, Perfesser. Always a pleasure to have yer drop by."

"I'm sure. I have news for you. Dr. Lee's dead. There's no one to sell bunyip blood to any more. You're wasting your time."

"If yer says so. Maybe yer comin' the raw prawn with me, maybe not. Reckon it don't matter much either way. I gotta git outta here."

"Fine with me. All I want are the bunyips. Leave them behind, and you can take Freddy's truck. That'll give you a good head start on the authorities."

"Well, now, that sounds awful invitin', Perfesser. Jist put yer shotgun down there on the ground, an' I'll hop in Freddy's ute an' drive away."

Paul knew the danger in following Nate's instructions, but did so anyway.

Nate slid to the ground and released Maude, then aimed his pistol squarely at Paul's head.

"Yer a bloody fool, Perfesser."

Paul froze. Nate edged forward to make sure he wouldn't miss. At such close range, the .45 pistol looked as big as a cannon.

"Say yer prayers, Perfesser, 'cuz yer about to meet whoever it is yer sends 'em to."

Paul closed his eyes. He was back on Grandma McDaniel's knee. "If you die saying a prayer . . . "

Please, God, forgive—

Plato appeared, his face wide-eyed with alarm.

Will I at least live on in the archives?

The bunyip lunged forward, seizing Paul's forehead with both hands.

Paul saw a burst of blue light. Then another light, this one glowing white hot, blinding in its intensity. The light grew ever brighter, first warming, then burning, and finally consuming him.

Nate corrected his aim and fired. His bullet split the air with a crack.

Bits of skull and brain tissue splattered the truck.

* * *

Freddy arrived in a police cruiser, lights flashing and siren blaring. He bounded out of the car ahead of the officer and knelt over the crumpled body. The mid-afternoon heat blazed at full intensity, and flies swarmed over every bit of exposed flesh. Freddy had to wave them away from the face to identify the corpse.

"Gawd, what a mess!" he said, shaking his head. "Fer a minute there, Perfesser, I was afraid it was you!"

"Well, that was certainly Nate's intention." Paul, who'd been sitting in the still-cool freezer compartment, walked over. "Stupid bastard had no idea what he was up against. He kept trying to look behind himself to see who was twisting his arm back and forcing the gun to his own head. About the time he felt his trigger finger pull, he realized that it was all being done from inside his own mind."

"So which of our little friends got t' do the honors?"

Paul looked into Freddy's eyes but didn't speak.

A blue flash.

"Bloody hell! All by yerself? I didn't know yer could—"

"I didn't either, not until the moment it happened. I guess the archives left me a parting gift."

"Gawd! D'yer suppose—?"

"I'm not even sure I could do it again. And I never wanna find out. This is our little secret, okay?"

The police officer walked over and knelt by the body. "S'pose you tell me what happened?"

"Sure," Paul replied, then caught Freddy's eye and cocked his head in the direction of a clump of gum trees lining a dry creek bed. "Give me a minute, first. I've gotta take a leak."

Freddy nodded his acknowledgment. "Reckon I need to siphon the python meself."

The two walked toward the trees.

"So where's the bunyips, mate?"

"Gone. They changed their minds. They decided they'd be better off on their own. And if you think about it, they'd be pretty stupid to trust their fate to humans."

"Yeah, they's right. We couldn't even get 'em to the airport without somethin' goin' wrong. So where's they headed?"

"They haven't decided yet. Maybe back to their old territory near Woolloona, maybe somewhere new. The archives have added a lot of maps from my memories, so they know where most of the water bores are around here. That'll give them a lot more possibilities than they used to have."

"Y'know, Perfesser, it's scary. They's bound to come across people sooner or later, an' who knows what'll happen then? On the other hand, I'm—"

"—glad that they're back in charge of their own fate. Me too. If there's one thing I've learned from all this, it's that our own decisions, however bad, are easier to live with than somebody else's."

"I'm jist sorry I didn't get to say good-bye."

"You will. To Maude, anyway. She's waiting for you in the trees down there. She'll catch up with the others later."

"She gonna be safe? Y'know, after ever'thing that's happened, I wonder if—"

"The bunyips have learned a lot." Paul pointed to the base of a tree they were approaching.

Freddy's jaw dropped as he observed the leering human figure leaning against the trunk. "Nate Townsend! I thought you'd kilt the bludger!"

He turned to Paul, who smiled calmly. "Don't worry, Freddy. You're here to protect us."

"But me bloody shotgun's—"

"—right there in your hand. See?" Paul pointed back at the tree.

Freddy looked up in utter bewilderment. Instead of Nate, he now saw an exact image of himself, shotgun in hand.

"What the—?"

The bogus Freddy dissolved, replaced by the sight of Maude doubled over with laughter.

"The bunyips can make us see whatever they want, Freddy. That should be enough to scare anybody away."

Freddy sighed in relief. "I know they's goin' away fer their own good. But I'm beginnin' to think—"

"—that humans are the ones who really need the protection. Yeah."

Maude grinned smugly as she nodded her head in agreement.

EPILOGUE

"Paul! Welcome!" Clarence stepped to the front of his cluttered mahogany desk to shake hands, then lifted a stack of papers from one of the maroon leather armchairs and dropped it to the floor. He gestured for Paul to sit.

"I'm so glad you had enough time to drop by. I understand you've made contact with the bunyips?"

Paul plopped himself into the chair. "Indirectly, at least. Freddy and I took one of our tour groups backpacking the northern Flinders last week. One night, while we were camped out, Maude sent me a vision."

"You didn't actually see her, then?"

"No. They were only a few miles away, but the bunyips have decided to avoid direct contact with people altogether. They haven't seen a single human during the entire fourteen months since they left the hospital."

"That's good news, all things considered. What else did you learn?"

"Well, remember that the Flinders themselves are well outside the bunyips' traditional territory, so that says something in itself. They seem happy as ever. They're eating well, and the population has grown to sixty, plus four dormant fetuses in the pouch."

"Great. How about you and Freddy? How's married life treating you two?"

"Couldn't be better. I'm happy as can be, and even Freddy's adjusting. I'm sure you can appreciate that life with Bronwyn would be as big an adjustment as any man could ever hope to make. Not only that, but Bronwyn just found out that she's pregnant too. She's due a couple of months after Sheila."

"Any chance your new responsibilities might drive you to a desk job? You know, the university here in Canberra is dying to get you. They'll even guarantee you tenure and a promotion to full professor within three years."

"No way!" Paul laughed. "For one thing, they couldn't even come close to paying what I already make. That Outback touring company Freddy and I started is a gold mine. More important, though, I'm happy. I get paid doing what I enjoy, and I'm surrounded by friends and family. Only a fool would change that.

"Sounds like you've become a bit of a bunyip yourself."

Paul's smile didn't lighten the conviction in his voice. "You have *no idea* how right you are."

"Hmmmmm. So tell me, what brings you to Canberra?"

"A little mystery has been nagging me." Paul pulled a bed sheet from his pack and unfolded it. "Bits and pieces of the archives seem to have found their way into my own memory. Then again, they might just be weird imaginings from my own dreams. But there's one particularly vivid set of memories, if that's what they are, that comes to me again and again. Every time I enter it, I see something new."

"And the sheet . . . ?"

" . . . is an exact map of the night sky as I see it during those dreams. I started it right after the first dream, and add to it every time I go back. The sky is always the same. I just add more details after each trip. Note the position of the full moon. At the time this drawing is made, it's undergoing a total eclipse."

Paul pointed to a series of numbers written on the lower right corner of the sheet. "Last month, I drove to the exact geographical location where the dreams take place, then got a fix on the latitude and longitude from a navigational satellite. Those are the map coordinates. If we pile all this information into one of the observatory computers, we just might come up with the precise date when the skies over that vantage point would match this configuration I've drawn. Then again, we might get a nonsense answer. In that case, we'll know I'm only dreaming."

Clarence paced the room slowly, then sat on his desk directly across from Paul, hands in his pockets. "Easily done, my friend. But before I suffer a heart attack from the shock of the result, why don't you tell me what you *expect* to come of this."

Paul stood up and walked to the window behind the desk. In his mind's eye, a herd of diprotodon grazed the manicured lawn below as a flock of giant emus strutted by. "I think we'll wind up with a precise date somewhere around 40,000 years ago."

"You're telling me that you think you have memories going back to the Pleistocene?"

Paul stepped back to his day pack, pulled out a small sketchbook, and handed it to Clarence. "Here are some of the animals I've been observing. I make these drawings immediately after waking up."

Clarence's eyebrows raised as he leafed through the book, and he let out a whistle of astonishment.

Paul continued, "Here's another mystery: An old aboriginal man talks to me in these dreams. I've learned his language so well by now that I can speak it when I'm awake. The old man tells me things that no one could possibly have known back then. He even manages to predict the eclipse just before it happens. I ask him where he gets his knowledge. His answer is always the same, that the Rainbow Serpent reveals it to him."

"Good Lord, Paul! What you're telling me is that you

not only travel to the Pleistocene in your dreams, but that you actually have . . . "

" . . . a window to the Dreamtime mythology of the aborigines. Yes."

The men gazed at each other in silence, each lost to wonder within his own mind.

ABOUT THE AUTHOR

Jim Schutte was born in central Kansas in 1950 in a third generation family of Dutch-American wheat farmers. Family economics and a stern grandfather dictated that he spend most of his adolescence behind the wheel of a 1953 Minneapolis-Moline tractor.

At Kansas University, after majoring in everything from English to entomology, he graduated with a degree in anthropology. From there he got his master's degree from the University of Wyoming in archaeology. After two field seasons in Mexico, he tired of digging up dead Indians and retrained in physical anthropology at Southern Methodist University, getting his Ph.D. in 1979. But his eclectic interests continued to carry him into other areas. He served postdoctoral research fellowships in cardiology and pulmonary medicine at the University of Texas Health Science Center at Dallas before finally deciding that his short attention span precluded an academic career.

Throughout his academic career, Jim remained interested in writing. His first publication was a brief satire of a scientific experiment involving marijuana, which appeared in *Playboy* in 1973. He described an alleged "experiment" which involved—among other things—the drycleaning and steam pressing of brain tissue in order to help determine the effects of drugs on it. Despite the utterly preposterous nature of the entire "experiment" several physicians and scientists actually took him seriously. *Playboy* later published a letter from a prominent professor of psychology who complained that "Schutte's scientific methods are archaic to say the least," and went on to say that he was "ashamed that people like Schutte are part of the growing scientific community."

From 1983 to 1991 he served as Southwest Editor for *Medical Economics* magazine, the nation's best-read publication for doctors. During one of his assignments he spent three weeks crisscrossing the Australian Outback while researching an article on the Royal Flying Doctor Service. During another assignment he took a camel safari across central Australia. From such research his first novel, *The Bunyip Archives*, evolved.

In 1991 he left *Medical Economics* to found and edit *The Malpractice Report*, a monthly newsletter dedicated to educating physicians in ways to reduce their risk of being sued for negligence.

In addition to editing the newsletter and writing novels Jim freelances magazine articles on topics ranging from travel to real-life adventure stories. He is also co-author of the nonfiction book, *Preventing Medical Malpractice Suits: A Handbook For Doctors And Those Who Work With Them.*